A NEW BEGINNING

ALEXA ASTON

 Created with Vellum

PROLOGUE

FIVE YEARS AGO...

Carter Clark awoke, his nose buried in Emily's hair, his arm securely about his wife. He inhaled the sweet scent of her shampoo and smiled. She had used it ever since they had begun dating in high school. They had been married three years now and were on their annual fall trip to Seattle, where they always took in a Seahawks football game. Emily was as crazy for the Seahawks as Carter was, maybe even more so.

He snuggled closer to her, thinking how they'd made this trip together for the first time during their second year in college. They had so much fun, it had become a tradition. They stayed at the same small bed-and-breakfast. Ate Saturday brunch at the same spot before the game on Sunday. The Seahawks should consider the Clarks good luck for them because the team had never lost a game when the pair had been in attendance. Today's opponents, the Cowboys, came in undefeated, while the Seahawks were three and two.

Carter's palm went to Emily's belly, and he thought of the baby that now grew inside her. They had waited to have children, wanting to be established in their careers and have some savings built up before adding to their family. Carter was a third-generation firefighter, stationed at the Salty Point firehouse, while Emily taught third grade at Maple Cove Elementary, where his mother served as principal. His dad was the chief at Carter's firehouse. One day, he hoped to hold the same position.

They had only told three others about Emily's pregnancy. She was ten weeks along now, and they were holding their good news until she reached twelve weeks. They had told his parents—but not hers. His dad was hands down the best poker player Carter had ever faced, his stoic face made of granite, giving nothing away. His mother, diplomatic and empathetic, probably knew more secrets than anyone in the Cove because so many confided in her.

His wife's parents were the exact opposite—malicious gossips. Sometimes it surprised him how they could have given birth to such a sweet, shy woman as Emily. Her father operated the local gas station, while her mother owned Serenity Salon. Both places were a haven for town gossip, and Emily had been the one who told him they would wait before they revealed to her parents that she was pregnant. They had wanted to share their good news, though, and had done so with his folks and his closest friend, Dylan Taylor.

Dylan had left the Cove right after their high school graduation, joining the military. He now served halfway around the world as an MP for the army, and Emily said it would be fine to tell him. They Face-Timed with Dylan last weekend and shared about the baby. His friend had been genuinely happy for them. Carter only hoped Dylan would return to the Cove one day. The two of them had been inseparable from childhood, playing Little League and Pop Warner ball together, attending the same church, and eventually, double dates. Dylan had dated Willow Martin, a girl he had truly loved. But Willow was an artist and wanted to spread her wings beyond the Cove. She now lived in Europe and painted for a living and had not visited the Cove in more than five years. Sometimes, Carter wondered if Dylan would ever come back to their small town, knowing it would always remind him of Willow, the girl he loved who got away.

Emily began to stir, and then her fingers lightly danced along his forearm. Soon they were making tender love, and he was in awe of his wife. She was smart, kind, and already a fantastic wife. She would make for an even better mother. He couldn't wait to be a father himself. His parents had been terrific role models, and Carter planned to emulate their parenting style, thinking he and his sister, who now lived in San Francisco, turned out pretty darn well.

As they lay entangled in the afterglow, Emily said, "I can't believe this is the seventh time we've made this trip. The Seahawks should pay us to do so every year when they play their toughest opponent. We do have a proven track record, after all."

"Tomorrow's game will be a challenge," he agreed. "Ready to get up and attack the day? You can shower first."

She rose slowly and got that funny look on her face he had seen all too many times in the past few weeks. Quickly, she made a mad dash to the bathroom, and he heard her vomiting. Her morning sickness had been a regular nuisance, one that never bothered her until after she got out of bed each morning. Her obstetrician had assured them that this was natural and soon the nausea would subside. Despite being sick every morning like clockwork, Emily had already put on five pounds. Carter knew her pregnancy would begin to show soon since Emily was petite and small-boned. His mother, who was five-nine, had said no one could tell she was pregnant until her fifth or sixth month each time, but that Emily would show much more quickly.

He reached for the TV remote and turned on ESPN's *Game Day*, which was broadcasting from the State Fair of Texas, where perennial rivals Oklahoma and Texas would battle it out on a sunny day. He heard the shower start and relaxed a little, knowing Emily was now fine.

She emerged half an hour later, dressed casually in leggings and a long pink tunic, her short hair pulled back from her face with a headband.

"Your turn," she told him, going to her purse and removing a package of Saltine crackers. "I'm going to nibble on these before we head out to brunch."

"How is your stomach today?"

"So-so. I hope I'll be able to enjoy our favorite place to eat."

He rose from the bed and went to kiss her lightly on the lips before entering the bathroom. Soon, he was showered, shaved, and dressed in jeans and a polo shirt. They both slipped into jackets since the October day was cool. He hoped the rain would stay away this weekend.

They headed out and talked about how they would spend their day. After brunch, they usually hit Pike's Market and then Kerry Park, a small park on the south side of Queen Anne Hill. Emily loved tradition, so Carter figured they would go to the same places in order to please her.

They had to wait half an hour for a table at the

brunch place, but they snagged one outdoors in the sunshine. It was in the mid-fifties, with no breeze, and felt pleasant. He went for the French toast and bacon, along with three eggs and a bowl of oatmeal and side of fruit. His wife ordered her favorite brunch food, Eggs Benedict. Dairy hadn't set well with her during this first trimester, and Emily had sipped milk and eaten yogurt sparingly. He worried about the hollandaise over the Eggs Benedict, but when their orders arrived, she dug in and seemed to really enjoy the meal.

"Maybe I'm turning the corner, just like the doctor said," she said brightly.

He took her hand and raised it to his lips for a tender kiss. "I wish I could gobble up all this sickness you're experiencing."

"You may be stoic when it comes to being ill, but I wonder how you would react to your belly growing four times its usual size, much less having to give birth."

He chuckled. "God knew what he was doing when He let women be the ones to carry and bear the kids."

"I think God should've made us alternate," Emily said, a twinkle in her eye. "Women produce the first and men have the second kid."

He laughed aloud. "Then I think we would see a ton of only children on this planet."

Carter signaled for the check and paid it, and then they strolled down the street, their fingers linked. They reached Pike's Market, taking in all the sights and smells. He thought the scent of fish might bother her, but she didn't mention it. Instead, laughing and clapping as they watched the men sling the fish around.

He bought her a bouquet of fresh flowers, as he

always did, and then they walked to the nearby Victor Steinbrueck Park for a few minutes before calling an Uber to take them to Kerry Park and its fantastic views of the Space Needle, Elliott Bay, and Mount Rainier in the distance.

They leisurely strolled through the park, stopping to take a few selfies, not a care in the world, no place to be except with each other.

"Will we even take this trip this time next year?" his wife asked. "The baby will only be about four months old."

"It's tradition. Of course, we'll continue coming here each year. At least until we're in our eighties or nineties," he declared. "Then we might need to slow down."

"I guess we'll have to let your parents keep him or her. You know that I don't trust mine to do so."

They hadn't learned the gender of the baby yet and would find out soon at an upcoming sonogram.

"Sometimes I wonder how my parents even raised me," she said. "My mother doesn't have a maternal bone in her body. She probably has no idea how to change a diaper anymore. I rarely saw Dad when I was growing up because he was always at the gas station. Even though he owns it, he thinks he has to be there fifteen hours a day." She chucked. "Probably so he won't miss out on any gossip."

"You know my mom and dad would be happy to keep the baby," Carter told her. "They are really excited about this grandchild."

"I hope so," she said. "After all, your sister already has given them two."

"Yes, but they live too far away. Mom and Dad will have a blast spoiling a grandchild who only lives five minutes away."

They continued moving through the park and then Emily came to a sudden halt.

He saw a funny look cross her face. "What is it? Are you going to be sick?"

"No," she said softly and then winced. She pulled her hand from his and both her hands went to her temples. She began massaging them with her fingertips and flinched.

"A sudden headache just came on. It's... blinding..."

He clasped her elbow gently. "Do you need to sit down? There's a nearby bench. Or do you think you can make it back to the B&B so you can lie down?"

A whimper escaped her lips, and Carter knew it was serious. He scooped her up and carried her to the bench, which was about twenty yards away. He sat, cradling her in his lap.

"What can I do, baby?" he asked, feeling helpless.

By now, tears poured down her cheeks. Emily bit her lip. "Something's wrong, Carter. Really wrong. It's like... someone has plunged... a knife into the top of my head."

He jerked his phone from his pocket and dialed quickly.

"911. What's your emergency?"

His firefighting training kicked in as a calm descended over him. "I have a pregnant female. Twenty-five years of age. Ten weeks along. She's complaining of a massive headache. Says it feels like a knife has plunged into her skull."

"Where are you, sir?" the dispatcher asked.

Carter glanced about. He named the park and described their surroundings in as much detail as possible.

"I have emergency first responders headed to you now, sir. Please stay on the line."

"I'm putting you on speakerphone and setting the phone beside me. My wife needs me."

He held Emily, feeling helpless as her hands went to her head, the heels of them pressing into her temples.

"Oh, make it stop," she pleaded. "Please. Please. The baby..."

She went limp in his arms. Quickly, he placed her on the grass. He felt for her pulse and found none.

"She's unconscious," he shouted, hoping the dispatcher could hear him. "I'm starting CPR."

Even as he did so, he heard the wail of a siren in the distance and somehow knew they weren't going to arrive in time. Still, he pumped away, singing *Stayin' Alive* under his breath. He checked her airways again and her pulse.

Nothing.

Carter heard the dispatcher talking to him, but he couldn't make sense of her words. All his attention was focused on Emily. He was still pounding on her chest with the heels of his hands when an EMT nudged him aside and took over.

But it was too late. Carter's gut knew it.

His wife was gone.

They tried resuscitating her for several minutes as he dully watched. Then one of them looked at the other and slightly shook his head. It was over.

"I'm sorry, sir," the balding EMT said. "We need to take her to the hospital so they can pronounce her death."

"I'm a firefighter. I know," he said in a monotone.

Carter took Emily's hand and walked beside the men as they rolled the stretcher to the ambulance. He got into it, never letting go of her hand. He stroked her cheek, thinking she looked as if she were merely asleep. There would be no more yearly trips to Seattle Seahawks games. No more baby. No more decades together, growing old and loving one another.

His mind went blank and stayed that way until they arrived at ER. He accompanied his wife's body inside, where one of the EMTs spoke to a physician. They rolled Emily to a section off to the side and pulled the curtain.

The doctor checked for vital signs and finding none, called the time of death. "I'm very sorry," he said. "Your wife looks to be young and in excellent health. We'll perform an autopsy to find the cause of death."

"I think... it was an aneurysm," he said. "She complained of a massive headache. It came on abruptly. She was in agony for a short time—and then she was gone." He swallowed. "She was pregnant. It was... our first."

The physician's sympathetic gaze almost caused Carter to lose it. "Then it's a double loss, which makes it all the more tragic. I realize this is a painful time for you." He made a few notes on a chart and said, "I can give you a few minutes alone with your wife, then we'll take her so the autopsy can be done. There will be some paperwork for you to fill out afterward."

Carter stood at Emily's side, his heart torn in two. This woman had been a playmate from their kindergarten days. They had grown up together, partnering in science lab and entering math competitions. She had cheered at his football and basketball games in high school. They had fallen in love.

And now she was gone.

He continued holding her hand, stroking her hair, until they came for her. He pressed a final kiss upon her brow and whispered, "I love you—and our baby. I always will love you, Em."

After they rolled her away, a nurse sat with him, helping him with the paperwork. A woman in her early fifties appeared, introducing herself as a grief counselor. He let her talk on for a while, nodding without listening to her. Finally, she left.

The nurse returned, giving him information about the autopsy, which would be performed Monday morning. After that, he would be free to return with Emily's body to Oregon.

Numb, he stumbled from the ER, walking for hours. He finally called an Uber and went back to their B&B. He had left the happiest man in the world and now returned a broken man.

Carter wandered about the room, picking up items Emily had left strewn about. He glanced to the bed where they had made love a final time. He collapsed on it, sobs rising from his chest, feeling as if he wanted to die so he could be with her.

His cell rang and he removed it from his pocket, seeing it was his mom. He didn't feel like talking to anyone, but if he had to, his mom was the perfect person.

"Hello?" he said shakily, swallowing, trying to think how he was going to break this news.

"Carter?" Her voice sounded strained. Then a choked sound came across the line. Fear pooled in his belly.

"Mom?"

He heard her sniffing. "Carter, I don't know how to tell you this. Your father... he... he was killed fighting a fire. He's gone. Gone."

His world, already askew, came crashing down.

CHAPTER 1

FIVE YEARS LATER—BROOKLYN, NEW YORK

Tenley Fielding hung up from her call, the elation she had at hearing her friend Willow Martin's news quickly fading. Willow, one of her college roommates, had recently returned to the small town she grew up in on the Oregon coast. She had reconnected with her high school boyfriend, now the sheriff of Maple Cove, and they planned to marry as quickly as possible in a courthouse wedding. Willow had a track record of choosing the absolutely wrong men for her, and every single lover she'd lived with had cheated on her. Which was pretty insane, because Willow was tall, auburn-haired, violet-eyed, and drop-dead gorgeous. At least she was getting her happily-ever-after.

Unlike Tenley.

She knew now that she had married Theodore for all the wrong reasons, the biggest being that she didn't love her husband of four years.

She never had.

What she had been looking for was a father figure. A man who would approve of her and take care of her. Tenley's parents divorced when she was four, and her dad had dropped off the face of the earth. She had never seen him after he moved out of their middle-class home in Costa Mesa. Her mom had ripped up every picture that existed of him. Now, Tenley only had a vague, shadowy image of him. If she sat next to him on the subway, she would never know it.

Her mom smoked like a chimney and died of lung cancer when Tenley was a freshman in college. It had taken scholarships and balancing several part-time jobs to put herself through school. She was a hustler, though, having known poverty after her dad left. She grew up wearing Salvation Army clothes that never fit properly and had her school breakfast and lunch paid for by the state. She learned quickly to eat her fill—because usually nothing waited for her at home.

Her strong work ethic, coupled with her intelligence, helped her finish her double major degree in English and marketing at UCLA. When she graduated, she wanted as different a life as she could find, accepting a job at a New York publishing house and moving cross-country a week later. For three years, she rose quickly, thanks to her multitasking skills and the ability to think quickly on her feet. In business, she projected confidence.

Her personal life was another matter.

She'd never had a boyfriend in high school or college because she worked so many hours outside of school. The little free time she did have, she spent with Willow and their other roommate, Sloane, a network journalist on assignment in Africa now.

When she met Theodore at a party, she was drawn to him. He radiated self-assurance and was clever, as well as good-looking. That was what impressed her. His vitality and confidence. Tenley knew if she were with a man like that, he would take care of her.

Theodore made her feel secure and safe. When she found out he came from old money, she almost broke off their relationship, feeling she would never fit into that world. At work, she knew what she was doing. Her professional demeanor and confidence helped her to soar. Personally, it was a different can of worms.

She worried that she would say or do the wrong thing around his family and friends. Wear the wrong clothes. Use the incorrect fork. She voiced those concerns—and Theodore had laughed. Told her how silly she was. How she was worthy of any man. He convinced her she had the intelligence, looks, and style that would make her fit in anywhere, even his uptight, judgmental world.

He pressed hard. They were engaged after only four months. His parents expressed concern at the speed of their relationship, but Theodore was a strong personality and told them he knew what he wanted.

And what he wanted was Tenley Thompson.

Without hesitation, she signed the prenup agreement his parents' attorneys placed before her. Didn't even read it. She did so willingly because she knew she wasn't some gold-digger marrying Theodore for his money. No, she wanted his companionship. The protection he offered her. No more coming home alone to her empty, cramped apartment. She would have her husband. They would enjoy each other and eventually have children. The days of worrying about paying an electricity bill would be gone. She could relax. Be herself. Start the book she'd been promising herself she would write, which her crazy hours at the publishing company had forced her to place on a back burner.

They wed in a small ceremony, though no expense was spared. Went on a Tahitian honeymoon. Tenley didn't even have a passport, but Theodore had her application fast-tracked, telling her the Fielding name could open any door. She left her sixth floor walkup, and they purchased a luxury loft of four thousand square feet in Brooklyn's Dumbo area, home to art galleries and tech startups and some of New York's wealthiest up-and-comers.

Then it all unraveled. So slowly that she didn't realize it at first. Theodore convinced her to leave the publishing house for an opportunity to work for the Borough of Brooklyn in their promotions and marketing department. She glanced down at the new ad campaign she was working on. She enjoyed her work but found something lacking. It wasn't as rewarding as her time spent at the publishing house.

Theodore slowly began remaking Tenley, without her realizing it. He began suggesting clothes for her to wear until nothing that felt like her hung in her closet anymore. He didn't like Willow or Sloane, not bothering to hide his contempt for her friends the few times they had been together. Slowly, he isolated her, even suggesting she work from home a few days a week and discouraging her from any kind of socializing with her office mates. She was no longer included in after-work happy hours or invited to weddings or baby showers.

She was an island.

Many times she came home to an empty house. Theodore worked long hours as a stockbroker and went to several social events weeknights, trying to snag new clients and investors. He had made it clear he didn't need her help in these endeavors. Oftentimes, he would text her, telling her he was staying at his pied-à-terre, the small, Manhattan condo he had lived in before their marriage. He'd maintained ownership of it after their marriage, often sleeping there instead of coming home. When Tenley questioned him, he told her it was close to work and excused it with saying he was tired or he had an early business meeting the next morning.

She got to where she didn't care whether he came home or not. The time alone was well spent, plotting and starting her novel. When Theodore asked once what she did in his absence beyond work, she told him she was toying with writing a novel. He declared fiction a waste of time and discouraged her from pursuing the project.

Tenley never mentioned it to him again.

Her husband had gone to his office this Sunday afternoon, leaving her alone as usual. Her dreams of Sundays spent going to brunch, doing the *Times'* crossword puzzle together, or going to a movie or theatre matinee had vanished after the first few months of marriage. More and more, she wondered why Theodore had bothered to marry her since he ignored her most of the time.

Only after they wed did he tell her he was not interested in having children or even pets. She wanted both and voiced her opinion. He shut her down, hard and fast.

Could that be grounds for divorce?

Tenley had admitted to Willow in a recent conversation that she had made the mistake of her life. She hadn't elaborated, but she suspected her friend knew it involved Tenley's marriage to Theodore. The idea of divorce had increasingly overtaken her thoughts.

She decided now was the time to research it.

She lifted her laptop from the table, leaving her work stuff, and settled into a comfy chair, placing her feet on the matching ottoman. A quick Google search brought up several sites dealing with how to obtain a divorce in New York. Numerous grounds for divorce were touched upon, most of them not pertaining to her situation. Theodore hadn't abandoned her. At least physically. He wasn't serving a prison term. Neither of them had committed adultery.

She paused at that, wondering if that were actually the case. With so many nights spent away from her in Manhattan, was Theodore truly being faithful to her?

Chewing the end of her pen, Tenley wondered if she should hire a private investigator to follow Theodore. See who he was with and if anyone accompanied him back to the pied-à-terre. They had a joint bank account, but she had a separate stash of cash she added to on a regular basis, never knowing why she did so, or why she kept it a secret from her husband. Maybe she should use some of those funds to hire a PI. Or a divorce lawyer.

"Hmm. Cruel and inhuman treatment," she said to herself, wondering if that argument might apply, reading through the legal definition according to the State of New York. It included physical, verbal, sexual, or emotional treatment by the Defendant, against the Plaintiff, that endangered the Plaintiff's physical or mental well-being and made living together unsafe or improper.

Theodore had hit her a few times. He always claimed it was an accident. He had a hot temper and waved his hands around a lot, striking out and sometimes making contact with her. He'd blackened her eye one time. Scratched her cheek with his ring. He'd even pushed her once. She'd broken her fall, throwing her hand out, spraining her wrist. Every time she had made excuses for him. Every. Single. Time.

The more Tenley read, the more depressed she

grew, thinking how much time things could take and how costly a divorce would be. Theodore made ten times what she did and would certainly hire the best lawyers in the city. His family connections would open the door at any law firm he chose to have represent him in the divorce petition.

And what if he contested it? Though the website said that New York had become a No-Fault state and the granting of a divorce was inevitable—even if one party didn't want one—it could take a long time to obtain. Even with a no-fault divorce, they would have to be separated a full year and resolve any issues—including support, spousal maintenance, and equitable distribution of their marital assets. With the prenup Tenley had signed, she doubted she would be entitled to anything beyond her portion of salary banked in their joint account.

With a no-fault divorce, one of them would have to state that their relationship had broken down irretrievably for at least six months. She could do that. Her heart told her the marriage had died long ago. But would Theodore go along? No divorce had ever occurred in his family. He had even joked once how they were bound together because his mother would never accept a divorce in the family. That had been shortly after their marriage, and Tenley hadn't thought anything of his words. She had been idealistic, thinking they would never have problems so major as to result in one of them divorcing the other.

She needed to talk to a lawyer and see what her options were. It had to be someone that she could trust. If word got back to Theodore that she was planning to take legal action against him, he would fight her tooth and nail, making her life absolutely miserable.

The one bright spot was that she could leave the state once she had begun proceedings. Her residency in New York for the past nine years established her as a citizen, but the website said she could depart the state once someone other than herself had served Theodore with the divorce complaint.

Would Willow take her in?

Yes, her friend was getting married soon, but she was living in her grandmother's house now, even completing renovations on it. The house was a large, two-story home with numerous bedrooms. If Willow would allow Tenley to live with her, even for a few weeks or months, she could try to get on her feet. She would need to see if her office would allow her to telecommute fulltime. She was on excellent terms with her boss and thought that a strong possibility. It would be a big ask of Willow—and Dylan, whom she'd never met—but the idea gave her hope. Living on her own in New York, she wouldn't be able to save any money for lawyers or private investigators.

Tenley decided to go for a walk. Though the mid-December day was gray and dreary, no rain was in the forecast. Though a native Southern Californian, she didn't mind the cold, like so many other New Yorkers did. A walk across the Brooklyn Bridge and back would help clear her head.

She changed into an old pair of sweatpants that she'd kept and only wore when Theodore wasn't going to be home. She put on tennis shoes and a UCLA sweatshirt, the one item she had insisted on keeping in her wardrobe and threw her coat on top of that. Putting on hat and gloves, she was ready for the brisk temperatures.

Leaving the loft, she headed straight for the bridge, walking at a quick pace. Not many people were out as she climbed the stairs to reach the bridge. She spied a few joggers ahead of her and the usual bikers with their sleek helmets, bent low over their handlebars. She crossed the bridge on the pedestrian walkway used by walkers and runners and reached the Manhattan side less than half an hour later. Thirsty, she walked along Centre Street and stopped at a frank cart for a bottled water. She downed it and then went back to the bridge, this time returning at a more leisurely pace.

When she reached one of the benches scattered along the walkway, a woman rose. She wore a knee-length, navy wool coat and dark sunglasses, despite the overcast day.

"Tenley? Can we talk?"

Warily, she asked, "How do you know my name?"

Slowly, the woman removed the sunglasses, and Tenley recognized Cecilia Montgomery, a minor Manhattan celebrity from old money, who designed posh handbags which started at two thousand dollars and only went up in price from there. Tenley had never owned one. Material things weren't important to her as they were to Theodore, though he had gifted her with what he termed the *appropriate pieces* to enhance her look. A Cecilia Montgomery bag had not been one of them.

"Hello, Cecilia," she said, still wondering how this stranger knew her name.

"Mind if we walk? I've been sitting here a while, waiting for you to return."

She had been so in her head on her walk that she hadn't been aware of anyone following her—but apparently Cecilia Montgomery had been and decided to wait for Tenley here instead of chase her across the Brooklyn Bridge.

"I suppose."

The attractive woman fell into step with her. "You're wondering how I know you. We were at a cocktail party together a few years ago but never spoke. I see Theodore making the social circuit, but you don't seem to accompany him very often."

Insecurity flooded her now, walking beside this elegant, beautiful woman. The kind of woman Theodore should have married.

"No. I'm not as social a creature," she said. "How do you know Theodore?"

"He's my husband."

CHAPTER 2

S hock reverberated through Tenley. "Your what?"

Cecilia's brittle laugh brought chills to Tenley. "You heard me."

She wondered if the woman were drunk or on drugs. But her eyes were clear as she studied Tenley. "Go on."

"Teddy and I went to prep school together. Our parents were friends. I've known him my entire life."

"You're lying," she accused. "Anyone that knows Theodore knows he would never go by Teddy."

Cecilia's brows arched. "Really? So he makes you call him Theodore. I only thought that was for business. Hmm."

She did not like the sound of that *hmm*.

"Let me give you the Sparks Notes version," the dark-haired beauty said. "Spring break. Senior year in college. Our friend, Pip Morrow, was getting married after graduation. He and his wife would then start law school together that fall."

Tenley had met Pip Morrow. The wife was now Pip's ex-wife and dating someone in the mayor's office.

"Go on."

"I was at Smith College. Teddy and Pip were at Yale. Several in our circle used to vacation together. Ski over Christmas break. Do fun-in-the-sun in spring break. Summer in the Hamptons."

The life this woman described sounded so foreign to Tenley. She had never gone on a single vacation until her honeymoon. Worked every school vacation, pulling double shifts, since she didn't have school and could do so.

"We decided to do Vegas for once. A five-day bachelor party at the Skylofts in the MGM Grand. You know, our own private section of the hotel. Suites. Luxury amenities."

"All paid for by your parents," Tenley said dryly.

"Who else? Anyway, it was five days of constant partying. We began drinking on the flight out and never stopped."

"So, guys and girls went?"

"Yes," Cecilia confirmed. "Our usual crowd. We drank. Bed-hopped from room to room. Gambled. Maybe we even saw a few shows. I can't remember now. It was ten years ago. The point is, on the night before we left, Teddy and I got married at some cheesy Vegas chapel. Elvis officiated."

Tenley assumed it was someone licensed to perform weddings in the state who was dressed as Elvis Presley. She started to ask what this had to do with her, and then it hit her.

What if Theodore had never legally ended his first marriage?

Excitement filled her. She hadn't bother to research an annulment—because she hadn't thought it applied to her. She swallowed, her heart pounding.

Sounding bored, Cecilia said, "We laughed about it the next day. I tucked the marriage license into my carry-on, and we never mentioned it again. I went back and finished my last year at Smith. Teddy had already graduated from Yale. It was as if it never happened."

"You're telling me that you and Theodore are still legally married? That my marriage to him isn't a valid one."

"That's exactly what I'm saying, Tenley. And I need that marriage now."

She frowned. "I don't understand."

"Teddy and I—and most of the group we ran with —grew apart as we went through our twenties. I run into a few of them at fundraisers or cocktail parties, but it's not like we hang out together anymore. Teddy and I did have a pretty torrid affair about five years ago. Intense as all get-out. But it flamed and burned. Ever since then, we haven't really spoken. We just nod at affairs when we see one another."

It would have been not too long after his affair with Cecilia when Tenley and Theodore had met and begun dating. She couldn't help but wonder if this long-ago, semi-forgotten marriage was the reason he had pushed her into them marrying too quickly.

"Why do you want to be married to Theodore?"

"I need Teddy. I married two years ago. Foolishly, I thought it was love. My attorneys warned me, but I refused to make Andrei sign a prenup. He's Romanian and quite the macho stud. I didn't want to offend his masculine pride by forcing him to sign." Cecilia sighed. "Truth be told, I thought he might walk away from me if I did so."

"What's changed?"

Cecilia assessed her. "You're smart. I'll give you that. Andrei has been putting a great deal of my money up his nose. He was working as a high-end fashion model. Print ads. Runway work. But cocaine has made him unreliable."

An image flashed in her mind of Andrei, the most famous male fashion model who walked the runway shows in New York and was only known by one name. Tenley hadn't heard about his marriage to Cecilia Montgomery. Then again, celebrities weren't actually on her radar. Still, even ninety-year-old grannies knew who Andrei was from all the billboards of him plastered in Times Square alone.

"Andrei hit me the other night. That's when I knew I had to get rid of him. But without having signed a prenup, he'll walk away with a great deal of *my* assets. The State of New York may call them marital assets earned during the marriage, but I'm the one busting my ass, designing and selling my brand."

They had reached the end of the bridge and moved down the steps to reach the sidewalk in Dumbo.

"My attorneys have told me to come clean with Andrei. Tell him we're not legally wed. I've even spoken to a reporter who's guaranteed to tell my side of the story in a favorable light. If I'm married to Teddy, Andrei isn't entitled to a dime. Once he figures it out, I'll give him a little money to make him go away."

"But I'm in the way now," Tenley pointed out, her thoughts whirling.

"That you are. You aren't seen much with Teddy. If you want out of your marriage without a lot of fuss, I can set you up with an attorney. Not my team, of course. That wouldn't be quite kosher, would it? But they have someone in mind. She's a real shark."

If what Cecilia said were true, then Tenley could actually find herself single again very soon. She could put all her unhappiness behind her. Break away and start over.

Cecilia said, "I'm sure you were in love, Tenley, just like I thought I was. But I'm not going to see my name and brand flushed down the toilet, Andrei dragging me down with him. I've worked too hard."

"How do you think *Teddy* will react to all this?" It felt funny calling her husband that boyish nickname. He had insisted she always call him Theodore. Not even Theo, for short.

The true Mrs. Fielding shrugged. "I don't know. Frankly, I don't care. I don't want to be stuck with Teddy. Don't get me wrong. He's gorgeous. Smart. But a little too smug and uptight for me."

Tenley shook her head. "You'll divorce him?"

"I will. And since we've been apart for years, the money I've made from my handbags should be considered my property, not his."

"You do realize that you're both bigamists," she pointed out.

"True," Cecilia agreed. "But that's the beauty of my deal with the reporter. You see, she'll play it off as a foolish, impulsive act by two friends who were slightly tipsy."

She frowned. "I thought you said you'd been drinking nonstop."

"We had. But that might be grounds for an annulment between us—and I don't want that to interfere with my annulment from Andrei. Teddy and I didn't even remember we got married, we were so drunk. Until the next day. And this enterprising young journalist did some tremendous digging, unearthing this marital relationship between us. She'll play it like we were tipsy but knew what we were doing. Then we were embarrassed and just swept it under the rug, hoping to forget about it and get on with our lives."

She knew news could be manipulated in so many ways. With Cecilia's money and a reporter telling the story from a young, impressionable woman's point of view, it would be an easy sale to the rest of the media. The resulting scandal would probably jack up her handbag sales, as well as garner her sympathy.

"My lawyers say they can smooth things out. Neither of us will do any kind of time for being bigamists. Maybe we'll have to pay a fine. Definitely, community service."

"I'm in," Tenley said firmly. "I want an annulment. When can I meet with this attorney representing me?"

Cecilia smiled, looking like a sleek shark. "I guess things weren't going so well in paradise, were they?"

She ignored the question. "When?" she pushed.

"Now, if you'd like." Removing her phone from the beautiful leather handbag she carried, Cecilia pressed a button. "She's in. And she signed a prenup. We're almost there."

They continued walking. A few blocks from Tenley's loft, a black town car pulled up to the curb and stopped.

"This is our ride," Cecilia informed her.

A driver was already out, opening the door. Cecilia climbed inside the vehicle, and Tenley followed. Seated inside was an attorney she recognized from the news. The woman had represented nothing but women in high profile cases, including celebrity divorces.

"Hello, Tenley. I'm Sylvia Driver. Your divorce lawyer. Give me a dollar," she instructed.

Frowning, Tenley pushed her hand into her coat

pocket and brought out a few bills. Handing a dollar to the lawyer, Sylvia smiled.

"Now, I'm officially representing you and our private conversations will be under the attorney-client privilege umbrella, thanks to this retainer. Miss—Mrs. Fielding—will be paying for the rest of my services. Let me tell you what I have in mind."

Sylvia concisely and thoroughly outlined what would take place over the next few weeks.

"An annulment will establish that your marriage is not legally valid. Grounds for an annulment, then, are very different from a divorce. In your case, we will only have to prove that your supposed husband, Theodore Fielding, is a bigamist. That he was still married to someone else—in this case, Mrs. Cecilia Fielding, at the time of your marriage to him. The court will declare, with the proof provided, that a valid marriage between you and Fielding never took place. You will receive a certificate of annulment, and you will be free to remarry at a future date. That marriage will be considered your first."

"So, I've been living in sin the past four years?" Tenley said drily.

"Call it whatever you want. I'd like to believe that you'll think of it as a mistake we easily erased. A very sad misstep which you were led to take by a lying, cheating asshole." Sylvia smiled. "Do you have any problem with that, Tenley?"

She returned the older woman's smile. "Not one, Sylvia. Not a single one."

"I have been in close touch with the firm representing Cecilia in this action, as well as the reporter. She may or may not wish to get a few quotes from you. I'd let her interview you if she wishes to. She knows you're an innocent party in this, and her claws will be retracted."

"That's good to know."

"If you are amenable, we will file all the necessary documents first thing tomorrow morning," the lawyer continued.

"The sooner, the better. I guess I'll need to leave the loft."

"That won't be necessary," Sylvia assured her. "I'll file something that will allow you to remain there. Fielding can stay at his pied-à-terre. He already spends quite a bit of time there anyway."

"He's cheating on you, by the way," Cecilia informed her. "Has been for at least the past four months. That's how long I've had him watched."

Tenley's gut tightened. She swallowed the bile that rose in her throat.

"You'll garner quite a bit of sympathy in the press," Sylvia assured her. "I feel certain I'll be able to get you the loft in a settlement. You can keep it if you wish. It's a seller's market now, though, and I think you could walk away with a pretty penny if you decided to get rid of it."

"I'll have to think about that." She hesitated. "We have a joint bank account. My salary is direct deposit. I have a fear Theodore will close the account and take what's in it, leaving me with nothing."

Sylvia patted Tenley's knee. "Don't worry about that. I'll have his assets frozen, joint or otherwise."

"What am I supposed to live on in the meantime with the account frozen?"

"I'll front you some money," Cecilia said. "You can consider it a loan."

"I can't ask you to—"

"You didn't ask," Cecilia interrupted. "I'm offering."

"Okay," Tenley said reluctantly.

Sylvia spoke for a few more minutes, asking for Tenley's e-mail and cell number and providing her business card.

"Cecilia's attorneys and I know the right people, Tenley. This will make a huge splash in the news and run its course after a few cycles. We're going to move very quickly on the annulments for you and for Andrei and then move on to a divorce for Cecilia from Fielding."

"How fast?"

Sylvia thought a moment. "It's about two weeks until Christmas. I think by New Year's, you'll be a free woman."

CHAPTER 3

The last day of the year was dark. Storm clouds gathered outside Tenley's window as she stared out across Dumbo. She needed to leave in a few minutes to meet her boss, Diane Nichols, at the office.

The last few weeks had been insane, with the news first breaking about Cecilia Montgomery's secret marriage to Theodore Fielding years earlier. The press had a field day, and Tenley had not left the loft after her name became public, ordering food to be delivered, as well as a few groceries. The guy who delivered her groceries, however, had been a reporter. One who had paid off the deliveryman and accepted the box to hand to her. Tenley had let him in. Immediately, he bombarded her with questions. She had ordered him to leave, throwing out Sylvia Driver's name, saying she would sue him for every dime he had.

Hearing the famous attorney's name was enough to chase the reporter off.

She hadn't opened her door to anyone after that, becoming a hermit as she worked from home and got her exercise by doing a little yoga and pacing the loft for an hour or more each day. The only exception had been when Sylvia contacted her, telling Tenley that Theodore and his attorney would be coming over to collect some of his clothing and personal items. She had visited the pied-a-terre a couple of times in the past and knew Theodore had plenty of clothes there. The lawyer had been a dream to work with, kind and understanding yet firm and professional. It was Sylvia who fronted money to Tenley instead of Cecilia. Tenley would pay back those borrowed funds once the loft sold.

Sylvia had been good enough to come, along with a huge guy whom she termed an assistant, but who Tenley suspected was hired muscle. They arrived an hour before Theodore and his lawyer did, and Sylvia had instructed Tenley not to utter a word to Theodore, especially if he baited her.

She didn't have to worry about that. Her non-husband merely glared at her when he entered the loft and then went straight to the space designated as their bedroom. She could hear suitcases being unzipped and assumed he packed clothes. While he did so, his attorney told Sylvia that his client had purchased all the furnishings in the loft and would be removing them the next day. Tenley wished she could have sold tickets to the show that followed. Sylvia was a bulldog with a bone, and by the time Theodore and his attorney left, Sylvia wore a triumphant smile. Theodore's lawyer had told him to make sure to take with him any personal items he wished to keep because the entire contents of the loft and ownership of the property belonged to Tenley now.

She had left it to Sylvia to sell the loft, and the older woman told her she worked closely with a trusted realtor in these matters. She even told Tenley they had a buyer for the loft and everything inside it, from furniture to dishes to linens. The sale would close less than a week into the new year. She had asked if the buyer needed to see the loft and was told no. Frankly, she didn't care who this buyer was. All Tenley wanted to do was get out of this place.

She glanced at her watch and saw it was time leave for the office. Although it was a Sunday, Diane had asked for Tenley to meet her this afternoon. Her boss had suggested that Tenley not come in during all of the circus occurring in the media, telling Tenley she would be a distraction.

She slipped into her all-weather coat and belted it, claiming her umbrella from the stand next to the door. She took an empty box with her, figuring she would be taking her personal possessions when she left today. Diane had not told her she would be let go, but Tenley knew it was happening.

Stepping from the loft, she locked the door and raised her umbrella, glad that Sylvia suggested changing the locks to keep Theodore out. It was a little over a mile to the office, something she had enjoyed walking on the days she went in. Many New Yorkers had a long commute and were tired by the time they arrived at work.

She entered the building and smiled at the guard on duty, signing in.

He gave her a sympathetic look. "I'm going to need your employee badge, Tenley," he said apologetically. "Then I'll call up and let Diane know you're on your way."

"I understand," she said, his words confirming what she already knew.

Making her way to the bank of elevators, she rode up to the sixth floor and was soon standing at the glass doors, waiting for her boss to let her in.

Diane appeared and gave her a smile, then unlocked the door, allowing Tenley to step inside.

"It's good to see you, Tenley," she said, warmth in her voice. "Come on back."

They went to Diane's office and had a seat. They had passed no one else. It didn't surprise her, since it was New Year's Eve and a Sunday.

"I'll lay all my cards on the table, Tenley," Diane began. "I fought to keep you—but there are people above my pay grade who axed that."

"It doesn't surprise me. The Fieldings have a lot of political and economic influence in this city. In this state," she corrected.

"The whole situation is a clusterfuck," Diane declared. "I think in a way, you are fortunate to be able to remove yourself from it. I'll say this in confidence— and deny it if you ever repeat it—but I never liked your husband. I think he's getting exactly what he deserves."

Not only had Cecilia and Theodore been exposed to the public as bigamists, once the annulments had been filed and quickly shuttled through the system, Cecilia and her team of attorneys had filed for divorce from Theodore. Since this time of year was a slow news cycle, the press had eaten up all the gossip surrounding the situation, attacking like vultures. Tenley had fared the best of the four parties involved, having a low profile to begin with.

"I'm sorry that I have to let you go," Diane apologized again. "I will give you a glowing recommendation, however. Just let me know whom to send it to. I don't care if I have to talk to three hundred prospective employers. You are creative, talented, and have a wicked work ethic. I wish I could clone you and run the office with those clones."

Diane paused. "Do you have any idea what you'd like to do?"

"Other than leave New York?" Tenley said, a wry smile crossing her face. "This town is Theodore's and his family's territory. I don't think I would get a fair shot at any position I applied for here."

"You're from California, aren't you?"

"Yes, but I'm not sure if I want to go back there either." She hesitated. "I've been working on a novel. I've been given the loft that Theodore and I lived in as part of my settlement. The proceeds from its sale will last me for quite a while if I'm careful."

"So, you want to finish your novel and see if that goes anywhere?"

She nodded. "I've always wanted to write. Theodore discouraged me from doing so, saying it was beneath me and not worth the time I'd have to put into it."

"Well, we all know Theodore Fielding is an ass, as well as a bigamist. When you finish writing it, send it to me. I know a few agents and even some people in publishing. I feel I really owe you, Tenley. I hate letting you go."

"That's a nice offer—and I'm probably going to take you up on it. For now, it's get-out-of-New-York for me. I'm actually headed to the Oregon coast. A little town called Maple Cove. One of my college roommates and best friends lives there. She's offered me a place to stay while I'm working through everything. Hopefully, I can get this book finished while I'm staying with her."

Diane stood and offered her hand. "I wish you the best of luck." She grinned. "And if some day, you were to write a *roman à clef*, I would be the first to buy it."

She hadn't thought of writing about what she'd

been through and thinly disguising it as fiction. Right now, it was so raw she couldn't even consider it. But who knew? Writers used all kinds of incidents in their own lives as fodder for their books.

She shook Diane's hand. "I already turned in my badge downstairs. Let me go to my cubicle and clear out a few personal things. I assume I'm already locked out of company e-mail?"

"That was my next step. Removing privileges to e-mail and the backdoors into the website. I can give you a few minutes to go through your e-mails, but I need to be out of here in an hour."

"I'll be gone long before then, Diane. Thank you for being such a wonderful boss and for going to bat for me. I hope you didn't lose any standing profession-ally by doing so."

"If I did? Screw 'em."

Tenley left her boss' office and headed to her workspace. She turned on her computer and logged in to her employee account. While it was processing, she took the two picture frames from her desk. One was of her, Sloane, and Willow, and she placed it inside her box. The other was her and Theodore. She opened the frame and removed the picture, tearing it into pieces over and over before tossing it in the trash. The frame followed. She wanted no reminders of her time with him. Opening her drawers, Tenley collected a few random items. An extra pair of black pumps. Two of her favorite lipsticks. A tube of hand lotion and tin of breath mints.

She scrolled through her e-mails. Many of them were from journalists who had found her through the company site and begged her for an exclusive inter-view. She deleted those quickly. Some e-mails were from people she'd worked with, both here and at her former publishing house, all but one sympathetic and wishing her the best. Once she had cleared those, she logged out for the final time and turned off her computer. Picking up the cardboard box, she returned downstairs. She'd already said her goodbyes to Diane and didn't want to see her again.

She rode the elevator to the lobby and signed out, wishing the weekend guard a Happy New Year.

Outside, she opened her umbrella since it was raining heavily and trudged back to the loft, which she could no longer think of as home. When she reached it, she slipped her hand into her coat pocket and removed her key ring, starting to insert the key into the lock, when she was spun around out of the blue. She dropped her box, items spilling everywhere.

Then her gaze met that of Theodore Fielding's.

"You think you're so clever. Changing the locks. You and that bitch attorney."

Tenley wanted to crawl within herself but did not want to show this man any sign of weakness. She had taken the high road in all matters, not contacting Theodore and allowing everything to go through their attorneys. Now, though, she wanted to stand up for herself.

"If you had hired a better attorney, you wouldn't be here," she flung back.

"We had a prenup. I shouldn't have had to pay you a dime."

"And you knew going into our so-called marriage that I wasn't in it for your money."

She couldn't say she had loved him, and so she kept silent.

"I don't know why I married you," he spat out. "You were the absolute worst lay I ever had."

His words stung. She had only had a few dates before she started seeing Theodore and had been embarrassed to confess to him that she was a virgin at twenty-six. He had been quite charming, telling her he thought it was sweet that she was so old-fashioned and had saved herself for marriage. Their lovemaking —at least to her—had seemed very basic and perfunctory. He had never excited her. She didn't think she had ever had an orgasm during sex with him. As their marriage progressed, he had spent more and more time away from her, never initiating sex.

"If you would have taken the time to show me more, I might have pleased you. You bragged about having so much experience, but I don't think you had much more than I did. I'm glad our marriage has been dissolved. You are a lying lowlife, *Teddy*."

He slapped her. Hard. The sting on her cheek burned, filling her with shame. Tenley bit her lip and said, "Go."

Theodore glared at her a moment and then walked away.

Kneeling, she gathered the scattered items and placing them in the soaked box. All of a sudden, she felt someone hovering over her and quickly stood.

She didn't recognize the man before her, but she knew he had to be a photographer from the looks of him. They all seemed to have that lean, hungry look about them as they chased the next picture opportunity.

"Are you all right?" he asked quietly.

"Yes," she replied. "I suppose you're going to publish that. Did you get the slap—or just my reaction?"

"Both," he informed her. "Theodore Fielding is one of the biggest bastards on the planet. You deserved better than him. You need to go right now to the nearest police station and file assault charges against him. I've got the photographic evidence to back you up. I'll even testify as an eyewitness."

For a moment, she actually considered doing so, wanting to punish the man who had hurt her so deeply, wasting over four years of her life. But she had her annulment in hand. She would be closing on the loft in a few days. After that, she would be flying to Portland, ready to start her new life.

"I think I'll pass," she told him. "I'm ready to close the book on this sour chapter in my life. If I press charges, things will only keep dragging on. I can't keep you from publishing the shots, though. Have at it."

"You're a class act, Tenley Thompson," he said, admiration in his voice.

She realized he had used her maiden name, which she had reclaimed when the annulment came through. Legally, Tenley Fielding had never existed. She was now Tenley Thompson once again, her old self.

New name. New year. A new Tenley.

Or at least she could try to find the old Tenley—and go from there.

CHAPTER 4

Carter awoke well before dawn. For the first day in over a month, he had nowhere to be and nothing specific to do. He pillowed his hands behind his head and let his thoughts wander.

He thought back to a few nights ago. New Year's Eve. Dylan and Willow had held a party at their house to celebrate their recent marriage. He was glad his friends had both returned to the Cove after years away and discovered their love for each other had never died. Though a few in town whispered about their lightning-fast romance, Carter couldn't blame the couple for wanting to be together and not waste another minute apart. They were taking their second chance and squeezing the joy from each minute of every day.

He, better than most, understood that philosophy of life. After losing Emily, he realized how precious life truly was and that it could end in a split second. While he was grateful for the years he had with Emily, both before their marriage and during it, he knew it would be hard to give all his heart again to someone else. Recently, he had mentioned to both Dylan and

Willow his desire to dip his toe back into the dating pond, though prospects in the Cove were lean. People either left the Cove for a more exciting life or they stayed here with someone they had dated in high school, leaving a miniscule number of available single women.

The only two unattached women he did know were cousins, Ainsley and Rylie Robinson, and Carter looked upon the pair as little sisters. While both were attractive and fun to be around, he doubted any kind of romantic attachment would develop with either of them. No, he would rather keep them as the good friends they had become and continue to socialize with them, Dylan and Willow, and his new friend Gage.

Gage had moved to Maple Cove last summer, and he was still a bit of a mystery to most people. A former Navy SEAL, Gage had merely said he was tired of the military and ready for something different. His parents had vacationed once on the Oregon coast, and he remembered it to be a beautiful, soothing place. Gage had driven up and down the seaside towns of the state, settling on Maple Cove, and had opened his own business, serving as a personal trainer to individuals and holding group exercise classes outside. Carter hadn't thought Gage would be able to make a go of things and was pleasantly surprised when the Cove and a couple of the surrounding towns took to the idea. Now Gage had a full slate, teaching group classes in the Cove, Salty Point, and Crescent Cove, as well as training individuals.

Carter finally rose and felt a little at loose ends. Usually on his off days from the firehouse, he worked construction projects for Pete Pulaski. With the focus on the recent holidays, not many people had hired

Pete and his ever-changing crew, which included several firemen from the Salty Point Firehouse where Carter was assigned.

He decided to take some time for himself this morning and assembled a quick backpack with water and snacks as he brewed a pot of coffee and ate a quick bowl of cereal. He poured the coffee into a large thermos and went to his truck, driving to a favorite trail he hadn't hiked since the summer. After hiking for several hours, he returned home and hit the shower, deciding to try a new recipe today. Emily had been a terrible cook—the only thing in which she had taken after her mother—while Carter had learned to cook the basics during his years at the firehouse. He enjoyed trips to the grocery store and planning and cooking meals for his fellow firefighters. He excelled at simple meals and received regular praise for his spaghetti and meat sauce, meatloaf, and baked chicken. Cooking intrigued him, though, and he had started trying more ambitious recipes when he came home after a long day working with Pete's crew. He decided he would try a new spin on coq au vin today but would need some items from the store. He consulted his recipe book, one which was a wire-bound blank slate. Any recipe he tried and liked, he recorded in this book. He jotted down the items he would need to purchase and grabbed his keys.

When he got into his truck, his cell dinged, and he pulled his phone from his pocket to read the incoming text.

Need a favor ASAP.

The text was from Willow. She had always been one of his favorite people in the Cove, along with her grandmother, Boo, who had recently passed away and left her house to Willow and her older brother Jackson, a defense attorney in L.A. Instead of texting, Carter called.

"What's up?" he asked after she answered.

"I'm double-booked. It's my own fault. I reversed two days in my head. I was thinking Tenley was coming in tomorrow, but she's not. It's today."

He knew Tenley Thompson was one of Willow's college roommates who was coming to visit from New York. Willow had mentioned the visit, and he was eager to meet one of her friends. Carter had wondered if this Tenley was an artist like Willow.

"Please tell me you're off today, Carter, and you can pick her up from the airport. My scholarship committee is meeting this afternoon about the same time Ten's plane lands. It's the judging for the finalists. We're making our decision on the winner today."

Carter knew how much this contest meant to Willow. Boo had been an artist as Willow was, and funds from the estate had been earmarked for a rotating scholarship. Willow had tapped a few people from the community, including his mom, to help serve on the selection committee. Applicants had filled out a form and submitted online pictures of their artwork. Willow had mentioned that once the committee narrowed down the field, the finalists would bring their pieces so the committee could view and judge the art in person. His mom had talked excitedly about her former students entered in the contest.

"As a matter of fact, I'm free as a bird. Nobody seems to want any renovations at their houses this time of year. Pete told me he probably wouldn't give me a call for another couple of weeks. I'm all yours."

"You are a lifesaver. I really owe you one, Carter. By the time you and Tenley return to the Cove, my meeting will be done and we'll be able to notify the winner. I'll text you her flight information and picture so you'll recognize her. You'll have to check and see which baggage claim. That's where we'd planned to meet."

"Text a picture of me to her, as well," he suggested. "Being a jaded New Yorker, she may not be trusting of a stranger who approaches her, offering a ride to the Cove."

Willow chuckled. "Actually, Tenley was raised south of L.A. Near Disneyland. She only went to New York after we graduated from UCLA. I'll still text her your picture, though. Do I even have one of you?"

"I'll send a selfie now," he told her. "Since I'll be wearing the same clothes as the picture you send, that should be confirmation for her that I'm an okay guy."

Carter ended the call and snapped a picture, texting it to Willow. Moments later, her text came through with the airline's flight number and ETA. The next text was of Tenley herself.

She was stunning.

He went to the airline's website and input her flight number and destination, finding her arrival time was in three hours. It would take him a little over an hour to reach the Portland airport. With some time to kill, he would go to The Gourmet Chef, a store he had discovered online and visited in person twice. There was a new blue Le Creuset Dutch oven he had his eye on that he might purchase today.

He started the truck and noted he only had a quarter tank of gas. He would need to stop at Fred's station on the way out of Maple Cove. He had a distant relationship with his former in-laws. They had never been ones to celebrate holidays, and he and Emily had always gravitated toward his folks. Carter occasionally saw Fred when he gassed up and rarely saw Wilma, who owned the local hair salon patronized by women from the Cove and beyond. Carter preferred having his hair cut by a fellow fireman, whose dad had been a barber and passed along a few skills to his son.

He pulled into the gas station, which was self-service as most were, and got out of his truck. Inserting his credit card into the pump, he silently counted to himself, trying to predict when his former father-in-law would arrive.

Two gallons later, Fred strolled out to greet him.

"Hello, Fred," he said, keeping his eye on the turning numbers.

"Carter. How are you doing?"

"Not bad."

"Heard that the Tates are getting a divorce," Fred offered, starting up his gossip mill, as usual.

Carter shrugged, not taking the bait. Fred went on, mentioning a few other people in the Cove, while Carter grunted noncommittedly.

He finished filling his tank and placed the handle back into the pump, waiting for his receipt to print. He tore it off and said, "Good seeing you, Fred. Tell Wilma hello."

"Will do, Carter. You have a nice day."

Driving away, he was angry at the sick feeling in his gut. He didn't like his encounters with Fred and Wilma. They were shallow, spiteful people, and he thought the only reason the couple married was because of their names being the same as the famous cartoon Flintstones. It was always a starting point in a conversation. They reminded him of his time with Emily. Any time he saw one of them, it was as if the bandage were ripped off, scab and all, and he had to start the healing process all over again. It shouldn't be this way after five years. It should be all right for him to want to find someone else. If Emily were a ghost who now materialized beside him, she would be the first to berate him for not getting on with his life. He had been in a holding pattern for five years now. Carter decided it didn't matter what Fred and Wilma said—either to his face or behind his back. He would start looking to find someone.

Even if it were only a few casual dates to begin with. After all, he was thirty and didn't want to spend the rest of his life alone. Seeing how happy Dylan and Willow were had inspired him. Carter wanted what his friends had. He wanted to find love again. He wanted to be a husband and father.

He arrived in Portland seventy minutes later and headed for The Gourmet Chef. The store had a homey feel to it, as if it sprang from a French country farmhouse. He browsed the Le Creuset Dutch ovens and selected an azure one and then went to look at the various gadgets. Cooking gadgets fascinated him, and he wound up purchasing a cookie stamp and garlic press.

On his way to pay, he also saw some cute dish towels with a strutting rooster on them and something written below in French. He stopped a passing clerk and asked, "Do you know what that says?"

She smiled. "I do. It translates to *Men make hot chefs*."

Carter laughed. "I've got to get a couple." He pulled two from the shelf and added them to the items he carried.

The clerk checked him out, and he returned to his truck, putting the sack in his back cab. Glancing at his watch, he knew it was time to head to the airport. Once again, he checked the flight status and found the plane was landing ahead of schedule. The baggage claim was the same, however.

Carter started the truck and drove to the airport, parking and entering the terminal. By the time he got to the right baggage claim, it was already surrounded with people. He glanced and saw two different flights were sharing the carousel, one from Miami and one from New York. He glanced around, looking for Tenley, but did not see her.

Then he spied someone from behind that could be her and approached. "Tenley?" he asked.

She didn't respond and so he tapped her on the shoulder, again saying, 'Tenley?

She turned and he saw it was not the woman he was looking for. "I'm sorry," he apologized, quickly moving away because of the frown the stranger wore. He continued weaving through the passengers waiting to claim their luggage, and then he saw the woman from Willow's text.

She was even more stunning in person.

Smiling, he approached her, wondering if Tenley might be single.

CHAPTER 5

Tenley finally slid her Kindle into her tote. Trying to concentrate on reading a book was beyond her. Her head was filled with too much... stuff.

She placed her tote back under the seat in front of her and looked out the window. The plane was still cruising along at thirty thousand feet, so she couldn't see anything below.

Her thoughts drifted, going over the last few days. Watching the ball drop in Times Square on TV, ushering in the new year. Donating sacks of clothing she couldn't stand to a local women's shelter. Combing through her possessions and either throwing or giving away most everything, until she was able to pack everything she owned into two suitcases. She carried personal items in her tote, and her backpack contained her laptop and various chargers. It was liberating to think she was leaving her old life behind.

And eager to see what her future held.

Her list of priorities included finishing her novel and finding herself again. She had liked who she was in college and during her years at the publishing house. It was only after she met and married

Theodore and became so isolated that she began to change into someone she didn't recognize.

She glanced at the trashy tabloid she'd bought at the airport, with its picture of Theodore and Cecilia on the cover and a huge, jagged line separating them. As she'd promised, once Tenley and Andrei had their annulments in hand, Cecilia filed for divorce from Theodore. Or Teddy, as all the news outlets were calling him, taking their cue from the fashion designer divorcing him. Tenley knew Theodore must be furious at the pet name gaining such prominence. His mother, in particular, was fighting the good fight for her son, trying to paint Theodore as the innocent victim in the situation—and pretty much losing that battle if the memes which had popped up were to be believed.

Tenley didn't have a Facebook or Twitter account. She hadn't thought she had enough friends to create a Facebook account and knew she didn't have enough clever things to tweet about, so she'd never established either. Willow was the same. Her friend had no social media because she didn't care about things like that. It had taken some arm-wrestling before Remy, Willow's agent, had convinced Willow that she needed a website. It was pretty stark, with only pieces of Willow's art displayed on it and information to contact Remington Moore, her agent. No bio of Willow or any way to reach her.

Sloane was the exact opposite. Being in the news business forced her to have multiple social media accounts. Sloane had convinced Tenley and Willow to at least set up Instagram accounts. While neither of them posted anything, they both checked daily for what Sloane posted. Her friend's passion for people and the news she covered shone brightly on her Instagram account.

The tabloid article had gotten most of the story right, piggybacking off the journalist Cecilia had found to be so friendly. Teddy Fielding was painted as the villain in the entire escapade. Tenley knew the court date for the divorce had been set for mid-January, which was unheard of, since New York divorce law made couples jump through multiple hoops over an extended time. The speed showed just how much influence Cecilia and her family had in the city.

After the divorce hearing, a second date would occur for both Cecilia and Theodore to face bigamy charges. Cecilia had already told Tenley it had been decided in advance by the judge that she would receive two hundred hours of community service, while her ex would do five hundred. The thought of Theodore Fieldling picking up trash along the FDR Highway brought a smile to Tenley's lips.

Four bells chimed, which she knew had to be some kind of signal to the flight crew. Sure enough, the captain came on and informed them he was putting the fasten seatbelt sign back up since they would soon begin making their descent into Portland. Flight attendants went into action, collecting the last of the trash and empty drink cups.

Landing in Portland was a much different experience from flying into New York. No giant skyscrapers or Statue of Liberty. No bridges connecting the island to the mainland and other boroughs. A sense of peace washed over Tenley. Though she had never been to Oregon before, she hoped it might become her new home. She needed to live somewhere. With Willow having married and put roots down, it would be nice to live near one of her two best friends.

The landing was smooth, and the plane taxied along the runway to its gate. It finally came to a stop, and she unbuckled her seatbelt and reached for her tote. Pulling out her phone, she prayed she had a bit of juice. In her excitement to leave Brooklyn, she had neglected to charge her cell the night before and only saw how low it was as she Ubered to LaGuardia. She'd sent Willow a text before she boarded, confirming her flight number, and then turned the phone off after she got to her seat, having seen it was about to give up the ghost.

Powering it on, nothing happened. Dead. Well, at least Willow knew the correct airline and the flight number. They had agreed to meet in the baggage claim area fifteen minutes after her flight landed, knowing it would take several minutes before her luggage appeared on the carousel. Thank goodness for arranging that in advance. If not, she would have had to find an outlet in the airport and charge it a bit to let her friend know she had arrived.

Tenley stopped at the first restroom she passed, freshening up, even applying a new coat of lipstick. She dropped the tube into her new Cecilia Montgomery bag. A messenger had delivered the tote yesterday afternoon with a one-word message—*Enjoy!*

She planned to enjoy her new handbag—and her new life—to the max.

Tenley moved along the concourse, following the arrows to baggage claim, shifting her backpack now, slipping her right arm through so that it rested solidly against her back.

She located the carousel where her luggage would appear, seeing it shared space with another flight. The area was crowded, and many people gathered around the carousel as suitcases started to come out. Eagerly, she glanced around, looking for Willow, and was disappointed not to see her. Of course, the flight had come in almost fifteen minutes early, thanks to a tail-wind. Willow might still be on her way to the airport or parking the new SUV she was so proud of.

As she continued to scan the crowd, a man caught her eye. He was dressed in what she thought a typical resident of Oregon would wear—worn jeans, a flannel shirt, and a lightweight jacket. She noticed him not only because of his good looks but the fact he, too, seemed to be searching the crowd for someone. She watched him approach a woman, tapping her on the shoulder. Obviously, he had made a mistake from the women's frown, and he quickly retreated, winding his way through the crowd again.

She couldn't help but notice the woman had re-sembled her, with the same shoulder-length blond hair and height. Her spidey sense kicked in, that dis-trust of everyone around her that she had picked up during her years living in New York. She tamped it down, telling herself it was just a coincidence.

Tenley glanced again to the carousel, not spying her bags yet, thinking the ones there must be from the Miami flight. Then she saw a tall man who had sat on the aisle seat in her row lean over and claim a black suitcase. She turned her attention to the suitcases now coming out, knowing her luggage would be out soon. Then she had a prickling feeling rush through her, and she looked over. The handsome stranger was headed her way, a smile on his face.

She didn't know him. Instantly, her guard went up. Was he some kind of slick player trying to pick up women? Did he have a type—and was she his type? She faced him as he approached, one of those devas-tating smiles on his face, the kind that made women go weak in the knees.

"Hi, Tenley," he said as if he knew her as he reached her. "I've been looking all over for you."

"I don't know you," she said flatly. "How do you know my name?"

He pulled out his cell and touched the screen, turning it so that it faced her.

Her image stared back at her.

Fear rippled through her. "Are you some kind of stalker?" she accused. "Get away from me." She stepped back but she was flush against the airport carousel and had nowhere to go.

The stranger took another step toward her, and she felt threatened. Without hesitation, she slung her heavy tote into his head, knocking him off-balance, his phone flying from his hand and landing on the moving carousel.

"Security!" she shouted at the top of her lungs. "Security! I need help over here!"

The people near her quickly moved away, giving her a wide berth.

The guy had recovered and said, "My phone!" He took off, trying to reclaim it from where it sat on the moving conveyor belt.

She watched as two tanned uniformed security guards approached him. One latched on to his elbow, and she heard him say, "Step away from the carousel, sir."

"My phone!" the man protested and tried to break away.

The second security guard grabbed his other arm, and they pulled him back as she stepped toward them.

One of them asked her, "What seems to be the trouble, miss?"

"I think he's been stalking me," she said shakily.

"He has my picture on his phone. I don't know who he is, but he called me by name."

The stranger frowned, obviously not happy to be restrained, but not struggling. "There's an easy explanation for this, Tenley."

Her New Yorker instincts kicked in. "There's absolutely no reason for you to have my picture on your phone," she said sharply.

The other security guard asked, "Are you thinking about pressing charges?"

"Hey, come on. I was just asked to pick her up from the airport."

"Sure, you were," the first guard said. "If you'll accompany us to our office, we'll straighten this out." He glanced to Tenley. "You need to come along, too."

"Why? I need to get my bags and meet my friend," she insisted. "I don't know him. I don't want anything to do with this."

"I'm afraid you need to come with us, miss," the second guard told her, latching on to her elbow.

"Get your hands off me!" she demanded, trying to jerk away.

The guard held tight to her with one hand. With the other, he removed a radio from his belt. "We're bringing in two people who caused a disturbance," he said tersely. "Stand by. We may need help if they aren't more cooperative."

A teenaged boy with a bad case of acne appeared before them. "Uh, this was on the carousel. I saw it was that guy's." He handed it to the first guard, who thanked him.

The stranger who approached her met her gaze. "Let's go with them, Tenley. We've already caused enough of a scene. We can easily sort this out in private."

"I want it noted that I'm accompanying you under protest," she said and then remained silent as she and the other man were escorted through the terminal.

They reached a door, which one of the guards accessed by swiping his employee badge, and were led through a maze of corridors until they reached a nondescript room with a beat-up table and several folding chairs.

Another man awaited them. He had an air of authority about him and told them, "Have a seat."

She did as asked, sitting on one side of the table, while the man who'd approached her sat on the other side. Tenley set her tote next to her on the ground and slid off the backpack, resting it next to her purse. The man in charge dismissed the two security guards, telling them to go write up their reports and that he would speak to them later and put their statements into the report he created.

As they began to leave, she spoke up. "I need my luggage that's coming out. Everything I own is in those two suitcases."

"Give them your claim check," the authority figure suggested. "They'll pull your bags."

She dug inside her tote and passed the claim check over, and the two men left the room, closing the door behind them.

The remaining airport figure took a seat at the head of the table. "I'm Jim Fisher, head of security for this terminal. Let's see if we can sort out things. See if any charges are warranted and if the lady wants to file or not. Let's hear your stories." He pointed at the man. "You first."

The stranger said, "My name is Carter Clark. I'm a fireman at Salty Point. I was asked to pick up Miss Thompson at the airport. That's why I have a picture of her on my phone. Willow Martin, her friend, texted it to me so I would recognize her." He turned his attention from Fisher to her. "If you would've turned your phone on, you would have seen you also got a text with my picture."

My phone was dead when I got off the plane," she said defensively.

"Then plug it in," Clark said calmly.

Tenley looked to Fisher, who said, "There's a plug here you can use, Miss Thompson."

She searched her backpack and located her phone's charger, attaching it to the phone and plugging it into the nearby outlet.

"It will take a couple of minutes to get enough charge for me to open a text. *If* I have one."

"You do," Clark assured her. "Willow asked me to give you a ride to Maple Cove."

"Then if I call her, she'll confirm that?"

"She won't answer her phone," Clark said.

Tenley snorted. "How convenient. Why not?"

Clark ignored her and looked at Fisher. "My best friend is Sheriff Dylan Taylor of Maple Cove," he said, withdrawing his wallet and removing his driver's license. He set it on the table and pushed it toward Fisher. "Sheriff Taylor has known me since we were in diapers and can confirm my identity. He is the husband to Miss Thompson's friend Willow."

Suddenly, she got a sinking feeling that she had made a mistake. A terrible mistake. "Why wouldn't Willow pick up if we called?" she pressed.

"She got her days confused," Clark said easily. "Right now, she's in the middle of a committee meeting for the scholarship they will award in Boo's honor."

"You seem pretty glib," she told him, the uneasy

feeling growing as she stubbornly pushed it aside. "You have an answer for everything. You could've found out something like that online."

"I suppose so, but I knew they were meeting not only from Willow but my mom, Dorothy Clark, who's the principal at Maple Cove Elementary. She's one of the three community members Willow asked to serve on the selection committee. They've narrowed it down to the finalists, and they're deciding this afternoon whom the scholarship will go to."

She glanced quickly to Fisher, who was tapping on his phone. After a moment, he held up a finger and said, "I'm calling the Maple Cove Sheriff's Department." He paused and then said, "Yes, I'd like to speak to Sheriff Dylan Taylor. This is Jim Fisher at Portland International Airport."

After another pause, Fisher said, "Hello, Sheriff Taylor. I have a man here who says he's a friend of yours. A Carter Clark. Address in Maple Cove. Says he works at the Salty Point Firehouse."

Fisher listened a moment. "I see. He says your wife asked him to pick up her friend at the airport today. I merely need to confirm that with you."

Another long pause. Fisher nodded. "Thank you, Sheriff."

He put his phone on the table. "Mr. Clark is who he says. Sheriff Taylor confirmed Miss Thompson was flying in today but did not know Mr. Clark had been asked to pick her up. Miss Thompson, could you please check your phone now?"

She stood and retrieved the phone. Opening it, she saw she had a couple of texts from Willow. Opening them, she saw a message.

Totally messed up, Ten. My committee meeting is at the same time your flight lands. Have asked Dylan's best friend, Carter Clark, to pick you up and bring you back to the Cove. Texting his picture now so you'll know what he looks like. Can't wait to see you!

Carter Clark gave her a rueful smile as she glanced sheepishly at him. "I told Willow that you were a jaded New Yorker and wouldn't want to come with me unless she texted my picture to confirm with you. She sent me yours so I would know whom to look for."

He turned to Fisher. "This was just all a misunderstanding, Mr. Fisher. Hope you can see that now."

The head of security nodded. "I can understand Miss Thompson's concerns with a stranger approaching her."

"I'm sorry my phone wasn't charged," Tenley apologized. "If I would've seen the texts, none of this would have happened."

"It's always good for travelers to charge their phone before they leave on a trip, Miss Thompson," Fisher chided. "Next time, maybe you can be a little more prepared."

Fisher stood. "You folks have a nice day." He left the room.

Tenley and Carter both rose. She shook her head, embarrassment flooding her. She unplugged the charger, replaced it in her backpack, and slipped the phone into her purse, slinging the backpack over her shoulder.

Carter already stood at the door waiting for her. As she moved into the hallway, she saw her luggage sitting outside the door. Without a word, Carter raised the handles on both suitcases and taking one in each hand, began rolling the bags down the corridor, Tenley following. She couldn't help but notice his broad shoulders and tall, muscular frame. They returned to the main area of the terminal, and she caught up to him, touching his sleeve.

He stopped and turned, his warm, chocolate-brown eyes drawing her in. "Yes?"

"I am so, so sorry, Carter."

"For thinking I'm a stalker—or giving me a black eye? You packed a punch with that bag you slammed into my face."

Mortified, Tenley felt her cheeks burning. "I don't know when I've been more embarrassed—unless I take into account that time I learned that I was married to a bigamist."

Shock filled Carter's face. And then he died laughing. When she faced him silently, his laughter died.

"You're serious."

"I am," she confirmed. "A few weeks ago, I learned my four-year marriage was a sham."

His reaction surprised her. A slow smile crossed his face. "Now that sounds like an interesting story. Want a ride to Maple Cove, Tenley Thompson? You can tell me all about it."

Tenley's heart skipped a beat, caused by his steady gaze.

"I guess I owe it to you. Sure. I'd love a ride."

CHAPTER 6

Carter led Tenley out to his truck. He swung her suitcases into the pickup's bed, covering them with a tarp.

"In case it rains," he told her, liking what he saw.

She was about five-nine, with shoulder-length, golden-blond hair and sky-blue eyes. For a tall girl, she was curvy, with generous breasts and a sweet curve from her waist to her hips.

In other words, the exact opposite of Emily.

His wife had been short, small-boned, and her facial features almost elfin, with dark hair and dark eyes. Yet while Carter had thought Emily beautiful, he was incredibly attracted to Tenley Thompson.

"You can put your backpack and that rectangle you slammed into me in the cab," he told her.

"Cab?" she asked, looking clueless. "Sorry. I've never ridden in a truck."

He led her to the passenger side and opened the small door. "This is called an extended cab. Lots of trucks only have two doors and seats. The extended has extra seats behind the front ones. Sometimes the truck has a small door, like my model. Others, you have to open the big door and crawl into the back."

"Gotcha." She removed the backpack from her shoulder and handed it to him. Carter placed it on the seat.

"The Gourmet Chef?" she asked, indicating the sack on the back seat.

"Yeah. I did a little shopping in Portland before I came to the airport," he admitted, opening her door.

Tenley climbed in, setting the large black thing—which he assumed was her purse—on the floorboard. "I'll need to hear what you bought. I'm not much of a cook. I can boil water for Kraft Mac and Cheese and can handle a few other basics."

Carter closed her door and went to the driver's side. Climbing in, he started up the truck and pulled from his parking space.

"What basics?" he asked.

She laughed. He liked the sound of her laugh. Rich. Deep. Open. "Like brown a pound of ground beef, drain the fat, and dump in either a pack of taco seasoning, a jar of Prego, or a can of Sloppy Joe mix."

He laughed now. "You'd fit right in at the firehouse. Those are basic, filling meals. We eat those all the time. Empty a few cans of green beans or corn along with those, and you've got a meal."

"Do you do any of the cooking when you're on duty?" she asked.

"All the time. Except I aim for a step beyond basic. I serve meatloaf. Beef stew. Roasted and fried chicken. I do a pretty mean casserole, too. King Ranch is a favorite."

"I have no idea what that is, but I'd like to try it. Any man who shops at The Gourmet Chef has some skills. My former boss, Diane, was a great cook. Always bringing in things for us to eat. And always in Gourmet Chef bags. She knew her stuff. You must, too."

"I'll cook for you sometime," he volunteered, surprised he offered to do so, realizing he really wanted to. He felt at ease with her. It had been a long time since he'd been around a woman he didn't know. Carter didn't feel nervous or uncomfortable. He also hoped he'd put her at ease and decided to follow up on that.

"You really don't have to tell me about your asshole husband," he told her. "I mean, I'm assuming he's an ass because of what you said. But you don't really owe me any stories."

"No, I think I'd like to tell you. You don't seem the type to judge. I like that."

Her voice was slightly husky—and he liked *that.*

"You know I'm friends with Willow. She and Sloane Anderson and I were roommates at UCLA. I grew up poor and worked my tail off, claiming scholarships and working a myriad of part-time jobs to put myself through college. I wanted a change of pace after graduation and moved to New York. Worked for a big publishing house for almost four years.

"Then I met Theodore."

Just the way Tenley said her ex-husband's name gave him a chill.

"What wife calls her husband Theodore?" he ventured.

"Exactly," she said. "I thought after a date or two, he'd be Theo. Nope. He was Theodore until the end."

"That's already a strike against him," Carter commented. "And that's even before we get to the bigamy part."

She laughed again. "I like you, Carter. You're... refreshing. Nothing like most of the people in New York."

"I will take that as a compliment. Continue with your Mr. Asshole story. Or Mr. A, for short."

"All right," she agreed. "Mr. A was handsome, charming, and a stockbroker from a wealthy family. He rushed me into a quick engagement and marriage."

Carter listened as she recounted her marriage. Quitting her publishing job and taking one Mr. A approved of, near their Brooklyn loft. How he pulled away from her, attending social functions without her. Often sleeping in the city while she remained in Brooklyn.

"I realize now he really isolated me. I had no work friends. No friends or acquaintances in the neighborhood." She paused. "I've always wanted to be an author. I started a novel. He disapproved. He thought fiction was pedestrian and a waste of time. Never read a word I wrote. He couldn't stand Willow or Sloane. Not that I saw them that much, with Willow living in Europe and Sloane constantly traveling to report on the next story. Willow told me early on to dump Mr. A and when I didn't, she was a good friend and kept quiet and remained supportive. Sloane told me to try and enjoy the things we had in common."

She shrugged. "The trouble was, he never wanted to do anything. I thought marriage would be long walks and meals in restaurants. Sunday mornings enjoying coffee and bagels, reading *The New York Times*. Shopping together and seeing movies or plays. Having kids." Tenley paused. "None of that. Theodore—Mr. A —was all about work. And his side pieces, which I suspected he had but didn't care about as time went on."

"How did you learn about his... other wife?"

Tenley chuckled. "Now that would make a juicy book."

She went into detail about her first meeting with Cecilia Montgomery and what the handbag designer had revealed. Hiring Sylvia Driver. The tabloid press and photographers loitering outside her loft. The ultra-quick annulment, thanks to old money connections, and then Cecilia filing for divorce.

"That's how I wound up here," Tenley finished. "With the sale of the loft and its furnishings, I could pack what I owned and go anywhere I wanted. I decided to come to Maple Cove and lick my wounds for a bit. Let Willow fuss over me some. Try to pick up where I left off in my book. It was a little hard, trying to concentrate on writing with my life in chaos."

"What's your book about?" he asked, curious.

"Maybe that's for another day after I've slugged you and you have matching black eyes," she teased.

He liked her. He really liked her.

"Do you know how long you'll stay in the Cove?"

"No. I haven't a clue. California hasn't been home in a long while. My dad left when I was young. My mom died of cancer my first semester in college. Frankly, if I like Maple Cove, I'd love to stay on, just to be close to Willow. Of course, if I do that? I'll have to find a place to live. With Willow and Dylan being newlyweds, I don't want to wear out my welcome. I mean, I've never even met Dylan. We did FaceTime once so I know what he looks like. But I also know how they spent years apart. They don't need a third wheel around the house for too long."

She shifted in the seat, facing him more. "How long have you known Dylan?"

Carter grinned. "We used to stay in the church nursery as infants. We're six weeks apart. Pretty much grew up doing everything together. It was hard on both of us when he left for the army after high school graduation."

"Willow said his parents were killed."

"And Grace, his sister. She was the sweetest kid. An artist like Willow. Dylan told me he just had to get out. There were too many memories here. Besides, Willow was headed off to UCLA and then Europe, doing her artist thing. Dylan wound up traveling the world on the army's dime."

"Only to come back to Maple Cove," she mused. "I'm glad Willow also returned and they realized they still loved one another. I've never seen her happier."

"Same with Dylan," he said.

"What's being a fireman like? I'm sure there's special training. Is it always something you wanted to do?"

"You need a high school diploma or GED. I decided to get my associate degree at community college first. I needed to grow up a little bit. But it was always in my blood. My grandfather was a fireman at the Salty Point Firehouse. That's the next town over from the Cove, about twice the size of where we're heading. My dad also was a fireman and served at Salty Point."

"So, you followed in their footsteps. I love that kind of history. Is your dad still at your station?"

"No," he said quietly, a lump growing in his throat. "He died five years ago fighting a fire in Crescent Cove. That's the other side of Salty Point."

Tenley placed her hand on his shoulder, causing electricity to ripple through him.

"I'm so sorry, Carter. I didn't mean to bring up something so painful."

He shrugged. "I'm fine. The job is hazardous. Dad

was always careful, but a burning beam fell on him. Struck him in the head and back, trapping him. Even if someone could have pulled him to safety, he would have been badly burned, his back most likely broken. I like to think he went fast, doing the job he loved, rather than suffering for weeks in a hospital bed and dying in agony."

She squeezed his shoulder and then removed her hand. Carter wanted to snatch it back and kiss it. Hell, he wanted to kiss her. She had beautiful lips, the bottom one plump and tempting him to sink his teeth into it.

He shook his head, trying to clear it.

"Are you all right?"

"Yeah. Fine."

He turned his conversation to the passing scenery. By now, they were ten minutes out and would be arriving in the Cove soon. They remained silent until they hit the town limits, and he began a running commentary of the places they passed. Carter took her around the square, pointing out Ainsley's bakery and Rylie's antique store, as well as Sid's Diner and Crust 'n Stuff.

"Best pizza for miles," he proclaimed.

"Better than New York pizza?" she challenged.

Laughing, he said, "New Yorkers own it. I'm sure that's why it's so good."

"Ooh, then I'll have to try it."

"I'll take you if you want," he offered, his palms suddenly growing sweaty and his heart beating in double-time.

"I'd like that," Tenley said, unaware of how she was affecting him physically.

They cruised through town and then left it.

"We aren't stopping at Willow's?"

"Boo's house—her grandmother's—is just outside of Maple Cove. It's up ahead on the right."

He pointed out Gillian's driveway first.

"I'm familiar with Gillian," Tenley said. "We've met in New York a few times. In fact, she came to The Runyon Gallery a couple of months ago when Willow's agent set up an exclusive showing there. Gillian is so kind. It will be good to spend more time with her."

"Here's the turn," Carter pointed out, driving just past the mailbox and then turning into the long drive. "Woods to the right separating Boo's from Gillian's. No house on the other side." He paused. "I've got to stop calling it Boo's. She was such an icon in this town. It's still hard to think she's gone."

"I had the pleasure of meeting Boo a few times over the years. She was feisty and fun."

"That was Boo," Carter agreed.

He parked his truck behind Dylan's SUV. Moments later, Willow came flying out of the house, Dylan following at a more leisurely pace.

Willow hurried toward them. Tenley flung open her door and jumped out, meeting her friend. The two women threw their arms about one another, hugging as if they hadn't seen one another in decades.

Carter eased from behind the wheel and headed toward the house, Dylan meeting him.

"Had a little trouble?" Dylan asked, studying Carter's face. "Is your eye swelling?"

By now, the two friends had separated and came toward them.

Tenley must have overheard Dylan's remark because she said, "Guilty as charged, Sheriff. I gave Carter his soon-to-be black eye. It was a big misunderstanding—and all my fault. I think I'm going to be making it up to him for quite a while."

"We can hear about it over dinner," Willow declared. "If you'll get Tenley's luggage, we'll head inside. I've made Boo's chicken tetrazzini. There's plenty of it."

"Let me get my purse and laptop," Tenley said, heading back to the truck.

"Is that a Cecilia Montgomery bag?" Willow asked as her friend removed her purse, clearly impressed.

"It is. She sent it yesterday," Tenley confirmed.

"And she's carrying bricks in it," Carter said, rubbing the side of his face. "I should know."

Tenley slung the backpack over her shoulder. "I did hit him pretty hard."

"Hard? She practically knocked me down. And almost cost me my cell phone."

Dylan laughed. "I see it's going to be a lively dinner," he said, lifting one of Tenley's suitcases as Carter claimed the other.

Carter followed his friends inside, wondering if Tenley's arrival might coincide with a new chapter in his own life.

CHAPTER 7

Tenley awoke to darkness and reached for her phone on the nightstand. It was a little after four, but that meant it was after seven New York time. She set down the phone again and tried to go back to sleep. It would take her body clock a few days to adjust to West Coast time.

She thought back to last night and how good it had been to see Willow and meet Dylan. They had shared a lovely dinner, and then Carter left and Dylan excused himself so they could have girl time. It was easy for Tenley to see just how much her friend was loved. The small touches. The looks that passed between the married pair. She couldn't be happier for Willow, who had been through so much emotional turmoil over the last decade.

Her thoughts drifted to Carter Clark and how much she had confided to the handsome fireman about the past month of chaos in her own life. She had shared with him even more than she had Willow or Sloane. Perhaps it was because he was a sympathetic stranger and didn't seem judgmental. Or it might have been because he was one of the good guys.

And she was drawn to him...

That frightened her. He had not mentioned a wife or girlfriend, and she hadn't asked. The fact she was coming out of such a tumultuous time in her life made her want to steer clear of any kind of romantic entanglement, but once she got her head on straight—and if Carter Clark were single—it was possible there might be something there to explore.

Knowing she wouldn't be able to fall back asleep, Tenley rose and decided to go make coffee. She knew Willow was an early riser and usually went running. She didn't know Dylan's habits, but the Maple Cove sheriff seemed quite fit. Maybe she could have coffee ready for both of them while they went on a run together. She had never been a runner herself. She liked to walk. She really hadn't until she moved to New York, which was definitely a walking city. On the opposite coast now, perhaps she would do more than walk. Willow had mentioned all of the great hiking trails in the area, and Tenley thought that might be something she might enjoy, as well as walking the beaches. She thought it incredibly sweet that Willow and Dylan had found Shadow, their rescue dog, on one of those trails. The lab was a cuddler and had spent much of last evening on the sofa between them as they talked, his head in Willow's lap.

Tenley puttered down the stairs and saw a light already on in the kitchen when she arrived. Dylan was lifting a coffee pot, and the smell of freshly brewed coffee filled the air.

"Morning, Tenley. Coffee?"

"Please."

She seated herself at the table and he brought her a mug of steaming joe.

"Sugar or cream?" he asked.

"Both if you have them."

He retrieved creamer from the refrigerator and indicated a small bottle on the lazy Susan. "That's stevia. Willow has made a believer of me. It's a natural sweetener, and she claims it's better for us."

"Willow has always been into health," she said. "A lot of that came from Boo."

She squeezed a small amount of the stevia into her coffee after Dylan warned her how strong it was and then added the hazelnut-flavored creamer and stirred with the spoon he handed to her. Taking a sip, she sighed.

"Willow told me that the Pacific Northwest has some of the best coffee she's ever had."

"Yeah, you go into Seattle or Portland, and there's a coffee shop on every corner. Some of them not even Starbucks," he joked. "I try to always use fresh beans. I keep them in the fridge, if you're first downstairs and want to make the coffee. Or if you just want a single cup, there's a Keurig over there. Pods in the drawer beneath it."

Dylan joined her, doctoring his coffee. "I'm glad you've come to visit, Tenley. Willow has really been looking forward to this."

"I don't want to overstay my welcome," she told him. "You are newlyweds. I don't want to get in your way."

Last night, Willow had shared they were eager to start a family, but Dylan had asked that they give themselves at least a year together to enjoy and build their own relationship before they started trying. Being aware of that, she did not want to stay with them too long.

"I know that you left your previous job. Willow says you're a writer now?"

"Writer, yes. Author—not yet."

"There's a difference?"

"A writer can write all day, but an author is someone who's been published."

"Have you submitted your work to any publishing house?" he asked, his interest genuine.

"Not yet, but my old boss in Brooklyn has a few connections and asked me to send the finished manuscript to her. There's always the indie route, as well. Indie publishing, where you do it yourself."

"Mind if I ask what you write?"

She had never talked about this to anyone beyond Willow and Sloane, but she already felt comfortable with Dylan.

"It's YA. Young Adult fiction. It's also got a strong fantasy element."

"You mean like something like *The Hunger Games*?"

"Yes, that's YA, though that trilogy was more dystopian in nature. When I started off, I thought this novel would be a one and done. Now I realize after doing some intense outlining that it's likely to be a trilogy. It could even go beyond that. That will make it harder to pitch," she revealed. "Publishing companies these days take very few chances on new authors. They like the tried-and-true names. James Patterson. Nora Roberts. John Grisham. To take a chance on a newbie could cost them a lot of money, especially one's whose first book ties to other books. Because of that, I may wind up having to publish it myself."

"What does that involve?" he asked, clearly curious about the process.

"I'd need to find a good developmental editor. One who really looks at the plot and characters and makes suggestions that strengthen both. I'd have to take those notes and do rewrites until I was happy with the flow and pace. Then I'd have to locate a line editor, who would literally go line-by-line, checking for sentence structure. Word choice. The tone and emotion of the piece. Once those corrections are made, it would need to be proofread for typos and grammar mistakes. It's easy for a typo to slip past you. Our eyes are used to seeing words the right way, and as we read, we subconsciously fill in or correct what's wrong."

"That sounds like a lot of work."

"It is. Sometimes the developmental editor can also line edit for you. If you aren't given a ton of notes, the rewrite can actually be pretty fast. I tweak as I write, writing a couple of chapters before I go back and tighten up things. I'm hoping that by doing so, I won't have an extensive rewrite once the manuscript is completed. But that's just the actual writing."

"There's more?"

"If I go indie and publish it myself, yes. The book has to be formatted for e-book and paperback versions. A cover has to be designed for both of those versions. With this being a trilogy, I might even want to have all three covers designed at the same time by the same graphic designer, just for consistency. Then there's all the marketing. I won't even go into that."

"Sounds as if you've really researched this."

"I have. I always like to be prepared. Sloane calls me a Boy Scout for that very reason."

She took a sip of coffee and added, "I'm a little over halfway through with it now. At least this first book. I'd like to finish it up while I'm here. Here doesn't have to mean in this house, though, Dylan. I am at loose ends and if I like Maple Cove, I may want to stay. It would be great to be close to Willow and an auntie to your little ones."

He grinned at that thought. "I want you to stay with us as long as you want, Tenley," he assured her. You won't be in the way one bit. Boo's house is large."

"That's generous of you, but I know as newlyweds, you want to share meals together without a third party around." She smiled at him. "And I've seen those heated looks you've given my best friend. You probably are still working on christening every room in this house, if I'm not mistaken.'

He roared with laughter. "Well, we're working on it. But I promise not to run around naked since you're staying with us."

She chuckled. "That's why I think I should find some little place to stay after a week or so. Just to get familiar with the area and see if I do want to remain here."

"My offer stills stands for you to stay here as long as you wish. If you do want to find a small place, however, you might want to take over where I was living before Willow and I got married. It's a bit of a dump, I'm afraid, but private, all the same."

"Where is it? Is it still available?"

"It's on the town square, above Sid's Diner," he told her.

"Carter drove me around the square yesterday on the way here. I remember the diner being on one of the corners."

"Most of those businesses have rooms above them. I'd say a good majority of the owners use them for storage and business purposes, but Sid of Sid's Diner lived above his place before he and Nancy got married years ago. Sid's gone now, and Nancy—who was a teacher—took over running the diner. It's got one large room that serves as the den. The couch is nothing to write home about. There is a small kitchenette, and then a bedroom and bath. I can vouch for the mattress. It's comfortable. I'd told Nancy she needed to replace the couch. If she did that, it would be a great place for you. Everything would be within walking distance in town, and you'd be able to meet a lot of people that way. I can tell you the Cove is a good place to live, Tenley, and we would be pleased if you decided to stay."

His words triggered an image of Carter Clark which she quickly shook off.

"I'll consider it, Dylan."

"Consider what?" Willow said, as she entered the kitchen dressed in running clothes, her long hair pulled back in a high ponytail.

"Dylan was telling me about the space over Sid's Diner," Tenley said.

"Why?" her friend asked, frowning.

"I may want to rent it."

"Double why?" Willow asked. "You just got here, Ten. Of course, you'll stay with us. You've seen how large the house is. If you think you'll be in the way, you won't."

"But what about all that newlywed sex? The loud moans of ecstasy. The—"

"Enough!" Willow cried, stopping Tenley from going further. "Your room is at the opposite end of the hall. And I'm not that loud," she protested.

"Or so she says," Dylan said dryly, handing his wife a cup of coffee.

"I know this wasn't the most convenient time for me to come for a visit," Tenley continued. "We planned this before your marriage and my annulment happened."

"I don't care," Willow said stubbornly. "You're staying. End of discussion."

"I do want to stay for a week or so." She paused. "I'm actually thinking of staying longer."

Her friend's eyes lit up. "You want to *move* here."

"Maybe."

Willow squealed, throwing her arms about Tenley. "This is fabulous news. For us to be on the same continent is great. The same time zone, amazing. But the same town? I love it!"

"I want to get to know the area," she said. "I'll stay here a week or so. Then I'd like to move to Dylan's old apartment on the square. I'd be close to so much stuff. Maybe get to know people. See if I wanted to stay in the area."

"Oh, you'll want to stay. The Cove is fabulous. I thought so as a kid. Now that I'm back? I appreciate it even more as an adult. And you'll meet some more friends tonight at Game Night."

"What's that?"

Willow was drinking her coffee, and she indicated for Dylan to answer.

"I used to get together with some friends once or twice a month on a Friday night. It really depends upon Carter's schedule because it rotates. But we eat dinner. Play some games. Have a few drinks. Talk. Laugh."

"I'm in," Tenley declared, not remembering the last time she had simple fun.

"We're supposed to host tonight," Willow said, already finished with her coffee and rinsing her mug before placing it in the dishwasher. "But Carter told me when he dropped you off yesterday that he wants to cook for us. He's coming over early. Around four, I think."

Her heart skipped a beat. "I knew he cooked. He mentioned making meals at the firehouse."

"He had to learn," Dylan said. "Emily was a horrible cook."

"Emily?" she asked, her voice growing suddenly tight as she recognized the *was*. Maybe Carter was divorced.

"Emily was Carter's wife," Willow told her. "She died about five years ago."

"A sudden aneurysm," Dylan added. "They'd been married about three years."

Sympathy filled her. "That's awful."

"It was," Dylan agreed. "I was still stationed overseas and hated I couldn't be here in person for Carter. He and Emily were high school sweethearts. They got married after she graduated from college"

Great. Carter had a longtime relationship with Emily and then married her. Losing her tragically would have affected him to his soul. Even if she were interested in beginning something with him, Tenley threw on the brakes. She didn't want to compete with the ghost of a dead wife. Already, she knew Carter was a really nice guy. He would be the kind who would still love his wife, dead or not. Better she knew now and friend-zoned him.

"That's very sad," she said. "It's good you're here now and that you're still friends." She paused a moment. "Who else comes to Game Night?

"Two cousins whom I adore already," Willow said. "Ainsley owns the local bakery."

"You mentioned that name before. Didn't you run into her in Paris?"

"I did. She was studying there and left to come back to the Cove. She opened Buttercup Bakery. And let me tell you, she rivals the best pastries I ate in France. Rylie owns an antique store on the square. She used to visit the Cove in the summer each year. You're going to love them, Ten."

"And Gage," Dylan reminded. "He moved here last summer. Left the military and is now a local personal trainer."

"Hmm. I've never had a trainer," she mused. "That might be something I can do for myself."

"Talk to Gage about it tonight," Willow suggested. "He's a little quiet but a lot of fun."

Dylan glanced at his watch. "We need to get going, Bear, or I won't have time to get in a run and make it to work."

"I didn't mean to keep you," Tenley said. "See, this is me getting in the way of your routine."

Willow embraced her. "You are not in the way. We'll just run a route that's a bit shorter this morning. Make yourself at home. We'll be back in an hour or so."

The couple waved goodbye and went out the back door. Tenley took a seat at the table again and sipped her coffee, mulling over everything she'd learned just now.

Resolve filled her. She would put her attraction to Carter Clark on the back burner. Way on the back burner. Like, not even on a simmer. Even though Dylan hadn't mentioned it, the handsome widower might even be dating someone. If not, she was too raw to even consider a relationship now. Nope, Carter— and Gage—would hopefully become friends. Good friends. She was here to finish her novel and see if building a life in Oregon appealed to her or not.

Tenley found the cereal and poured it into a bowl, adding milk to it. She also found the orange juice and poured herself a small glass. Pulling her phone from the flannel pajama bottoms she'd slept in, she scrolled through her personal e-mail and then hit several news sites. She found a report Sloane had filed and watched it, proud of the work her friend was doing.

Then she opened a document on her phone and began speaking, jotting down some new ideas she'd had for her trilogy. She'd transcribe her notes later. They involved a new character that wouldn't be introduced until the final book in the set.

By the time she finished, Willow and Dylan returned.

"I think I'll go for a walk now the sun is up," she told them. "I've read movement spurs creativity, and I've got a critical scene coming up. I want to walk and think about it."

Tenley went and changed into sweatpants and a long-sleeved T, pulling a light jacket over it. She left the house and took a path Willow suggested down to the beach near Boo's house. She found a fallen log and sat on it, watching the waves roll in and out. Unfortunately, she couldn't get into her book.

Because her thoughts kept returning to a brown-eyed fireman and his devastatingly sexy smile.

CHAPTER 8

Carter gathered his supplies and went to his spice rack, adding jars of oregano, basil, and parsley to one bag. He had never looked forward to Game Night more than tonight.

Because of Tenley Thompson's presence.

He had texted Willow and let her know he wanted to be the one who provided dinner this evening for the group. Usually, they did takeout from one of the local restaurants, especially Crust 'n Stuff, since pizza was a perennial favorite.

Tonight, though, Carter wanted to show off his cooking skills to Tenley. He had thought more about her in the past twenty-four hours than he had anyone or anything since Emily's death. He didn't feel he was being disloyal to his wife's memory. Of everyone he knew, Emily had been the most kindhearted and generous in spirit. She would have urged Carter to find a new love and begin a new life. He realized that he hadn't been ready before now to do so. That he'd needed those years without Emily to discover more about himself and truly get over her death. While he would always love his first wife, he believed he could find love again. Being a good husband to a second wife wouldn't mean he was disloyal to his first. If Emily had taught him anything, it was that love had no limits.

Becoming a father was also very important to him. Dylan had confided that he and Willow were eager to start their family but had decided to hold off for a year in order to let their second chance relationship grow and solidify. Carter would do the same whenever he found his special someone.

His gut told him Tenley Thompson was the one.

He had been the same in his sureness when it came to Emily. They had played in the sandbox together and grown up in the Cove, moving in the same circles. Then one day, it hit him—he was meant to be with Emily. He never looked at another woman after that. They had dated their final two years in high school and went off to community college together. After two years, he left with his associate degree and trained to become a fireman, while Emily went to the University of Oregon in Eugene and earned her teaching degree. He had told her if she met anyone while away and wanted to explore dating him, she should take that opportunity. Emily had been just as certain of Carter, though, as he was about her. They had known they would marry after her graduation. He was older now. Hopefully, a little wiser. But he had always been someone who trusted his gut. It told him to take the opportunity and explore a future with Tenley.

He might have to tread softly at first, however. Tenley had been quite open with him in telling him about her sham of a marriage. He knew she had been hurt deeply by the man who married her, and it would take her time to heal from such a terrible experience. He only hoped that Tenley would give him—them—a fighting chance. He would take his cues from her, but for now, he believed proximity was the key. He would take every opportunity and use every excuse to be around her as much as possible.

Starting today.

Carter moved his groceries to the truck and then returned to his kitchen for the bakeware and pans he would need. He already knew Boo had a huge pot to boil the pasta in and would use that, but he really liked the two nine-by-thirteen baking dishes he was taking, as well as his frying pans.

He made the short drive from the bungalow he and Emily had bought a year after their marriage and pulled from the highway into the long drive leading up to Boo's house. He supposed they would always call it Boo's.

Cutting the engine, he saw Tenley sitting on the porch as if she waited for him. Then he realized she was engrossed in her laptop and thought she probably was working on her novel. He was curious about it, just as he was curious regarding everything about her. He got out of the truck, and Shadow—who had been lying on the porch at her feet—trotted down to greet him.

Carter knelt and petted the dog. By the time he stood, Tenley was striding toward him with her long legs in a pair of jeans that were molded to her every curve. Usually, a tall girl such as Tenley was thinner, but she had amazing curves that he longed to explore.

"Can I help?" she asked brightly. "Willow said that you were making dinner for Game Night."

"You can help me bring in the groceries and if you have time, you can sit and keep me company while I work."

"You certainly brought a lot with you," she noted, as he began handing her cloth bags.

"I brought the food and a few pans and mixing bowls."

They gathered everything from his truck and brought it inside to the kitchen. Tenley excused herself, saying she needed to retrieve her laptop. She was gone about five minutes, and he figured she had closed out and saved her document and taken the laptop to her bedroom. He had unpacked everything in her absence and filled the large pasta pot with salted water, putting it on to boil.

"What are you making for us?" she asked.

"Tonight, we are having manicotti."

Her eyes lit up. "Yum. I love Italian. Of course, you're competing with my memories of New York Italian cuisine. Little Italy in Manhattan has some of the best food I've ever eaten. I lived in Brooklyn, and they also had some great little Italian mom-and-pop joints."

"Well, this is my spin on Italian. Usually, manicotti doesn't have meat in it, but I like a meat sauce over the stuffed shells. I hope you'll appreciate my interpretation of the dish."

He heated two frying pans, placing one pound of ground beef in each, and began assembling everything else he would need on the new, large island that was a result of the updates Pete's crew had done last month.

"This is my first time cooking here since Willow had the kitchen renovated. This island will come in handy."

"What did it look like before?" she asked.

Carter laughed. "Way different. I worked on both the kitchen and bathroom renos."

She frowned. "You told me you were a fireman. Are you a volunteer fireman instead? I'm confused."

"Thanks to the schedule fireman have, many of us work second jobs or even have our own businesses. I don't want to put the effort into what it would take to run a business—the marketing, keeping the books, dealing with taxes—but I am pretty handy. I work for a guy in town named Pete Pulaski, who's a contactor. He uses several guys from my station on his jobs."

"How often do you work for him?"

"It varies. When I first came to firefighting, we were running a twenty-four/forty-eight schedule, meaning twenty-four full hours on duty, followed by forty-eight full hours off. A couple of years ago, we moved to a model used by more firehouses throughout the country. It's a four-day, twelve-hour shift. Then I have four full days off. Today was my second day in that grouping. I have seniority, so I'm on the seven-to-seven day shift when I work."

"Why the change from one day working and two off to four and four? she asked, her curiosity evident.

He stirred the browning meat. "Studies showed being on twenty-four full hours was mentally and physically taxing for firefighters. Twelve-hour shifts of four days at a time had been tested other places and seemed to be the way to go. I think my dad would've approved."

"So these changes went into effect after he passed?"

"Yes. His number two, Arthur Raintree, became the new chief. Chief Raintree is the one who pushed for the switch in hours."

"You mentioned your mom yesterday. Willow did, too, when she was telling me about the scholarship Boo set up. That your mom was one of the members to serve on this first selection committee. Are you close to her?"

"We are extremely close." He chuckled. "Then again, Mom is close to most everyone in the Cove. She's just one of those people whom others enjoy confiding in."

"I can see that, if you're anything like her." She bit her lip and then said, "I probably disclosed more to you yesterday than I should have."

"I'll never repeat a word you shared with me, Tenley. I realize you're at a vulnerable time in your life, with everything you've been through recently. If you need an ear, though, I'm here. I know you made a trip to the Cove to visit Willow and will confide in her, but I'm open to whatever you have to say and hope you don't regret what you shared with me yesterday."

She studied him a long moment, those sky-blue eyes the window into her soul. "No regrets on my part," she assured him. "I've told you I may be interested in staying in Maple Cove. If I do, you'll be the first friend I made here."

"I like hearing that." He grinned at her. "As a friend, I'm going to put you to work now."

He gave her onions and bell peppers to chop. The water now boiled, and he added the manicotti shells to it. Carter placed paper towels on the counter to drain them and sprayed his two casserole dishes with a light coating of olive oil. While Tenley worked on chopping vegetables, Carter mixed up mozzarella and cottage cheese.

"Is that what you'll stuff the shells with?" Tenley asked.

"Yes. I always like to put a little sauce in the bottom of the pan, layer the shells in, and then pour the meat sauce atop them."

"I see you brought two pans. You must be making an awful lot of manicotti."

"Well, we do have three hungry men coming for dinner. Who knows? Your appetite might be as large as mine," he teased. "Any leftovers, I'll send home with Gage. Though now that I think about it, he may not want them. This dish probably has too much fat for him to eat off it more than once."

"Willow said Gage is a trainer. I suppose he eats clean most of the time."

"He does. Game Night is the exception. I may just let Willow and Dylan keep the leftovers."

"That doesn't seem fair. You're going to a lot of trouble preparing this meal for us."

"They're hosting, though. I don't mind."

"If there are leftovers, you should take them for yourself. That way, you wouldn't have to cook anymore during your final two days off. Are you working for Pete either Saturday or Sunday?'

"No. Things slowed down between Christmas and New Year's and are still slow at the beginning of the year. Pete did tell me he's starting to get a few calls. I guess some people look around and make some New Year's resolutions to update their homes, so I'm hoping construction work will start up again soon. In the meantime, I have two more days free."

He decided to nudge her a bit and added, "I'm probably going hiking tomorrow. You know what? You should come along and see some of the area."

"I haven't really done much hiking in the past, though I love to walk. Walking is something that de-stresses me," she told him. Smiling, she added, "I would like to go with you, however."

"It's a date," he said, and then noticed she winced at his use of the word *date*. Trying to smooth things over, he said, "It's nice to have plans with a new friend. I'm happy to show you the area."

She recovered quickly and smiled. "I appreciate it. As I mentioned, I don't want to tread on the intimacy of the newlyweds. If I can get out of the house for a few hours tomorrow, that would give them some privacy."

"Maybe we could even take Shadow with us," he suggested. "I love dogs."

"Do you have any pets?"

"No. but maybe it's time I thought about getting one."

"I've thought the very same thing," she said. "My... Theodore didn't like animals. Or children. I didn't find that out until after we were married." She paused. "I suppose I dodged a bullet by not accidentally becoming pregnant."

"Do you want children?" he asked softly.

She nodded. "I thought by now I would have at least one," she admitted. "I'm thirty."

"That's still plenty young enough to have kids," he assured her. Impulsively, he took her hand and squeezed it. "You're right. You did dodge a bullet by learning about your ex when you did and getting out of your non-existent marriage. You can find someone who is a better fit for you, Tenley. A man who'll appreciate you and give you the children you deserve." He squeezed her hand once more and then released it, turning back to stir the meat.

He drained the fat from the beef and then added some water and several spices. She stood next to him, watching his every move.

"I've never been much of a cook. Then again, I've never really tried. Watching what you're doing, though, I think I could make this recipe."

"I know you could. Take the tongs and go ahead and start removing the shells from the boiling water," he said. "Place them on the paper towels to drain."

He finished adding the canned tomatoes, onions, and bell peppers to both frying pans, stirring and allowing the mixture to simmer. He added a dash of sugar and a tiny bit of garlic after sampling it.

"Sugar. Hmm. Is that your secret ingredient?" Tenley teased.

"I have found a dash of it to add some interesting flavor to the sauce. I read about it on a cooking blog."

"You really are into this cooking thing, aren't you?"

"I really am," he admitted. "I picked up how to cook the basics when I first came to the firehouse. There are guys who like to cook and ones who like to clean. But food just took on a new life for me once I was the one preparing it. I've started following a few people online." He grinned sheepishly. "I even tape a few cooking shows. *The Pioneer Woman. Chopped.* They have some really clever tips. I enjoy making food, especially for others. I like the process. The end result."

"You should start your own food blog, Carter," Tenley said enthusiastically. "I know people would follow you. You're smart, good-looking, and articulate. Hey, you could vlog."

"What?"

"Vlog," she repeated. "It's a video blog. Or you could simply write your blogs, including recipes, and then insert a video into that."

"I know a little about computers, but I'm not that tech-savvy. Besides, I would need someone to film me. I can't ask anyone to give up that kind of time."

"Oh, I could easily help you with this. My last job was working for the Borough of Brooklyn. I helped design marketing campaigns and various graphics. It would be easy. I'd love to show you how."

"You're on," he told her. "How about hiking tomorrow morning and then a tech lesson tomorrow afternoon? And I will feed you as a reward if you'd like to stay for dinner," he added.

A slow smile spread across her face. "I would like that. Very much."

Carter taught Tenley how to stuff the manicotti shells with the cheese mixture, first whipping an egg and drizzling it over the cheese mixture to give it added moisture. He covered both pans with foil and put them in the preheated oven.

"Now all we do is wait for the others to arrive."

Tenley moved to the kitchen table and lifted a bottle of wine.

"Willow said this would be one of the bottles we would drink with dinner. That others would bring some, as well. Would you like to get a head start?" she asked, mischief dancing in her eyes.

Although he usually was a beer drinker, Carter decided it was time for that to change.

"Pour away," he told her.

CHAPTER 9

Tenley knew from Willow that everyone would be arriving between five-thirty and six. She found the corkscrew and opened the pinot noir as Carter located two wine glasses and placed them on the island.

She poured them both a generous amount while he filled the sink with hot water and dishwashing detergent. As they allowed the wine to breathe, she wiped down the counters, and he washed and rinsed the pots and pans he'd used, placing them on the drying board. Not many men cooked, and if they did, they rarely cleaned up.

She picked up a dish towel and began drying a mixing bowl. He took each piece she dried and placed it in one of the cloth bags he'd brought.

They finished up and both took a seat at the island on stools next to one another.

Carter held up his glass. "Here's to a great sous chef and new friend."

They clinked glasses and she said, "I didn't contribute much. Sous chef is a title I don't think I deserve."

"Stick with me long enough, and maybe you'll earn it," he teased.

She sipped the pinot noir. "Mmm. This is really good."

"It's from a local winery. They're all over Oregon. I'll take you to this one if you'd like to visit it. They have weekly wine tastings. Even classes on how to make wine and how to become a wine connoisseur. Most vineyards have places for you to picnic and several an event center to hold weddings and receptions and various parties."

He paused. "Maybe when your book comes out, we'll rent space and hold a big party in your honor. Mind if I ask what it's about? You mentioned YA but didn't really give me any details."

"Yes, it's YA. Young adult. It's got elements of fantasy woven through it. Although I think some adults might really like it, as well."

"Like *Lord of the Rings*?"

"More like Merlin and Morgan Le Fay. Are you familiar with Arthurian lore?"

He smiled broadly. "I was a nerd in school. Science and history were my two passions. The Middle Ages fascinated me the most. I'll tell you now that I've heard we're playing Trivial Pursuit tonight, and I'd make a great partner. I've got green and yellow covered."

"Well, I'm good at brown and pink," she countered, referring to the colors that represented literature and entertainment, while he'd mentioned science and history.

"We'd be unstoppable if we team up," he said. "Promise me you'll be my partner tonight."

"Sure," she agreed, her heart starting to pound loudly. Her mouth also went dry as his warm smiled washed over here. Tenley lifted her wine glass and sipped again, hoping that would help calm her sudden nerves.

But her awareness of him continued to grow. She caught a hint of his woodsy cologne. His knee brushed against hers. She watched his mouth as he talked and wondered what it would be like to kiss him. She was really out of practice at kissing. Theodore hadn't liked kissing. In fact, he hadn't really been into much foreplay. He always rushed sex, going for immediate satisfaction. For him.

Something told her Carter Clark wouldn't rush a thing. That he would enjoy taking his time with a woman.

"I'll be happy to be your partner," she added. "Sounds like we'll have a real chance at winning. What do we win?"

"The dessert of our choice at the next Game Night. Ainsley always bakes something fabulous. Last time, Gage won. He's a chocoholic, so whatever she brings tonight, he'll have asked for chocolate."

"What should we ask for?"

He laughed. "I like your confidence and attitude. You're assuming we'll win. That's a great mindset. As far as dessert goes, I like any kind of sweet. Cakes. Pastries. Cookies. Pies. Tell you what—I'll let you make the pick when we win."

Willow entered the kitchen. "Smells good, Carter. Italian?"

"It is," he told her.

"You made lasagna once. That was really good."

"This time it's manicotti. I hope you'll like it."

Willow laughed. "I like anything I don't have to cook. And you know Dylan will inhale anything in front of him."

"Can I pour you some wine?" Tenley asked. "Sorry we broke into the bottle before everyone got here."

The doorbell rang, and Willow said, "Yes to a glass. I'll get that."

She left the kitchen, and Tenley poured a glass of wine for her friend.

"I'll get two more glasses," Carter said. "Both Rylie and Ainsley will want wine over beer."

As he brought two more wine glasses to the island, Willow returned with two women who favored each other quite a bit. Both looked to be about five-seven, with beautiful periwinkle eyes. One had dark blond hair and was lean, while the other was brunette and curvy.

"I'm Ainsley," the blond said, setting down a Tupperware tub on the island. "The baker." Ainsley gave her a friendly hug.

"Ah, you're the one I'm supposed to tell which dessert I want for our next Game Night."

Ainsley burst out laughing. "Don't tell me. Carter has already talked you into being his partner and has promised you that your team will win."

"That he has," Tenley said, laughing.

"I'm Rylie," the brunette said, also giving her a quick hug as she placed a bowl of greens on the island. "It's so nice to meet you. Willow has mentioned both you and Sloane several times. It's great to meet you."

"I saw both your places of business on the square yesterday. Carter picked me up at the airport and drove me back to Maple Cove."

He handed the two newcomers glasses of wine. "Enjoy. And if you're going to stay, Tenley, you've got to start calling it the Cove. If we hear Maple Cove, we know it's an outsider."

"You might stay?" Rylie asked, her eyes lighting up. "Do tell."

The doorbell rang again. Carter said, "I'll get it, but my advice? Don't answer that question until Gage comes in, else you'll have to tell the story all over again."

He disappeared and a few moments later returned with a guy who definitely looked ex-military. He was very fit, tall and muscular, with hazel eyes and dirty-blond hair

"Gage Nelson," he said, offering a hand to Tenley, a twelve-pack tucked under his arm and what she figured was an eight-pack beneath his shirt. "Please to meet you."

"It's good to meet you, Gage. I hear you're trying to whip the citizens of the Cove into shape."

"One body at a time," he said, laughing. "And clients in the next couple of towns, too."

The kitchen door opened and Dylan came through it. "I see the gang's all here."

The timer dinged and Carter moved toward the oven, grabbing oven mitts. "Manicotti's ready but needs to sit a few minutes. I'll stick the bread in the oven to warm."

Tenley liked the organized chaos that occurred as plates were brought out, along with silverware and napkins. She and Ainsley were given the task of setting the dining room table.

"Willow couldn't wait for you to get here," Ainsley revealed. "She was someone my cousin and I looked up to when we were growing up. I was a couple of years behind Willow in school. Rylie came and spent summers with my family. We both wanted to be as cool as Willow was. It's been nice getting to know her now that we're adults."

"She was cool in college, too. Had that bohemian vibe. Didn't really care what anyone thought of her, which only made her seem cooler. I'm thrilled to be here visiting her and Dylan. They are so much in love."

"They are," agreed Ainsley. "They were in high school, too. I'm glad they've had this second chance since they both left the Cove and then returned."

"She told me about what happened to Dylan's family and how he joined the military. How he's now the town sheriff."

"Dylan commands respect. He did even as a teenager. Together they are terrific. I hope I'll be lucky in love someday and find a man who loves me as much as Dylan does Willow." Ainsley smiled wistfully.

Tenley already felt close to this woman and slipped an arm about her. "You'll find him, Ainsley. And he'll have been worth the wait."

They rejoined the others in the kitchen, which looked like a scene out of *The Big Chill.* Everyone was in motion, putting something on the island. Rylie tossed the arugula and pear salad she'd brought, plating it. Gage was sliding the plates down the island. Dylan was handing glasses to Willow, who filled them at the icemaker and passed them to Carter, who poured iced tea into each one. She and Ainsley took the glasses to the dining room as Gage brought in all six salads.

"That's some skill set you have," Tenley told him.

"A SEAL can do anything he puts his mind to," Gage joked, barely smiling.

She remembered Tenley had said Gage was fairly serious, but she thought being around this light-hearted group was good for him. Dylan and Willow brought in the drinks. Carter appeared with the twelve-pack and a second bottle of wine that had been uncorked.

Returning to the kitchen, Tenley checked on the bread and removed it from the oven, placing it next to the two dishes of manicotti.

"Olive oil," Carter declared. "I forgot it."

"I have some," Willow told him as she entered the kitchen, opening a cabinet and handing it over.

Quickly, Carter poured some of the oil onto seven small plates and sprinkled a dash of pepper onto each.

"Ladies, if you'll bring these small plates into the dining room, I think we're ready to serve in here."

They formed a line. Carter helped it run efficiently, doling out portions of the manicotti to everyone and placing a slice or two of bread on the plate before handing it over. Soon, they were all seated at the large pine dining table, laughing and telling stories on one another, helping Tenley catch up with what was going on in the Cove in general and with her dinner mates in particular.

"I suppose I should share a little of my story," she said, as the conversation wound down and the last bites on plates were being taken. "Willow and I—along with our third Musketeer, Sloane—roomed together at UCLA. We each went our separate ways. Sloane stayed in California as a reporter for a local station before jumping to an overseas position with a big network. Willow departed for Europe to study and paint. I wound up in New York, first at a publishing house and then later working for the Borough of Brooklyn."

She paused, taking a swallow of wine. "I married the wrong man for the wrong reasons and paid the price."

"You don't have to talk about this, Tenley," Carter

said, touching her arm.

"I don't want to wallow in your pity—but I do want you know where I'm coming from," she said, smiling at Carter. "My marriage was already on the rocks when I found out my husband wasn't my husband at all. He had married years ago when on a bachelor party trip to Vegas. His wife, a friend of his since childhood, approached me with that news. Long story short? I got an annulment. Sold the loft we were living in. Got the hell out of New York and came to visit Willow."

"She may stay," Willow said eagerly. "So, everybody remain on your best behavior until she's committed and can't leave."

The group around the table laughed.

"What are you planning to do, Tenley?" Gage asked. "Whether you stay in the Cove or not."

"I'm writing a trilogy. I've always wanted to be a writer. I thought this was my chance. The sale of the loft has given me some freedom and a nice pile of cash I hadn't expected. Obviously, with no true marriage there was no divorce, so no alimony. I quit my job in Brooklyn and am giving this writing thing a try. I definitely needed a change of pace and scenery. So far, I like what I've seen of this town."

"The Cove is very friendly," Rylie shared. "I didn't grow up here, but I visited it a lot. I'm glad I opened a business here. I do get a little of the tourist trade, but most of my sales come from true antiques shoppers. I also have some furniture I place on consignment and can even order a few new pieces for customers if I don't have anything that appeals to them. In fact, I just ordered a new sofa and wingback chair for Nancy Mayfield. She's going to replace that beat up one you suffered sitting on Dylan. She's hoping some new furniture will help rent out that apartment more quickly."

"Dylan told me about that place," she said. "I might be interested in leasing it for a few months while I decide if I want to stay."

"I want you to stay here with us," Willow complained.

"Dylan has promised me there'll be no naked running through the house while I'm staying," Tenley said. "But I don't know how long he can keep to that. That's why I need to line up somewhere else, Willow. I can't deprive your sex-starved husband."

Carter and Gage roared at that observation. Willow turned bright red.

"I hope you will stay, Tenley," Ainsley said. "Why don't we get Game Night started? Maybe you'll see how fun we are and never want to leave the Cove."

Everyone took their dishes to the kitchen. Willow insisted on loading the dishwasher. Tenley knew how particular her friend could be about things such as that, and she offered to refill or refresh drinks for everyone. Dylan and Gage went to set up the game, while Carter wrapped up the leftovers and placed them in the refrigerator

As everyone filed from the kitchen, she found herself lingering, waiting for him.

He closed the refrigerator door and smiled at her, causing her pulse to leap.

"Ready to trample the competition?" he asked, wrapping a friendly arm about her shoulders and leading her from the kitchen.

Tenley longed for more contact than his arm but said, "You've pretty much guaranteed me a win, Carter Clark. Let's go get it. And I want a Boston cream pie as our prize."

CHAPTER 10

Although Tenley was already stuffed, she eyed the plate of sliced brownie squares that Ainsley brought to the den. They had gathered around the coffee table, where the Trivial Pursuit gameboard had been set up. The two boxes of cards containing questions were on opposite sides, and she learned they would take turns reading the questions.

Gage claimed the first brownie and bit into it. "Delicious," he declared. "I say whoever wins tonight should demand Ainsley make these brownies next time." He grinned. "Or just throw the game and lose to me—because I'll ask for these babies every time."

Rylie shook a finger at Gage. "You hate Trivial Pursuit. No way would we let you win this." She looked to Tenley. "Gage says he's only good with the geography questions, which is pretty much the truth."

"I do know geography after my days hauling my ass all around the world for our country. As a Navy SEAL," Gage explained to Tenley, "I have literally been on every single continent. I think maybe I should find a partner and go on *The Amazing Race*. Now, that's one game I know I would dominate."

"With so many of us, we better partner up," Dylan suggested, "though we do have an uneven number tonight."

"I claim Tenley as my partner," Carter said quickly, giving her a warm glow inside.

Willow looked at him and then burst out laughing. "You knew we were playing Trivial Pursuit tonight, Carter Clark. We all know you're an expert at the science and history questions. You scoped out the situation and discovered Tenley would be the perfect balance to you." She looked at the others. "Tenley will wipe us up when it comes to the arts and literature and entertainment categories. She reads voraciously and knows a ton about pop culture."

"And rooming with Willow, I learned a lot about art," Tenley revealed. "So yes, I think Carter and I will be a formidable team. We're the ones to beat tonight."

Rylie said, "Nothing like throwing down the gauntlet. Gage, why don't we pair up? I know Dylan and Willow will do the same. That'll leave Ainsley the Brain to compete on her own."

Her cousin smiled. "I don't mind in the least. After all, I was the valedictorian of my high school graduating class. I know a little about a lot of things—and that can get you far in Trivial Pursuit."

"You should have some help, though, having to play solo," Dylan told her. "Maybe we'll give you three different times you can use one of us as a lifeline. Ask one of us a question to help you out since you're going it alone."

"I will take you up on those lifelines, Sheriff. Sounds fair to me."

Everyone claimed a brownie, while Gage started on his second one, saying, "Any brownies left over go home with me."

"I thought you were the clean eater," Tenley pointed out.

"Score!" declared Carter, high fiving her. "I told her you only ate what the rest of us do on Game Night. Surely you don't want to put all those ooey, gooey brownies into that hard-bodied temple of yours, do you?" Carter looked to the group. "We should do Gage a favor and make sure that there aren't any leftovers to tempt him."

They all burst out laughing, and Tenley was swept up in the camaraderie. She hadn't felt anything like this in a long time. If ever. She had always worked so hard, and these past few years being married to Theodore had kept her from simple social outings such as this. She had accompanied her ex to a handful of social occasions, mainly cocktail parties and fundraising dinners. She could not imagine Theodore and any of his friends or acquaintances sitting around munching brownies, sipping wine as they played a board game.

Yet this is exactly where she wanted to be. With these people. She glanced around the circle as playing pieces were being chosen and felt as if she had come home.

Despite how some of them had played down their knowledge in certain areas, the game proved quite competitive. She and Carter took an early lead, thanks to her claiming the slice of pie in both the brown and pink categories, where she excelled. Dylan and Willow were hot on their heels, while Ainsley took the lead on her own, using no lifelines to get there. Gage grumbled good-naturedly about partnering with Rylie, telling her he was going to trade her in for her cousin next time since they trailed everyone.

"Next time, *I'll* team with Ainsley," Rylie said, laughing. "Then we will totally rock this board."

Gage came through, earning two pie slices of his own in science and geography and soon the game was in a dead heat. Every team had completely filled their pies and it came down to a luck of the roll as to which team could land on the center first and answer a question of their choice. Dylan and Willow were first, Willow asking for an arts and literature question, hoping it was something from the arts. It wasn't, and neither Dylan nor Willow knew the answer of Robert Browning.

Carter glanced at Tenley. "You would've gotten that one."

"I would have," she agreed.

Their next roll, they actually hit the center and consulted one another on which category to pick.

"I think we should go with history," Carter said. "I know I'm good at it, and you've been able to answer several of those tonight. I think as a team, it's our strongest category."

"I agree with you," she said. Looking to Ainsley, she added, "This is for Boston cream pie."

Ainsley chuckled. "You two had already consulted on the winning dessert before we even started? That's pretty cocky."

"No," Carter said. "Just extremely confident." He looked to Gage, who was to read their question.

Gage cleared his throat. "What sport's hall of fame enshrined Abraham Lincoln for having a stellar record of just one loss?"

Tenley saw Carter frown in thought, but she immediately knew the answer. "Wrestling," she said.

"Wait!" Carter cried. "This is for the game. We need to talk about it."

"No, we don't. I'm right," she said, brimming with confidence.

"It wouldn't matter," Dylan said. "The question has already been answered. No do-overs."

Carter nodded. "I trust you." He looked to Gage, who's face had remained neutral during the discussion. Slowly the corners of his mouth turned up into a smile, and he announced, "Tenley is right. The correct answer is wrestling. Winner and champions—Tenley and Carter!"

The group applauded their win and congratulated her and Carter. Tenley felt such a part of these people in this moment. Carter threw an arm about her shoulders and kissed her cheek. The whiff of his cologne caused tingles to rush through her.

"Boston cream pie, baby," he told Ainsley. "I don't think I've ever seen one of those at the bakery."

"You wouldn't have," Ainsley teased. "Because your weakness is cannolis and cookies. You bypass everything and head straight to that part of the display case anytime you come in."

"Guilty as charged," Carter admitted. "But I am looking forward to that Boston cream pie. Come to think of it, I've had a donut filled with it. I know the pie will be great."

"It's almost nine," Willow noted.

Immediately, everyone stood and began cleaning up. It surprised Tenley because nine would be early with a New York crowd. Then she realized these people had a different lifestyle than what she came from. Since Ainsley owned a bakery, she must get up incredibly early to have items ready for the breakfast rush. She didn't know if Dylan worked weekends or not, but she knew he and Willow enjoyed a morning run together and might be up early to do that. Gage, being a personal trainer, probably had numerous clients both Saturday and Sundays and would need to get a jump on the day. And Rylie owned a shop on the square. Saturdays were probably one of her busiest days.

She helped to bring in dishes and glasses to the kitchen, and Willow placed those items in the dishwasher and started it.

Carter had taken out the last of the manicotti, ready to divide it up, but Willow told him to take it home with him.

"It was the best manicotti I've ever had," Tenley told him. "You've made a believer out of me. I'll want it with meat sauce in the future."

"If we're still going hiking tomorrow morning, we can go home and heat it up for lunch if you'd like."

"Oh, are you going hiking?" Rylie asked. She named a few of her favorite local trails and told Tenley to put them on her list and try them over the next few weeks.

"You named five or six. That's too many for me to remember," she protested.

"Let's exchange numbers. I'll text them to you," Rylie said, and they input each other's cell numbers. Ainsley got in on the action and also traded cell numbers with Tenley.

"You'll also have to come by my antique store," Rylie continued. "In fact, we need to plan a girls' night."

"I'd love that," Tenley said, having warmed to both Rylie and Ainsley.

Everyone took their leave except Carter, who lingered. He said, "I'm not sleepy. Are you?"

Sleep was the last thing on her mind as he looked

at her. She was more aware of him as a man than she ever had been Theodore.

"No, I think I'll stay up a while. Want to keep me company?"

"Sure."

By now, Dylan and Willow had returned from seeing their other guests out and excused themselves, going up the stairs, Shadow trailing them.

Tenley and Carter took a seat on the sofa, close, but not *too* close to one another.

"I want to hear about your book," he told her. "Other than *Lord of the Rings*, I have to admit I wasn't much of a reader. I don't think I read an entire book all the way through school. I would grab Spark Notes and then pump Dylan about plot and character before we would have a test over novels. I just couldn't get into things like *The Scarlet Letter* or *Moby Dick*."

"I hope what I'm writing will capture the attention of people who don't like to read. I'm creating a new world in my trilogy. World-building can become pretty complicated," she told him. "It's a way to invent new rules for a society and turn a reader's usual thinking upside down."

"I'm not quite sure what you mean."

"Are you a horror movie fan? Vampires?" she asked.

"Now you're talking! I don't think there's a vampire movie I haven't seen. From *Nosferatu* and Bela Lugosi's *Dracula* to the *Blade* trilogy and *30 Days of Night*. *Let the Right One In*. Even the *Twilight* series. I've seen them all."

"Vampires have a lot of rules. It's their world, and writers have continually reinvented that world. Can a vampire walk in the day or not? I watched *The Vampire*

Diaries—and those vampires had rings that allowed them to do that. Does garlic work against them? Or crosses? Can they see their reflection in a mirror or not? Those are the kinds of rules I'm talking about, and different writers of vampire tales have put their own spin on that. The writer introduces the reader to that world and its rules. That's what I'm doing in my fantasy."

"Tell me what it's about. You've only spoken in very broad terms before."

Tenley took about twenty minutes, walking Carter through a group of her three main characters, who each would be the lead protagonist in his or her own book in the trilogy. She explained the powers they had and a curse that was central to the world she had envisioned.

"This is the kind of thing I would read," he told her. "Even now, all I usually pick up is *Sports Illustrated*, but this is fascinating, Tenley. Tell me a little about the plot of each book," he encouraged. "You've talked character and world. I want to hear what happens to these people."

Over the next hour, she shared with him various events and how she had used Joseph Campbell's *Hero's Journey*—from to the call to adventure and magical mentor, to despair and finally rebirth.

"I want each book's protagonist to complete a good portion of his or her journey as an individual but still leave the final chapter of every book slightly open-ended so readers will continue with the series and see how it's resolved overall."

They began tossing ideas back and forth, and she was amazed at how creative Carter was and how quickly he understood her world.

She yawned suddenly and apologized. "I think New York time is kicking in for me," she apologized.

"I should've thought about that. I'm sorry for keeping you up so late, but everything you shared is just so exciting. Why don't we leave a little later tomorrow morning? Say nine? That'll give you enough time for shut-eye, and you can grab some breakfast. If you want, I'll bring some snacks and waters."

"It sounds like a lot of fun," she said. "Thank you for offering to take me on my first Oregon hike."

They moved from the sofa, and he claimed his manicotti from the refrigerator, having put all the pots and pans he brought with him in his truck earlier. She unlocked the front door and opened it, feeling the cool night air.

She looked at Carter and saw something in his eyes. She thought he might kiss her as he leaned closer to her and realized she wanted that to happen, which surprised her. Then he brushed his lips against her cheek instead. Disappointment flooded her.

"Thanks for partnering with me tonight, Tenley. I'll see you tomorrow morning."

He stepped onto the porch and headed down the stairs and to his truck and waved goodbye. She returned the wave and closed the door, leaning against it a moment.

She had so little experience with men and didn't know if she had read his signals right. Or had she sent signals of her own that kept him from kissing her?

Tenley decided that tomorrow if Carter did not make a move, then she would. She wanted to kiss him. Badly.

And she planned to do so.

CHAPTER 11

Although Tenley had found it hard to fall asleep, when she awoke, she felt refreshed. Her first thought was of Carter Clark. Her mind advised her to friend-zone the handsome fireman.

Her heart told her otherwise.

She rose and found a sweater and jeans for the hike, hoping Willow would have some kind of footwear she could borrow because she didn't think her loafers or sneakers would be appropriate, and they were the only shoes she had brought with her.

Tenley showered and pulled her long hair back into a low ponytail, fastening it with a clip. She decided to eat a light breakfast and headed downstairs to the kitchen. The house seemed quiet and she figured Willow and Dylan were out for a run. She put a hazelnut pod into the Keurig and toasted a slice of bread while the coffee brewed.

She had just sat at the table when the door opened and her hosts entered the kitchen.

"Morning," Dylan greeted as he went to the refrigerator and retrieved bottles of water. Handing one to

Willow, he downed the other one within seconds. He kissed his wife. "I'm heading up to the shower, Bear."

Dylan exited the kitchen and Willow took a seat at the table, drinking her water at a much slower pace than her husband had. Then she frowned, sniffing the air.

"I thought you were going hiking this morning with Carter."

"I am."

Willow pursed her lips as she studied Tenley and then said, "Most people shower after a hike. Not before one."

Defensively, she said, "I hadn't showered since yesterday morning. I felt like it."

"You added perfume," Willow pointed out. "Am I sensing something between you and Carter? Because if I am, I'll do whatever I can to encourage it."

"No, we're just friends," Tenley insisted.

Willow gave her one of those Willow looks. "He stayed a long time last night. I heard when his truck left."

"We were talking," she insisted. "He's interesting. It's been a long time since I had someone to talk to like that. I was telling him about my book. He actually had some pretty cool ideas. We bounced things back and forth between us."

"Have you told him about Theodore? I know you mentioned to the group last night about your annulment."

"Yes. We actually talked about it on our way from the airport." She smiled ruefully. "I probably shared with him more than I should have about my situation."

"You wouldn't have done that if you didn't trust Carter." Willow took Tenley's hand. "Carter is definitely one of the best guys I've ever known. Absolutely nothing like the asshole you sort of married. I know you'll say it's too soon to even think about getting involved with another man. But speaking as a woman who just dived in to a relationship without thinking about the consequences, I can highly recommend Maple Cove men." She grinned.

Willow paused. "You know I was coming off a horrendous breakup with Jean-Luc after I arrived in the Cove. Actually, I was coming off a decade of bad choices in men. But I didn't let that stop me, Ten. When it's right, it's right. If you have feelings for Carter, explore them. If they don't pan out, he will be a loyal friend to you. I guarantee it."

"I'll admit that I am confused," she said. "He does seem like a terrific guy, but I don't know if I can trust my instincts anymore. I leaped without looking into marriage with Theodore when I should have taken my time to get to know him—and us as a couple—better. I stayed with him far longer than my gut told me to. In fact, I was making plans to leave him and file for divorce when Cecilia dropped into my life and things went upside down."

"You realize the annulment and her political influence to get you one so quickly was a gift," Willow pointed out. "Because of it, you have a blank slate as far as marriage goes."

"That may be the case legally, Willow, but I did go through a ceremony with Theodore Fielding. I did live with him for four years. That's hard to erase in my head."

"Well, I can guarantee you that Carter Clark is no bigamist. He only had one serious girlfriend, and he ended up marrying her. I would say trust your gut and see where things go with Carter."

"Do you think he's still hung up on his wife?"

Willow considered the question before answering. "I think losing Emily in such a quick manner scarred him emotionally. Recently, though, Carter talked to both Dylan and me about putting himself back out there once more. I think he needed time to heal from the experience, but now he's ready to give love another try. I can't think of two people who would be better for each other." She squeezed Tenley's hand and released it. "Besides, I told Dylan before any of this annulment stuff came up that you and Carter would be good together."

"What?"

Her friend nodded. "It's true. We talked about how Carter wanted to start dating again, and I told Dylan it was too bad that you were married because I thought you and Carter would click." She smiled. "And now you aren't married and both of you are here in the Cove. Let's just let things unfold, Ten. No need to rush. Just explore a friendship first and see if anything more follows."

"I do think it's thoughtful of him to take me hiking today. I'll also have lunch at his place afterward. Then I should be home."

"I'm not your mom. You don't have to report in to me. If you want to spend the enter day with Carter, do so. I'll be getting together with the members of the scholarship committee. We're going to do a prize patrol run to our winner's house."

Briefly, Willow told Tenley about the recipient of the scholarship in Boo's name and how the student was a sculptor, as Boo had been.

"On his application, he said he wanted to go to either UCLA or Rhode Island School of Design because of their sculpting programs. He comes from pretty modest means, so this scholarship can help make his dream a reality."

Willow rose and added, "I think I'm going to hit the shower myself."

Tenley took her dishes to the sink, rinsing them and placing them inside the dishwasher. She asked, "Do you have any kind of hiking boots I might borrow?"

"I do. Let me get them for you. I'll bring them to your room."

Once Tenley tried on the boots, she thanked Willow for the loan. "It's nice that we still wear the same shoe size. I suppose my rather small collection of shoes has more than doubled as long as I'm staying here. It's too bad we don't wear the same size in clothes."

Willow chuckled. "I'm still a tall drink of water, while you have those nice curves to your frame."

"I'm going to need to do some clothes shopping. I got rid of just about everything Theodore had convinced me to buy. If I stay in Oregon, I know it will be a much more casual lifestyle."

"There's no *if* to you staying, Tenley Thompson. The Cove is for you. I know it. You already fit in so well with the friends I've made since I've returned. Promise me you'll stay. Now that we're back together, I can't imagine ever being apart again."

"I'm leaning heavily toward remaining here," she told her friend.

"What we need to do now is get Sloane to move here," Willow declared, and they both laughed, knowing their friend enjoyed being a citizen of the world.

Tenley looked at the clock and saw it was almost nine. She slipped into the sleeveless down vest Willow had let her borrow and went to sit on the porch swing to wait for Carter. She didn't know what would happen between them today—or in the future.

But she was ready to find out.

~

CARTER REACHED for his phone to shoot Tenley a text and let her know he was on his way. Then he realized he didn't even have her cell number. He went to his truck, placing his backpack inside and then climbing behind the wheel. It felt good to be on his way to see a woman. And not just any woman.

Tenley.

He wondered if he was attracted to her because she was Emily's exact opposite. His wife had laughing eyes. Tenley's eyes were sad. Carter wanted to be the one who put the sparkle back in them.

He had enjoyed their conversation last night immensely. They had fun brainstorming ideas, tossing them back and forth as they discussed her fantasy trilogy. He wondered if she might let him read what she had already written and decided he would have to play that by ear.

He pulled from the highway into Boo's long drive and even from the distance spotted Tenley sitting on the porch waiting for him. She rose from the swing as he pulled his truck to a stop and cut the engine. Climbing from the vehicle, he went to meet her, his heart beating erratically.

"Good morning," he called.

She gave him a smile. "Good morning. I borrowed boots and a vest from Willow. Is there anything else I might need?"

"I brought a backpack with water and some snacks

in case we get hungry. Don't panic—but I also have bear spray. It's just a precaution. I haven't seen a bear in the woods since I was a teenager. I still like to be prepared, though."

"I'll hope the bears stay hidden. Aren't they supposed to be hibernating this time of year? After all, it is January."

He laughed. "That'll be the story we stick to. You ready to go?"

She nodded and he turned and went to the passenger side of his truck, opening the door and closing it after she got in.

When he slid behind the wheel, she said, "Rylie texted me a list of some her favorite hiking trails in the area." Tenley pulled up the texts and handed him her phone.

Cater skimmed the list and said, "We were going to hit the second one on here, but it's a great overall list. You'll need to hike each of these trails. Or as many as you can while you're here visiting. As long as I have your phone, I'm going to input my number. I wanted to text you this morning and give you a heads-up that I was on my way, but I realized I didn't have your number."

Quickly he scrolled to her address book and added himself to it.

He lifted his phone from the cupholder where it rested and said, "Put your number in my phone, as well."

She did so and then returned it to where it had sat.

He drove about fifteen minutes and then parked. She climbed from the truck before he could come around and help her out.

"The first thing we need to do is a little stretching,"

he told her. "I like to wake my muscles up before I begin a hike."

He led her through a series of stretches and then slipped the backpack over his shoulders. "Let's go this way," he suggested, knowing that the trail heading off to the right wasn't quite as challenging as the trail on the left. Since she had never hiked, he wanted to take it easy on her to begin with.

She surprised him, though, because she easily kept up with the pace he set, even after he increased it.

"You're in terrific shape," he observed.

"That's because I walked everywhere in New York. Yes, I took the subway when I had dozens of blocks to go, but a majority of the time, I walked. Several miles a day. To work. To a grocer's. To grab some take-out."

"Where did you live? I've never been to New York."

He listened as she told him about living first in Manhattan and working at the publishing house and then moving to Brooklyn and going to work for its borough.

"What did you do at both places?" he asked.

As they hiked, she shared some of the main tasks she was responsible for at each place.

"I feel like I'm talking your ear off. Tell me about being a fireman. You already said you earned your associate degree. What was the physical training like? What's a typical day like for you?"

"First, I had to be interviewed. Then pass a drug test and background check before I could report for the physical training. The topography varies across Oregon, thanks to the coastline, the vast forests, and the high desert that heads to the east and the mountains which dot the state. Different areas come with their own risks, be it wildfires, industrial fires, chemical spills, or major accidents. And that's in addition to learning how to fight fires in homes and businesses. A wildfire raging out of control across hundreds of acres has a different attack strategy than a fire burning in a two-story home."

Tenley grew thoughtful. "I guess I've never considered the various kinds of fires that have to be fought."

"I took basic coursework at the community college I attended, in addition to my other courses. It qualified me to be a volunteer firefighter in the state. Then I took it a step further with my Level 2 training. I've taken a leave of absence twice for short periods so I could earn certifications in fighting fires that burn with hazardous materials and Wildland operations."

He paused, not wanting to go into his reasoning, but not wanting to keep anything from her. "I also trained as an EMT. I actually go on a lot more calls in that capacity than I do as a firefighter. I perform CPR and use an AED. Do pharmacological interventions. I keep busier nowadays because of that specialty training. Life is never boring around the station."

Carter didn't mind Tenley knowing he was also an EMT. He just wasn't ready to talk about how Emily's death had driven him to earn the certification.

"Anyway, by the time I was hired at the Salty Point Firehouse—which is the next town over from the Cove and much larger—my dad was already the station chief there. I was so glad I was able to work with him for a few years and make him proud of me."

They reached a small clearing that overlooked the Pacific.

"Want to stop and soak up nature?" he asked her, wanting to shift gears and stop talking so much about himself.

"I'd like that."

They sat and he provided each of them with water.

Tenley passed on the granola bars he'd brought, but Carter unwrapped two and wolfed them down.

"What was it like when you finally started working under your dad?"

"I was following family tradition. My grandfather was the first fireman in the family, and he became chief at Salty Point. Dad followed in his footsteps. It was always something I knew I wanted to do from the time I was four or five. As far as having Dad as my boss, he was fair but firm. A stickler for the rules. He ran a tight ship, but it was still nice to be a part of such a group of men with him. Men who serve their community and sometimes sacrifice their lives for it."

"Do you have ambitions to follow in his footsteps and serve as chief yourself?"

"I do—and I don't. A part of me thinks it would be awesome to continue the family tradition, but I'm itching to try some new things. I've scratched that itch so far by working for Pete Pulaski's construction outfit. I've learned how to put in flooring. The best way to paint the inside and outside of a house. How to install kitchen appliances. Tile in the bathroom. Replace a toilet. I've thought about possibly getting my electrician's license. I don't think I want to own my own business, though, and I sure wouldn't want to compete directly with Pete because he's been good to me."

"You just need more," she said softly. "Perhaps you could do that through your cooking. Remember, I mentioned vlogging to you?"

"I don't know if I'm good enough to do something like that."

"You enjoy cooking, don't you?" she pushed. "You take recipes and toy with them, making them your own."

"Yeah. I do. But being on camera? And writing about it? I'm not too sure about that."

"Let's tape a practice segment today," Tenley suggested. "Just to give you an idea what I'm talking about. I can film you with my cell phone's camera. You don't have to be perfect. You just have to be you."

The thought of writing about cooking, and actually filming himself as he did so, intrigued him.

Carter rose and stuck out his hand. Tenley took it and he pulled her to her feet.

"I'm game if you are," he told her, keeping her warm hand in his.

Her large eyes studied him intently. "Are you game for *this*?"

Tenley pressed her lips to his.

Immediately, fire ignited within him. Carter pulled her into his arms, thinking he might never let this woman go.

CHAPTER 12

Tenley hoped she had not made a mistake by being the one to initiate a kiss between her and Carter. Part of her felt it was too soon to explore something romantic between them, but her sudden, growing feelings for this man left her feeling bold.

She did worry about the kiss itself because of her lack of experience in kissing. She had dated so infrequently before Theodore, and then once they married, kissing went on the back burner. She hoped her inexperience wouldn't show.

Carter's arms went about her, drawing her nearer to him. He radiated a comforting warmth that enveloped her as he returned her kiss without hesitation. She liked that he didn't dive right in but was taking his time, tenderly brushing his lips against hers. The scent of his cologne, mingled with the pine trees around them, stirred a deep yearning within her. She felt prized. Appreciated. Something she had never experienced with Theodore. He slowly teased her mouth open and eased his tongue inside, leisurely exploring her.

He tasted slightly of the honey granola bars he had

eaten, causing her to smile. One hand moved slowly up her back to cradle her nape, and he deepened the kiss. Tenley felt dizzy. Desire washed over her, something she was unfamiliar with, but instinctively recognized.

Carter had taken control of their kiss, but she wanted to be a more active participant, and her tongue began warring with his. Her body flushed with heat, tingles rippling through her limbs, as the kiss continued. She had never kissed anyone for this long before. She wanted it to go on forever. She clutched his shoulders to steady herself, her nails digging into them as they both fought for control now. The kiss was passionate. Thrilling. All-consuming.

Then Carter gentled it, his tongue easing from her mouth, his lips soft and yet firm against hers once again, brushing with a deliberate slowness that stoked the fire within her.

Finally, he broke the kiss, his eyes searching her face.

"That... was a kiss," he declared, wonder in his tone. "I haven't kissed a woman in five years." He smiled gently at her. "But it was well worth the wait, Tenley Thompson. Because I shared it with you."

Tears sprang to her eyes, and she saw the frown of concern on his face.

"Nothing's wrong," she assured him through watery eyes. "It's been a long time since I kissed someone myself."

He released her but took her hand and laced their fingers together. "I think we need to talk a little."

They took a seat again, and Tenley drew strength from him as she viewed their joined hands. She suspected he wanted to tell her about his marriage.

"I need to tell you that I was married before," he

began. "Emily and I grew up together in the Cove and dated in high school and beyond. Once she earned her teaching degree, we got married. She is the only other woman I ever kissed—and the only woman I ever made love to."

With his free hand, Carter cupped her cheek, his thumb stroking it. "But I have to say how much I enjoyed our kiss, Tenley. I know you've had a rough go of things recently, but if—and when—you're ready, I would like to make love to you."

She thought what a gentleman Carter Clark was, telling her of his past and letting her know that they might have a future together. Oh, Tenley didn't want to think beyond making love with him once, but she thought Carter was a man who, once he made a physical commitment, an emotional one would follow.

It should frighten her, but it comforted her instead. His words made her feel respected. Desired. Appreciated.

"I only had a handful of dates until I married Theodore," she explained. "I was always working so much, putting myself through school and then trying to get ahead at my publishing house. Theodore was the first man I had sex with."

She deliberately used that term instead of making love because she realized in her heart that was all it had been. No emotional investment on either of their parts.

"He's Mr. A. Don't call him by his name," Carter reminded her.

She smiled. "Mr. A was more interested in his satisfaction and pretty much skipped kissing. I figured it was because I wasn't very good at it."

Carter leaned over and kissed her softly. "I think you are spectacular at kissing. Maybe you weren't kissing the right man. Mr. A had a diamond and didn't even know your value."

He leaned in again for a lingering kiss, one Tenley felt down to her curling toes.

When he broke it, he said, "Just checking. Yes, you do know how to kiss."

Tenley burst out laughing, so comfortable and at ease with this handsome, giving man.

She gazed into his chocolate-brown eyes and softly said, "I would like to hope it's a *when* and not a question of *if* we make love. I usually don't jump into anything so rashly. I'm more of a realist than a dreamer, although I do dream of one day supporting myself as a writer. But I do want to make love with you, Carter. Whether it's today or next week or a month from now, we'll just have to see."

He smiled at her, bringing a rush of emotions in her. "I'll accept that answer and look forward to that time."

Carter brushed his lips against hers and then said, "I think it's important that you initiate that, Tenley. I know how chaotic your life has been and how emotionally raw you must be. When you're ready, tell me."

"I hope I don't sound too forward when I say this, but I believe that I need you to help me heal. I can't promise you what will come from this, Carter, but I'd like to start the healing process soon."

"It's hard to think on an empty stomach," he said lightly, pulling them to their feet. "I suggest we go back to my place and attack the leftover manicotti and then take things from there."

"Deal."

They turned to hike back to his truck, this time walking side-by-side and hand-in-hand. A calm descended over Tenley. She was an adult. Thirty years old. And for the first time in her life, she was experiencing feelings she never knew existed. She didn't know what would come when she and Carter made love. If it would be a one-time thing or beyond. She did not want to lose him as a friend, however, and when they reached the parking lot, she decided she need to tell him that.

"Carter, I know when we make love we are making a commitment to each other. Whether it's a short-term one or something longer, I don't think either of us can say at this point. I don't want to lose your friendship, though. It already means a great deal to me."

He framed her face with his large hands. "You won't lose it, Tenley. You won't lose me. We're both at a point in our lives where we need to move on. I needed several years on my own to find myself. To see who I was without Emily by my side. I'm comfortable now as the person I am. I want to take this step with you and see where it goes. Do I hope we'll be in it for the long haul? I'd like to think so. But that's a decision we'll need to make together. Regardless of what that decision is, I need your friendship. I value it, new as it is."

"Thank you for understanding, Carter. I don't think a man has ever listened to me. In fact, I think only Willow and Sloane have truly known me up to this point, but I feel I can lay my soul bare to you and not worry."

He lowered his lips to hers in a soft kiss filled with promise.

They drove to his house, a cute bungalow painted in navy and cream.

Carter led her inside and pointed out where the restroom was, telling her to take her time in freshening up. Tenley did so, studying her reflection in the mirror, trying to see if she looked differently from when she had left to go on their hike, which she believed had changed her life.

She joined him in the kitchen, where she heard the microwave going. Carter was drying his hands and smiled as she entered. He pulled out plates and silverware, setting the nearby café table for two, and then asked, "What would you like to drink?"

"Let's see what you have," she told him, opening his refrigerator and peering inside.

"That's iced tea in the pitcher," he told her. "There's also bottles of beer and water."

"Iced tea will hit the spot with me," she said, shedding the down vest and slipping it around the back of a chair.

They polished off the remainder of the manicotti, both hungry after their morning of exertion.

"This is even more delicious than last night," she told him.

"I think it's like a stew or soup. Better the second day after the flavors have had time to sit a bit."

"What are some of your favorite dishes to make?"

"I don't really have any favorites. I just enjoy cooking. The guys at the firehouse, though, like any casserole I make. I do several Mexico and Italian ones. I've gotten into soups lately, the hearty kind that can be a meal in themselves, along with a salad and some crusty bread. For the most part at the station house, I do fried chicken, meatloaf, spaghetti. Things like that."

"What do you have on hand right now? she asked. "I told you we were going to test an episode of your vlog this afternoon."

He thought a moment. "I do have the makings for chicken and mashed potatoes. Would that do? Of course, the chicken is frozen now and would have to thaw."

She reached across and took his hand. "I can think of a few things we can do while we wait for it to thaw."

His gaze met hers. "Are you sure you're ready to go here, Tenley? After all, we haven't known each other very long."

"I feel as if I have always known you, Carter," she said. "You have an honesty and sincerity about you that makes you an open book. Yes, I do worry some that it may be too soon, but I also believe we have forged a powerful connection between us. I'm eager to explore that connection, if you are."

"I know this isn't the time to bring it up, but I need to tell you that Emily died a very quick, unexpected death. She had an aneurysm that burst in her head and took her from me in a flash. One minute, we were laughing— and the next, she was gone. So I know better than most people how quickly things can change. How important it is to truly seize a moment and make the most of it."

He gazed deeply into her soul. "I know this, Tenley. I want to make love with you. I want to connect with you on the deepest level possible. We can figure out the rest afterward."

They stood together and he slipped his arms about her waist, pulling her close, kissing her. Then he led her to his bedroom. She saw the neatly-made bed and smiled, thinking it was so *him*. Going to one side of it, she drew back the comforter as he did the same on the other side. He came toward her, clasping her hand and leading her to a chair in the corner.

A slow grin spread across his face. "This may take a while," he told her. "I want to savor every moment with you."

Carter sat in the chair, pulling her into his lap. Tenley snuggled close and placed her palm against his face, thinking it important that she kiss him now, showing him she was committed to what they were doing.

The kiss simmered between them, heating to a sizzle. Her body felt on fire, his every touch a flame stoking her. If kissing him had her this turned on, what would the sex be like?

She was ready to find out.

Her fingers slid to the top button on his shirt, easing it through the buttonhole. She moved to the second one and did the same. The backs of her fingers brushed against his heated chest.

Carter broke their kiss. "Don't jump the gun," he told her. "We've got all afternoon. And night. I want to do this right, Tenley. For you. For us."

His words moved her. She believed he did have their best interests at heart. This budding relationship, so fragile and brand new, and he wanted them to take their time.

"All right," she said softly. "I'll follow your lead."

He kissed her again, harder than before. Her nipples tightened into hard buds.

He broke the kiss. "I'm not saying you can't act and only should react." He smoothed her hair. "But I gather Mr. A didn't see to your needs. He was all about himself. I want to do for you. Show you how attracted I am to you. Make you come so many times you won't know what hit you." He paused, kissing her swiftly. "Just let me love you, Tenley."

Her throat thickened with such emotion that she could only nod. This was a man who wanted to please her. Take her on a journey with him.

And Tenley was ready to keep step with him.

He kissed her again for a long time. At some point, he slipped the clip from her hair and ran his fingers through her long waves. His lips moved to her cheeks, his breath warm against them. To her temples. Her ears. His teeth tugged on her earlobe, causing a shot of desire to rush through her like lightning. He pressed soft kisses against her brow. Along her hairline. His lips reached her neck, licking the point where her pulse beat wildly out of control. He nipped at it, creating delicious shivers through her.

His hand began massaging her breast as he kissed her, and the nipple hardened with need. Carter unbuttoned the shirt she wore, parting it, his lips brushing her collarbone, scalding her.

"This needs to go," he murmured against her skin, easing the shirt from her and then her bra.

He studied her, bare to the waist now, heat in his eyes. She grew embarrassed at his intense scrutiny.

"Don't be self-conscious," he told her. "You are beautiful."

His strong fingers kneaded her breasts, making them grow heavy. His thumbs circled her nipples, so close and yet not touching them, and she moaned at the touch. Then he dragged a nail across each at the same time. Her breath hitched and a whimper escaped her lips.

"I need a taste of you," he told her, his mouth closing on one breast.

Carter devoured her, a man famished. Her core throbbed almost painfully as she clutched him, her fingers tangling in his dark brown waves, holding him closer to her. Yes, her ex had touched her breasts before. Perfunctorily. Carter's touches were filled with need and a desire to please her. He continued to suck hard, and Tenley gasped.

He moved to her other breast, treating it as reverently as the first. Molten heat ran through her veins. Her breathing grew shallow and rapid, her heart beating even faster. She couldn't wait any longer.

"I want to touch you," she got out. "Feel your skin against mine."

As he kissed her, she undid his buttons and pulled his shirt from his shoulders. He shrugged from it, and she tossed it aside, admiring her new view. His chest was broad, a light dusting of dark hair on it, the ridges of his six-pack incredibly defined. Tenley buried her face in his neck, catching the tang of his cologne and tasting the salt of his skin. She trailed her lips along his neck to his chest, her fingers dancing over his nipples.

"I want to suck them," she said, speaking so boldly that she didn't even recognize it was her.

Her tongue swirled about his nipple, and she heard the deep groan. His arms went about her, and she continued licking his skin, sweeping her tongue against his nipple and then grazing it with her teeth. That got a rise from him and he stood, taking her with him. She wrapped her legs about his waist as he carried her to the bed and placed her gently upon it, stripping her of her hiking boots and socks. Moving to her waist, he removed her jeans, slowly pulling them over her hips and down her legs until he tossed them aside.

Carter made quick work of what he wore, ridding himself of everything until he stood before her.

He was magnificent.

She could now see just how muscular his chest was. How flat his belly was. His legs looked like tree trunks, hard and large. His cock stood at full attention, drawing her eye, making her realize just how small Theodore's had been.

A giggle escaped at that thought. She tried to stifle it and failed miserably.

Carter joined her on the bed, hovering over her. "I hope I don't look that funny to you."

"No, you are amazing," she assured him. "I was thinking how Mr. A compared to you. He was a boy. You're a man, Carter. All man."

And all mine. For now.

He bent, his teeth snagging the top of her panties, slowly dragging them down. Tenley had never been more turned on in her life as he removed them, dropping them next to the bed. She swallowed hard, preparing herself for him to enter her.

But he didn't. Instead, he began kissing her again. Everywhere. Carter took his time. Touching. Kissing. Exploring. Her body trembled in need by the time he was finished.

Leaning over, he opened the drawer to the nightstand. "I hope these haven't expired," he muttered.

She saw he had pulled out a condom and said, "We don't need it. I have an IUD. I had actually forgotten I did. It's been that long since I've had sex."

He tossed the condom back into the drawer and closed it. His mouth covered hers in long, drugging kisses as his fingers stroked the seam of her sex. She gasped as he slid a finger inside her, stroking her deeply. He added a second and pressed his thumb against her, rubbing in a circular motion. Tenley felt a deep pressure began to build as Carter's tongue and fingers imitated one another.

Suddenly, she cried out, her body arching, warm sunshine spreading through her. Her hips rose as waves of the most unbelievable pleasure rippled through her, leaving her limp and spent.

"That was an orgasm," she managed to get out. "My first."

"What?"

"It had to be," she said, suddenly babbling. "I've never had one. I've never felt like that. I was flying high and I just exploded and the waves rocked through me and I—"

Carter silenced her, his mouth on hers, hard and insistent. Tenley gave over to the kiss, her arms going about him, wanting to get as close to him as she could.

Then she felt his penis pressing against her, entering her quickly, filling her to the brim.

"Oh!"

He paused. "Are you okay?"

She grinned up at him. "I'm better than okay. I'm fantastic."

"Let's see if we can improve on that."

He rocked against her.

"Definitely, an improvement," she said. "And I didn't think it could get better."

"Oh, it can. It will. Hold on, sweetheart."

Carter withdrew and pushed into her again. Soon, they danced an intricate dance meant only for them. She rose and met his every thrust as he kissed her into oblivion. The pressure she'd felt before built again and erupted in sweet ecstasy as Carter shouted something and buried his face against her neck.

He collapsed atop her, driving her into the mattress, and she relished the feel of being surrounded by this very masculine blanket. Then he rolled to his side. They faced one another, him still buried deeply within her.

He brushed her hair back from her face and gave

her the sweetest of kisses. "I thought your kissing was spectacular. But your lovemaking skills are through the roof, Tenley."

She felt herself flush with embarrassment.

"No, honey. Don't be self-conscious. You were amazing." He smiled. "I feel like Leo in *Titanic*—I want to shout that I'm the king of the world."

"Please tell me that's the truth. That you aren't trying to build up my fragile ego."

Carter shook his head. "You were incredible. *We* were incredible together." He kissed her. "I don't think we should ever leave this bed."

She snuggled close to him, burrowing so that her cheek nestled against his chest and his heart beat beneath it, steady and strong.

"I'll stay as long as you'll let me, Carter," she told him, hoping he might wish her to be with him forever.

CHAPTER 13

Carter held Tenley in his arms, listening to her even breathing. She had fallen asleep. He took it as a compliment, that she would feel so safe with him that she could drop off so easily.

His life had changed today. In *Star Wars*-speak?

There had been a disturbance in the force.

This was a good thing, though. For too long he had kept his head down and gone to work at the firehouse or spent days working construction with Pete. Fixed little things at his mom's house. Enjoyed the occasional Game Night with friends. But he was conscious of not wanting to think too much or too hard about where he was in life or where he might be heading. It was as if he'd been in a holding pattern ever since the day they'd put Emily in the ground. He functioned. He worked. Ate. Slept. Then repeated the process.

All the while, he had tamped down the loneliness that welled deep inside him. He had been used to having someone to come home to. Someone to talk with. Someone to curl up with in bed at night. His person for so long had been his wife. When she died, a part of him died with her.

But he had been resurrected, thanks to the sleeping blond in his arms.

Tenley was smart. He liked that about her. She was also very easy to talk to. Her experiences differed from his greatly. Where he had a solid, loving home life, she lacked that. His parents had supported him, paying for his college and sending Emily and him on a honeymoon to Disneyland in California. Tenley had hustled her way through college, giving up a lot of the usual experiences because she was working so much. Her life in New York had been radically different from his on the Oregon coast.

Yet somehow, they clicked. He had never been more relaxed around a woman. It seemed effortless being around her. Sure, they would run into problems down the road sooner or later. All couples did. But he believed they both valued communication and would work out whatever troubles arose.

He glanced down at her. Yes, he was in this relationship now. For good. The certainty which had filled him when he'd been with Emily was just as strong with Tenley, if not stronger. Of course, she would need more time to commit to him. He would keep quiet for now. Tenley would have to come to the realization on her own that they belonged together. Carter wouldn't force any kind of timetable on her. He would merely be waiting for her.

And he would do his best to be in her company as frequently as possible. He thought a large part of any issues she might have stemmed from her lack of trust. Mr. A had done a number on her, with his lies and deceit. Carter had to show her that he was nothing like the bastard who'd married her and then tormented her, pulling away from her physically and emotionally.

Good thing he was a patient man.

He let her sleep, his thoughts drifting to what life with Tenley would be like. He already knew she wanted children. He did, too. She would be an excellent mother, with her imagination and caring heart.

She began to stir. He kissed the top of her head, wishing they could stay this way forever.

"Carter?" she asked sleepily. "Did I drop off?"

"You did. Either I'm a magnificent lover who wore you out—or so boring that I couldn't keep you awake."

She turned, looking up at him. "I don't think I can judge you on a single performance. I'm going to need several more to compare it to."

He laughed. "All said with a straight face. I like that about you. Do you play poker?"

"No, but only because no one's ever taught me before. I'm pretty decent at gin rummy and hearts."

"With your smarts and that poker face, you'll be unstoppable."

He kissed her, and the kiss heated up in seconds. The slow exploration the first time they made love now became a frenetic coupling of sizzling passion. Carter thrust into her, hard and fast, enjoying the feel of her. The scent of her. The taste of her. He loved everything about this woman.

Love...

No, it was too soon to think about love. He slammed that door as he came, hearing her cries of passion as she called his name.

He cradled her in his arms, finding it impossible to stop kissing her. He had been attracted to Emily and they'd enjoyed a healthy sex life. Something was different with Tenley, though. A craving for her that pierced his soul. Maybe it was because he'd gone so long without sex. Maybe because she was the complete opposite of Emily. Whatever the case, Carter was seriously addicted.

She placed her palms on his chest and nudged him away, breathing hard. "I've got to catch my breath. Can lips get sore? Mine have never had such a work-out. Not that I'm complaining. Kissing you is..." Her expression turned dreamy.

"Is?" he prompted.

"Indescribably delicious," she teased. "But I want to film you."

"Doing this?" he teased in return, his mouth covering her breast.

Tenley eeked. "No," she said, laughing. "Cooking."

"Uh... I forgot to take the chicken out to thaw," he admitted sheepishly.

"That's what a microwave is for," she determined. "Take it from the freezer and hit defrost. I'm going to jump in the shower while you're doing that."

She rolled from the bed and he drank in the long, slender legs with beautiful calves, probably from her many walks. The curve of her hips called to him, and he also left the bed.

"Don't follow me," she warned playfully. "Chicken," she reminded. "Thaw the chicken."

He sighed heavily and padded from the bedroom into the kitchen. Removing the pack of chicken from his freezer, he unzipped the freezer bag and took out two breasts, two thighs, and two legs. Placing them in a shallow ceramic pan, he set it in the microwave and tinkered with the buttons. It would take about fifteen minutes before thoroughly thawed.

Fifteen minutes he could certainly be doing better things.

With Tenley.

He joined her in the shower, enjoying soaping her

smooth skin and kissing her until the water ran cold. They got out and took turns toweling off each other. She dressed in the clothes she had worn but told him to wait.

"I want to see what's in your closet."

Once dressed, she flipped through various shirts, removing a beige Henley. "This," she declared. "With your dark-brown hair and eyes, this will be a nice contrast. And jeans with it. You fill out a pair of jeans in just the right way."

He hadn't washed his hair, but it had gotten damp in the shower. Tenley insisted on blowing it dry, and Carter enjoyed the feel of her fingers running through his hair. She combed it and then stepped back.

"Yes, you're camera-ready," she proclaimed.

"I'm starting to get nervous," he admitted. "I'm not use to making presentations."

"Carter Clark, you rush into burning buildings. Nothing could be more terrifying than that. Well, maybe a zombie invasion. Running from zombies might be slightly more frightening. But talking about chicken? Nope, I'm not buying it."

They returned to the kitchen, and Tenley asked him about how he would prepare the chicken.

"The guys at the firehouse like it fried. Let's do it that way."

"Walk me through the process before you begin."

He did, telling her how he would prepare the chicken and what frying pan he would use. How to change the heat. When to turn it.

"Okay. I want you to just talk to me. Yes, I'll be holding my cell and point it at you, but I want it to be a conversation just like we had. Pretend I know nothing about frying chicken. Well, actually I don't, so that part will be easy. Just walk me through everything, from what you get out to the very end when you bite into it."

Carter took a deep breath. "Okay. I think I'm ready."

"I won't stop filming. If you make a mistake, own it. If you trip over your words—or your feet—roll with it. Vloggers aren't perfect. They're human. That's half of why people tune in. They want to see everyday people who are just like them, but it's someone who can teach them something new about something they didn't know about. Just do a little intro where you let us know you're a fireman, and then take it from there."

Tenley tapped a few things on her phone and held it up, nodding at him.

"Hi. I'm Carter Clark, a fireman stationed at Salty Point, which is along the Oregon coast. Fireman put out fires, but we also have to keep our station house running. We constantly clean and check our equipment. Exercise with weights to keep in top physical shape. Continually train, learning new methods. But we also have to take time out to eat and clean." He smiled. "Cleaning toilets is not my favorite thing to do, but I do enjoy cooking. I didn't know anything about it when I first became a fireman. Now," he said with pride, "the other firefighters clamor for my dishes."

Tenley nodded at him encouragingly, and he felt himself relax.

"Chicken is one of the cheaper proteins and goes a long way in feeding my station house—or your family. Leftovers are a plus. I like to bake and grill chicken. I use it in fajitas and casseroles. But today, we're going back to basics and talking about how to fry a chicken."

He began setting out the things he would need, talking as he went. He explained why he liked a cast iron pan for frying chicken over a nonstick ceramic one as he heated vegetable oil in it. He dipped each piece of chicken in cold milk and then placed it in a paper bag filled with flour, shaking it until the chicken was coated before liberally salting and peppering. He discussed why he preferred a paper bag over a Ziplock but admitted it was hard to find paper bags nowadays.

He continued to talk as he added each piece to the frying pan, reducing the heat after each piece had fried for two minutes on each side. He told a few stories about eating fried chicken as a kid and the first time he had fried one for his fellow firefighters.

"Burned the hell out of it," he said, chuckling. "But they were a hungry bunch and ate it anyway. Still razz me about it to this day, though."

Before he knew it, the chicken was done. He used tongs to remove all the pieces, placing them on a paper towel to soak up the extra grease. Then he remembered he was supposed to taste it, so he lifted a leg.

"The best thing about fried chicken?" he asked. "Eating it."

Carter bit into the leg, closing his eyes as he savored it. Opening them, he said, "Crispy skin. Tender and juicy on the inside. Just enough pepper to give it a kick of flavor. That's the way to fry chicken, folks."

He felt like something was missing, though, and so he added, "Thanks for joining me today. This has been the first episode of *A Fireman's Guide to Surviving in the Kitchen with Carter Clark*. Have a great day!"

He smiled at Tenley, and she lowered her phone. "That was incredible." She dashed over to him, throwing her arms about him. "You are a natural on camera, Carter. And where did you come up with that title at the end?"

He shrugged. "I just thought about how I'm a fireman. How surviving those first few meals I made was the whole point."

"Well, it's perfect. You're perfect." She kissed him soundly. "Let me try a bite."

He still held the leg and lifted it to her. She bit into it and sighed.

"This is terrific. And the thing is, your explanation was so simple, yet thorough. A novice like me could easily replicate what you did. You aren't intimidating, despite your size. You're friendly and laid back and I think this could really be something."

"I do, too," he agreed. "What should we do next?"

"Let's think about it. We could start a You Tube Channel for you. Claim a web address and create a website for you. Or go the blog route. Let you write a brief intro, including the recipe and instructions, and then embed the video there. It can be whatever you want it to be—but promise me that you'll keep doing this."

"I'd like to try."

"I want to also think about sponsors," she mused. "I need to mull it over. Let me work out the best format for it. You've obviously already got your brand down. You think about different recipes you'd like to make on camera. Oh, this is so exciting."

Carter placed the chicken leg on the counter. "I can think of something even more exciting. Kissing my girlfriend."

She looked up at him shyly. "Is that what I am? Your girlfriend?"

You're my everything.

But Carter refrained from speaking his thought aloud and said, "You definitely are, Tenley Thompson."

CHAPTER 14

Tenley showered and dressed, excited about the day ahead of her. She would be going into Portland to shop for a new wardrobe, along with Willow, Gillian, Ainsley, and Rylie. Both the bakery and the antiques store were closed on Mondays, since both were open Saturdays and Sundays. Gillian, who was an accountant and did the books for several businesses out of her home office, would see a couple of clients this morning in Portland and then meet up with them for lunch and the remainder of the afternoon.

She came downstairs and found Willow in the kitchen, sipping coffee and nibbling on a piece of toast.

"The coffee maker is still warm if you want to brew a cup," her friend said. "There's also cereal, yogurt, and fruit, if you'd like that."

"Yogurt sounds good," Tenley said, pouring herself a cup of coffee and then removing a container of Greek yogurt from the refrigerator and joining Willow at the table.

"Thanks for planning this outing today," she said.

"I had so much fun with Ainsley and Rylie on Game Night, and it will be good to catch up with Gillian, as well."

"You don't have to elaborate unless you want to," Willow began, "but I am curious about you spending all day Saturday and Sunday with Carter."

She took a sip of coffee, trying to gather her thoughts. "Carter is very easy to be around," she began. "Especially after all the drama I've faced lately."

She wasn't ready to share that they'd had sex multiple times over the weekend.

"He's interesting. Smart. Undemanding. And he feels like someone I can trust."

"Carter is all those things," Willow agreed. "He is very down-to-earth. He also is one of the kindest men I have ever met. I would trust Carter with my life."

"He wants to read what I've written so far," she shared. "I e-mailed it to him last night after he dropped me off."

"That tells me a lot about your relationship. You've barely told me what the storyline is. And you haven't offered to let me read any of it."

"It's not that I don't want you to. I definitely had thought of giving you the manuscript when I finished my first draft."

Willow studied her. "But you trust Carter enough to want his feedback now."

Tenley nodded. "I do. We've talked about my plot and brainstormed some ideas for not only this book but the two that follow. Carter believes I can turn this trilogy into a series." She paused. "It's nice to have a man believe in me so much. I realize now how I haven't trusted a man in a long time. If ever. I'm sure if I saw a psychiatrist, she would tell me it goes back to abandonment issues with my father, a man I can't even remember."

She swirled the spoon through her yogurt. "You know I haven't dated much, Willow, despite the fact that I'm thirty. Even though I was married for four years, I never really knew Theodore. I still don't understand why he wanted to marry me and then why he shoved me aside the way he did. It bruised my ego and hurt my belief in myself."

Willow squeezed Tenley's hand. "Theodore Fielding was a jerk. He's a chapter that you need to close the door on and forget about. You're in the Cove now. We take care of each other." She grinned. "And it looks as if Carter is taking care of you."

She felt the blush cover her cheeks. "He is doing a lot to restore my faith in the male species. He did tell me he had been married before and that he lost his wife very quickly to an aneurysm. He wants to move on, Willow. I think with me."

Her friend beamed. "Then I hope you give Carter every chance, Ten. Both you and he are two of my favorite people. It would be incredible if you wound up together."

They finished their coffee and both brushed their teeth before they climbed into Willow's SUV. Their first stop was to pick up Gillian next door. Tenley had enjoyed meeting the older woman over the years, knowing she was close to both Boo and Willow. Gillian had never married, but she had taken in Willow and Jackson as an honorary niece and nephew, and that had extended to Tenley and Sloane when Gillian had come in for one of Willow's art shows in New York. Nowadays, Tenley regularly traded e-mails with Gillian and looked forward to catching up with her today.

She got out of the car and greeted Gillian with a warm hug. "I'm so glad you were able to come shopping with us in Portland."

"It came at a good time for me. I had clients I needed to touch base with today anyway. I'll handle that business this morning and then be able to meet up with the rest of you for lunch. Then I can help shop-till-you-drop this afternoon."

They picked up both Robinson cousins on the square, and the next hour was filled with happy chatter as Willow drove them into Portland. They dropped off Gillian and promised to stay in touch by text as to where they would eat lunch and when, once Gillian was free.

Rylie gave Willow instructions on where to head next, saying, "It's a favorite shop of mine. Small, so there's not much variety, but the owner carries a lot of great, basic pieces that you can build a wardrobe around. What are you looking for today, Tenley?"

"Practically everything. A wardrobe completely different from what I left behind in New York," she said. "Theodore had me get rid of a lot of things I loved after we were married, saying I needed to dress differently. Not only for the job he helped me land, but because I was now married to someone of a different social class and standing. I prefer classic, tailored pieces, with a lot of casual wear. His tastes ran to ultra-feminine and frilly and was much too fussy for me. I got rid of almost everything in my closet and drawers, so think of today as me starting from scratch. The wardrobe I want to build is one that would be suitable for a place such as Maple Cove."

Ainsley's eyes lit up. "Are you thinking about staying in the Cove?"

"I am," Tenley confirmed. "I'm from California, but

my mom passed away a good dozen years ago. It was just the two of us because my dad walked out before I ever started kindergarten. I have no idea if he's dead or alive and really don't care." She glanced to Willow. "Willow has always seemed like my sister—along with Sloane—and I want to be close to her."

"And us," Rylie inserted. "I knew when we met you that we were all going to be good friends. It was the same when Willow came back to the Cove."

Ainsley said, "Let's talk about what you'll need. You're wearing a nice all-weather coat, but you'll also need a light jacket and maybe a shorter raincoat for outerwear."

"I am putty in your hands, ladies," Tenley said, laughing. "Dress me from the inside out."

They went to the shop Rylie was familiar with. It allowed Tenley to stock up on many basic pieces, including several crisp tailored shirts and tunics, along with a few sweaters and pullovers.

Ainsley made the next suggestion, taking them to a shop that featured casual wear and what Ainsley termed smart casual items.

"They have jeans and leggings, but they also have a few tailored blazers. I know you'll be working from home and will want to be comfortable as you write, but you'll have a few occasions where you'll need to throw a blazer over a more casual outfit in order to dress it up," Ainsley said.

By the time they left that store, Tenley owned three blazers in navy, black, and beige. She also had added several pairs of jeans and leggings in four dark colors.

"I just got a text from Gillian," Willow told them. "She's through for the day and ready to meet us at the sushi place Rylie mentioned. She'll Uber over there and meet us for lunch."

"I'm looking forward to West Coast sushi," Tenley said. "It's one of my favorite kinds of food, one which Theodore did not like. Carter told me to call him Mr. A, and not even use his name."

"I assume A is for asshole?" Rylie asked.

She confirmed that, and the women all laughed.

"So you're keeping company with Carter these days," Ainsley noted.

"I did during the last four days when he was off duty," Tenley confirmed. "He had extra time on his hands because construction projects have slowed down and Pete wasn't using him. We hiked three different trails that Rylie recommended."

"Which was your favorite?" Rylie asked.

She talked about where they had hiked and what she had seen.

They arrived at the sushi restaurant and found Gillian already there. She had claimed a large, circular booth, and the four women joined her.

They poured over the menus and made their selections and then Ainsley asked, "Are you hanging with Carter as a friend—or is it more? I sensed something between you at Game Night."

"Definitely more," she confirmed. "He's ready to begin dating again, and even though I didn't think I should, this soon after my annulment, he's quite persuasive."

"And quite good-looking," Ainsley added. "I could sense Carter becoming a little restless lately. I didn't think he was the kind who would go for a dating app. The single female population in the Cove is fairly limited. You arrived at the perfect time, Tenley."

"I know you and Rylie are friends with Carter. I

hope that I didn't step on your toes as far as he's concerned."

Rylie burst out laughing. "Carter is like a big brother to Ainsley and me. I can't fathom thinking of him in a romantic light. But I'm happy if you've found each other."

Their meal arrived, and she appreciated not only the good food but the wonderful conversation with these four women. They were all quick-witted and interesting to be around. It only confirmed her decision to remain in Maple Cove.

"What is your book about, Tenley?" Gillian asked.

She gave them a broad overview of the novel and the trilogy, including a few of the ideas she and Carter had bounced around.

"I'm a voracious reader," Gillian said. "I can't wait for it to be published so I can read it."

"You work with numbers, Gillian," Tenley said. "I'll bet you have a great eye for detail in books, as well. Maybe when I finish polishing it, you might want to serve as my proofreader before I find an editor to send it off to."

"I would be delighted to do so, Tenley," her friend assured her.

"When do you think you'll finish?" Willow asked.

"I really don't know since I've never written a novel before. I'm a little over halfway through now, but Carter and I brainstormed some great stuff. I need to go back and drop some breadcrumbs in the first half of the book in order for things in the second half to incorporate those ideas."

"It's great that Carter was able to help you think through some of your plot and characters," Ainsley said.

Willow chuckled. "Especially since, from what I

remember, Carter couldn't finish a book in high school. He was always pumping Dylan at lunch when we had a test coming up over a novel he hadn't read. I think it's great that you've become so close and you trust him to read your work."

"I am a little surprised how close we've grown," Tenley admitted. "I even have him vlogging, which he seems to think is far out of his comfort zone."

"What?" the group said collectively.

Tenley explained her idea to have Carter create a food blog and embed video of what he cooked—or simply become a vlogger.

"Carter does have a lot of charm," Gillian pointed out. "If he could get over a camera faced at him, I think he would do well."

"We shot a practice video this weekend," she told them.

"We've got to see that," Rylie said.

"World you like to now?" she asked. "It's on my phone."

They readily agreed, and she pulled up the video and hit play. Tenley had watched it herself three times and knew it by heart. This time, she watched these four women instead of the video, wanting to gauge their reactions.

When it ended, Ainsley said, "He is a natural on camera. He was so relaxed and informative."

"I liked that he was easy to follow," Rylie added. "I can cook a few favorite dishes, but I would love to expand my repertoire. I could do everything Carter did and make fried chicken on my own."

"That was my thought exactly," Tenley said. "I'm trying to decide how to help him go about launching this. I thought about him starting a website or blog. You can see that he's already branded himself well. I think people—both men and women, young and old—would watch and learn. In fact, I could even see him doing a cookbook."

"This is really exciting," Willow said. "The potential is great. More and more people are working from home and break up their work day. They could watch a Carter video and try his dishes themselves. I believe there's a huge market he could tap into. Why, this could mushroom and grow into a fulltime job outside of firefighting."

Tenley had thought the same thing, but knowing how much Carter loved what he did and how he had followed in the family's footsteps, she had refrained from mentioning that to him.

Instead, she said, "He could do this on the side instead of working for Pete. He could set his own hours. I've even thought of him creating a You Tube channel and gaining subscribers. He hasn't committed to anything just yet, although I did have him start thinking about recipes he might want to film. I said I would take care of figuring out the platform and presentation."

"This is a huge undertaking," Gillian noted. "I can help in any way on the financial end. I'd be happy to donate time. Walk Carter through how to set up a business."

She thanked the older woman and added, "Enough of food blogging. I think I'm ready to shop again."

They called for the check, paid the bill, and hit two more stores, one for outerwear and one specializing in outdoor clothing and footwear. By the time the day ended, Tenley had the brand-new wardrobe she had sought—and more importantly, she felt she had established firm friendships with the women who had accompanied her.

Maple Cove was definitely feeling like home, thanks to these women.

And Carter.

CHAPTER 15

Carter was eager to see Tenley. He had worked Monday through Thursday, his usual seven-to-seven shifts, and had seen her Tuesday and Wednesday nights. He'd taken her for New York pizza at Crust 'n Stuff on Tuesday and then for a walk around the town square, pointing out the various businesses to her and telling her a little about who owned them.

On Wednesday night, she had wanted to return the favor and take him out to dinner. He'd suggested the Bearded Barrel Brewery on the square. They'd ordered two different flights of craft beer and wings and nachos to nibble on as they sampled the light to dark beers.

They hadn't made love again. He wanted to give her a little time and space on that. It was important he showed her it wasn't all about sex with him. He truly wanted to get to know her as a person. The more they talked, the more he liked her. Really liked her. They both had strong work ethics and seemed cut from the same moral cloth. Tenley enjoyed talking politics and definitely had her finger on the pulse of pop culture.

She had shared more about her childhood with him, a hard time because her father had walked out and never come back. Never contacted her. It had been a struggle for her mother to put food on the table, and most of Tenley's meals were eaten at school via a free government breakfast and lunch program. She had been very honest about her mom's drinking problem. To Carter, it seemed she had raised herself. He admired the fact that she'd put herself through UCLA with a combination of scholarships, federal grants, and a series of parttime jobs. She didn't hide her ambitions from him either. She wanted to write full time and support herself through her books. If she couldn't, she still planned on continuing to write and publish, supplementing that with whatever job she could pick up in the area.

For now, though, she had a cushion of cash, thanks to the sale of the loft she had lived in with her ex. She had talked about wanting to visit with Nancy and see the apartment above the diner. He'd called Nancy a few hours ago, and she had agreed to show Tenley the place tomorrow morning at ten, after the weekend breakfast crowd thinned out and before the lunch rush started.

Carter only hoped Tenley might want to stay over tonight. Then they could go look at the apartment together tomorrow morning.

He was making dinner for her tonight and had agreed to allow her to film him again. It surprised him that he'd actually enjoyed the video they'd made of him frying up chicken. Tenley promised tonight they would talk about some ideas she had regarding his blog. If he could make some money off it, then he might give up working for Pete.

His doorbell rang. He hurried from the kitchen to

the front door. Tenley stood on the porch and turned and waved at Willow. Carter did the same, and Willow backed out of the driveway and headed home.

"Come on in," he said, closing the door behind her and taking her into his arms for a long kiss.

"Mmm," she said after he broke it. "It's fun to come home to you. Besides, you even cook. A girl can't ask for more than that."

"I'll even clean up if you want me to." He kissed her again, one hand cradling her nape and then pushing into her hair.

"I'll clean up," she insisted. "It's only fair. Besides, I've done nothing but sit all day, writing on my laptop. I finished three chapters. That's the most words I've ever managed in a single day. I was on fire."

He heard the excitement in her voice. She had completed another five chapters in the three previous days.

"Are you about two-thirds through?" he asked.

"I think so."

She began telling him about what she'd written today, as she'd done the last time she saw him. He was pleased that she had been able to incorporate a few of the ideas he'd pitched to her after he'd read what she'd already finished on the manuscript. It was good. Very good. He suspected she wouldn't have to go the indie route and that a major publishing house would sign her.

"I'll either have to dedicate this first book to you or thank you first in the acknowledgements. You've really contributed a lot."

"I'm happy to help." He kissed her once more and released her. "Come on to the kitchen. I'm ready to roll if you are."

"What are you making?"

"King Ranch casserole," he told her. "It's Ree Drummond's basic recipe with a few twists of my own. When he saw her blank look, he added, "She's the Pioneer Woman. From Food Network."

"Oh, I saw part of her show the other day when Willow was making lunch for us. Sorry I didn't remember her name. I'll admit I've never turned on that channel. I'm more of an HGTV viewer. I liked her, though. She was casual yet informative." She paused. "But I think you're just as good."

He indicated everything he needed for the new video, which spread out across the small island.

"You look ready. And very organized," she praised. "Eager to try again?"

"I am. You're going to love this dish."

Tenley punched a few buttons and lifted her phone, aiming at him and nodding.

"Hi, everyone. Carter Clark back with you in *A Fireman's Guide to Surviving in the Kitchen*. Have I got a tasty, filling meal for you today! My fellow firefighters like meals which stick to their ribs, and King Ranch casserole is a favorite of theirs."

He indicated the counter with a sweep of his hand. "There's a lot of stuff here, so don't be intimidated. A little chopping and mixing and tearing—and you'll have an amazing casserole to serve your family or guests."

Carter mixed the soups and tomatoes with chiles together, adding several spices and stirring them in.

"Cumin is a favorite of mine. A little underused in my opinion, but it will help give this casserole flavor," he explained, as he chopped up a couple of jalapeños, two red bell peppers, and a yellow onion.

"Mix this all together," he said, doing so and then setting the bowl aside. "Now for the fun part."

He opened a package of corn tortillas and tore them into pieces with his hands, layering the bottom of his greased casserole dish, covering every surface.

"I've cheated a little—and that's all right. Cooking sometimes takes more time than you have, so short-cuts are smart to take. I needed a whole, roasted chicken for this and didn't have the time to do so, working twelve-hour shifts at the fire station the last several days. Instead, Costco saves the day with one of their amazing, cheap rotisserie chickens. It's smart, though, to let it cool first. Now, I'll tear it up, just as I did the tortillas."

He demonstrated, using his hands to pull bits of the cooled chicken from the bone.

"This dish is all about layering," he told Tenley, his audience of one. He had found it easy to talk about what he did because he was only talking to her.

Carter layered veggies and some of the soup mixture over the tortillas and chicken, adding liberal amounts of cheese atop it. He continued to layer until all his ingredients were used, and then he covered the glass casserole dish with foil.

"Sorry. Forgot to tell you that I'd already preheated the oven. It's at three hundred and fifty degrees now. All you'll do is pop this into the oven and bake for forty-five minutes."

As he cleaned up, he told a story about the first time he'd made this casserole at the firehouse and what a hit it had been.

"We'll be back when the oven timer goes off," he said.

Tenley turned off the camera. "You are a natural, Carter. Once again, this was super simple. Yes, there were a lot more ingredients than there were with the chicken, but this recipe isn't complicated. The tip about picking up a pre-made chicken was fantastic."

He glanced around. "Kitchen is clean. I've already set the table. Looks like we'll have to find something to do for the next half-hour."

She took his hand and led him into the bedroom. "I guess we can try for fast and furious."

He grinned. "I'm game."

They both scrambled out of their clothes and clung to one another, her skin warm and smooth beneath his hands. She was ready for him in record time—and he had been ready for her for days now. Their coupling was fierce. Intense. Raw.

And they still had time to dress and rush back to the kitchen, finding they had four minutes left on the timer.

"Here, let me smooth your hair," she told him, running her fingers lightly through it, sending the good kind of chills through him.

Picking up her phone again, Tenley nodded and pushed record again.

"The timer's about to go off. I like preparing casseroles because you can mix 'em up and slip 'em into the oven—and have time to do other things. Like kiss your girlfriend. A lot." He grinned wickedly at Tenley, whose hot blush raced up her neck to her cheeks and hairline.

Laughing, he picked up potholders as the timer went off.

"This recipe does better with another fifteen minutes in the oven, foil off," he shared.

Pulling the dish from the oven, he set it on the stove and removed the foil before returning the casserole to the oven and setting another timer.

"With fifteen minutes, you have time to set your

table. Toss a great salad. Open a few cold beers. Maybe mix up some margaritas. I'm going easy tonight."

She kept filming as he put together a simple salad with greens, tomatoes, olives, and croutons, drizzling a little oil over it and tossing it. Carter went to the refrigerator and pulled out two beers, popping the top on one and bringing it to his lips for a long drink.

He told another story about the firehouse as he took the beers and salads to the table and opened a sack of tortilla chips, noting they were the perfect snack to accompany the casserole.

The timer went off, and he returned to the oven, pulling out the casserole. Tenley moved in for a close-up and then moved back as Carter plated the casserole for them. He dipped a fork into it and brought it to his lips, blowing slightly to cool the bite.

"And that's King Ranch casserole, folks. My girl-friend and I will have a great meal tonight and plenty of leftovers for another meal or two." He stared into the camera. "Anything that gives me more time to spend with her is worth it. This is Carter Clark with *A Fireman's Guide to Surviving in the Kitchen*. See you next time."

Tenley lowered the phone. "I don't know what turns me on more now. The sexy look you just gave when you mentioned me—or that terrific-smelling casserole that's making my mouth water." She paused. "Am I really your girlfriend, Carter?'

He pulled her into his arms. "You are, Tenley. And I couldn't be happier about that."

After a very long kiss, he escorted her to the small table in the corner of the kitchen. The bungalow was small and didn't include a dining room. He'd never missed having one, though. The café table had been fine. Until now. He realized he wanted a large dining room table, with plenty of chairs to seat family and friends.

He kept that to himself, though. Tenley still occasionally seemed to him like a deer caught in the headlights. He didn't want to frighten her away with talk of having a big family and holiday dinners. She was like a wild stallion that needed to learn how to be calm. He didn't want to break her spirit. He merely wanted her to learn to trust him.

As they ate, she told him more about the pages she'd written today.

"Are you ready for me to read what you've written this week?" he asked.

She bit her lip, causing desire to flicker within him. "Do you really want to?"

"I more than want to, Tenley. I'm dying to. And you know I'm not a reader."

"I want you to. Oh, this is hard, Carter. I'm so far into the story now. It's like I'm handing over my baby to you. What if you don't like it? What if you hate it? I'm like a mom who doesn't want a stranger to tell her that her baby is ugly."

"I'm not a stranger. I'm a trusted friend. I've already told you how much I've enjoyed reading what you've sent. I know I'm going to like the new chapters, so you don't need to worry about that."

She nibbled on her lip again. "I do want you to read it. I trust your feedback."

"When can I?'

"How about now?" she countered.

He frowned. "You don't happen to have your laptop with you? I guess we can drive back to Boo's and get it."

She touched his forearm, sending a rush of heat

through him. "I e-mailed it to you before Willow brought me over. If you didn't want to read anymore, I thought you could simply delete it."

He linked his fingers with hers. "But I want to. Very much. Let's clean up."

"No. I'll do that. Go open your e-mail."

He leaned over and kissed her lightly. "Okay."

Going to the second bedroom, which he and Emily had used as an office, Carter found the e-mail from Tenley and downloaded the document containing the new chapters from this week. He began reading.

And found himself lost in another world.

Ninety minutes later, he emerged. Tenley sat on the sofa, scribbling notes on a pad. She looked up anxiously. "Well?"

Carter came and sat next to her, taking the pen from her hand and placing it and the notepad on the coffee table before her. He took her hands in his.

"It was like entering another world. I got so caught up in it. The characters. The story. Time flew by. I can't wait to read more."

He saw the tension leave her body. "You really did like it?"

"I loved it. Your descriptions are so clear. I can see it in my head. Like a movie."

Tenley nodded eagerly. "I do that, too, when I write. Run a movie in my head. I see the action and capture it on paper." She hugged him. "Oh, Carter, I'm so happy that you've liked everything you've read."

"I think you need to send it to your friend now. You mentioned someone who had some connections in publishing."

"Diane Nichols, my old boss in Brooklyn. But it's

not finished yet, Carter. I'd need to go back and polish the pages I've already written."

"It's damn good now, Tenley. I think Diane should read it. Maybe float a few chapters around to her friends. See what happens."

"You really think so?" she asked, uncertainty spread across her face.

"I *know* so." He kissed her soundly. "Believe me. This is going to be huge. Maybe not *Lord of the Rings* huge, but big all the same."

Tenley hesitated, and then he saw she had come to a decision. "All right. I'll do it now before I wimp out."

She picked up her phone and typed a few things. Taking a deep breath, she tapped her screen. A loud whoosh of air followed. "I did it. She's got it."

"Now you need to forget you sent it," he advised. "Go back to what you're doing. Keep writing. "

"How do I *not* think about it?"

"By getting caught up in your next chapter. I think I should take you home and let you get started."

She shook her head. "Nope. I wrote three chapters today. Tonight, I want to curl up next to my boyfriend and watch some TV." She smiled, mischief in her eyes. "And maybe find another activity."

"Another activity?" he asked, capturing her waist. "I think you claimed the gold medal during our last activity."

"I think I'd like to be a double-medal winner tonight," she teased.

Carter stood and swept her into his arms. "Then let the games begin."

CHAPTER 16

Tenley finished with her makeup and brushed her hair, liking the turquoise sweater she'd dressed in today. Carter was picking her up soon and taking her to eat breakfast at Sid's Diner, then they would go upstairs and see if Dylan's old apartment, which was still available, suited her. While she had enjoyed spending the past week with Willow, she knew they both needed space. Willow needed to enjoy her newlywed status, and Tenley wanted to explore her growing relationship with Carter. She had not stayed over at his place and wouldn't have thought to ask him to spend the night with her while she stayed with Willow and Dylan. Not that they weren't all adults, but Tenley wanted to protect the newness of her relationship with Carter.

A man she already loved.

She would never say those words aloud anytime soon, though. It would be insane to do so. She hoped it wasn't infatuation or a quick, hot passion that flared between them. What Tenley hoped for was that it could be love for both of them. That Carter would give his heart willingly to her. Obviously, he had adored his wife and kept her memory close in the years she had been gone. Even though Carter had taken the first step by starting to date Tenley, it didn't mean he was ready for a serious romantic relationship, even if he did refer to her as his girlfriend.

That's why she had to keep her feelings to herself. She wouldn't share them with him—and chase him off—or tell Willow or any of her new friends. Tenley didn't even know if people could fall in love this fast, especially if they'd been through something as traumatic as she had. Yet her heart told her Carter Clark was the man for her.

She took a deep breath, expelling it slowly, trying to calm her heart. It raced just at the thought of Carter, as if she were a teenager with a massive crush. She had never had time for romance during those teen years or in college. She hadn't found anyone that made her pulse dance and her stomach flutter with an explosion of butterflies. Tenley realized now that she had done herself—and even Theodore—a disservice by marrying him, much less so quickly. Although wanting companionship and security had been important to her, she realized she had owed herself more. She hadn't loved her ex-husband, but she certainly wanted to love the next one, hoping it could be Carter. That she wouldn't be a rebound relationship for him—one intense and fun, but not meant for the long run.

She went to her phone to see if he'd texted her. He hadn't.

But Diane Nichols had.

Call me ASAP!!!

Tenley's mouth grew dry. She had taken Carter's advice and e-mailed Diane a copy of what she'd written so far, asking her if she wouldn't mind reading through the partial manuscript and giving some feed-back. It was eight-thirty in Oregon, which meant it was eleven-thirty in Brooklyn. Maybe Diane had some questions before she started reading.

Bringing up her contact list, Tenley touched her old boss's name, nerves zipping through her as she heard the ringing begin.

Diane picked up on the second ring. "Tenley! Tenley! *What the hell*?"

Her heart sank. "Diane, I—"

"How could you keep this from me? It was freaking fantastic!"

Her knees almost gave out, and Tenley sat quickly on the bed. "You've read it?"

"Read it? I *devoured* it! You are sitting on a gold mine. I knew you were organized and smart, but you are incredibly creative. This is fresh. So original. Why, I think it's got Hollywood written all over it. I'm talking big, Tenley. Like... *Star Wars* big. I mean, I know it's not a space adventure. I'm just trying to think of some-thing to compare it to. Maybe *Game of Thrones*? It's got a huge cast and that fantasy element. I know you'd mentioned to me once that you were writing YA, but this is beyond that. It would appeal to all ages. I don't think you should classify it as YA simply because the protagonist is a teenager."

Her heart was racing now. "You really think so?"

"Girl, I *know* so. I told you I had a few contacts in publishing and would pass it along, but this is too big to do that. Do you have an agent?"

"No. I didn't think I needed one. I thought I'd probably have to go the indie route when I published."

"No, no, no," Diane insisted. "You'll want a big house behind you. And you absolutely need an agent. Do you know any?"

"I do from my days working at Sutton Press in Manhattan, but they specialized in non-fiction. Biographies. How-to books. Health and wellness. Parenting books."

"Then trust me on this. You'll want my cousin as your agent. Elmo Nichols."

Her mouth grew dry. "Elmo Nichols... is your cousin? Diane, he's a huge name in the industry. You actually think he'll take me on?"

Chuckling, Diane said, "I've already talked to him. Don't kill me. I sent him your partial. I know I didn't have your permission, but when I got up at six this morning, I saw it in my e-mail and began reading. I was done by nine—and called him. Told him I had something exciting for him to read that was written by a friend of mine. He agreed. I thought it would be a week before he got back to me because he's swamped, but I just got off the phone with him. He'd read it all, Tenley. He speed-reads. He loved it! He wants to represent you. I told him I'd have to talk with you but agreed to pass along his number."

"Elmo Nichols..." Her head swirled at the prospect of one of the top literary agents taking her on.

"Will you call him now?

"Of course. I'm just... stunned."

"Elmo's a real sweetheart—until it comes to business. He would be your fiercest advocate if you sign with him. I'll text you his number."

"Thank you, Diane. I don't know what to say."

"Say you'll send me more pages when you write them," her friend joked. "I've got to know what happens. And tell me there's more than this one book."

"I have in my head that it's a trilogy now. But a... my friend Carter says he thinks it should be a longer series. He's read it as well, and we've actually brain-stormed some plot points together."

"Your friend is absolutely right," Diane said. "Go. Call Elmo. I'm texting you his number now."

Tenley hung up and waited for the text to come through. Her heart pounded so loudly that she worried she might be having a heart attack. She closed her eyes, taking deep breaths for a few minutes before she calmed enough to call Elmo Nichols.

"Elmo Nichols," a voice said crisply, not bothering with a greeting.

"Hello, Mr. Nichols. This is Tenley Thompson. I'm Diane's—"

"You are a very talented writer, Tenley. You're Tenley. I'm Elmo. None of that Mr. Nichols stuff. And we are going to make publishing history together."

Before she had a chance to say another word, the agent quickly began outlining the publishing houses he wanted to pitch to on her behalf.

"It'll become a bidding war," he promised. "High six figures. Maybe seven if there's more than this one book. Tell me there is."

"I envisioned it as a trilogy, but a close friend has urged me to expand."

"Give me an overview of the trilogy."

Tenley spent ten minutes talking about the resolution to the first book and then outlined what she wanted to write in the second and third books.

"I like it," Elmo said. "Now tell me about beyond that."

"I only have a few ideas," she began, telling him about what Carter and she had talked over.

A brief silence ensued. She waited, her heart in her throat.

"I think we discuss the trilogy and hold back on

the series potential. Not that what you just shared isn't good. It is. But it needs to be fleshed out more. And it would give us more bargaining power if we sign on for a trilogy. Then we talk expansion after Book Two comes out. Hold their feet to the fire. Get you top dollar."

"But I'm an unknown, Elmo," she protested. "No proven track record. I've never been published before."

"That doesn't matter. I know talent when I see it and what sells. I have a good idea what the public will go for. How fast can you finish this first manuscript? Diane said you left her office last month. Are you writing full time now?"

"Yes. It's gone very well since I moved to Oregon. Maybe the change of scenery helped, but I think I could be done in another two weeks. I don't have an editor yet, though."

"You don't need one. Sure, I see a few little tweaks that can be done, but whatever house we sign with will assign a top editor. You've got raw talent, Tenley. You write clean and it's damn creative. We won't worry about developmental edits or proofing yet." Elmo paused. "I keep saying *we*. I need to know. Are you in with me? I will fight for you tooth and nail. Rep you to the best of my abilities."

Normally, Tenley would ask to take time to mull over such a huge decision. Her gut told her that with Elmo Nichols being one of the biggest agents in the literary world, she needed to jump on this opportunity.

"I would be happy to be represented by you, Elmo."

"That is music to my ears," he said, a smile in his voice. "I can e-mail you a contract. Don't sign and return quickly. Look it over carefully. Have your lawyer look it over for good measure. But I can tell you now, Tenley, I believe we are going to make an incredible team."

"I'll text you my e-mail address."

"Send me the remaining pages when you finish. I may want you to fly to New York right after I shop it. If I can narrow it down to a handful of publishers, I think it would be good for you to meet the team you'd be working with."

"I can do that, Elmo," Tenley said, excitement filling her.

He told her he would send her the contract, along with basic information regarding his office and how he handled things, and encouraged her to look over his website to see which clients he represented and what publishing houses they were signed to.

After she hung up, she sat a moment, numb, overwhelmed by what had just happened.

Her cell chimed. It was Carter.

Be there in ten. Hope you're hungry. Diner food is the best!

She texted a thumbs up and went downstairs as the door opened. Willow and Shadow came in. The pup greeted Tenley with a lick to her hand, and she scratched between his ears.

"That color looks terrific on you," her friend said. "Are you still going to breakfast with Carter?"

"Yes. He's on his way." She paused. "I'm going to look at Dylan's old apartment after we eat."

Willow took Tenley's hands. "I have loved having you here, but I get it. You want to give me space, and you and Carter need some, too. How are things going between you?"

"If I say terrific, will that jinx it?"

Willow hugged her. "Not at all. Dylan and I are thrilled that you two are together. It's like all the pieces are falling into place, Ten. I'm so incredibly happy with Dylan. I'm painting better than I ever have. You're staying in the Cove and have found a good man. We just need Sloane to stop hopscotching all over the world and come pay us a visit."

"Willow, do you think it's too soon for me to be in love?"

Her friend shook her head. "Not at all, Ten. I told you how I always thought you and Carter would be good together. I don't think there's any magic timetable when it comes to love. For some people, it strikes instantly. Others grow slowly into it over time. Don't bother looking at a calendar. Look into Carter's soul. And your own. If your heart is telling you he's the one for you, then don't tune that out. Listen to your heart—and act on it."

The doorbell rang. Shadow barked once and ran to it.

Tenley hugged Willow. "Thank you. For absolutely everything. From back when we met that first day in the dorm until this moment. I love you, Willow."

"I love you, Ten."

She went and answered the door. The minute she saw Carter standing there, Tenley knew she loved this man and always would.

"Come on in. Let me grab my purse. I left it upstairs."

He slipped his arms around her, preventing her from leaving, and kissed her. "Now you can go."

Her heart light, Tenley hurried up the stairs and collected her tote. While she had wanted to share her amazing news with Willow regarding being signed by a top agent, she needed Carter to be the one who heard it first. She returned downstairs and they told Willow and Shadow goodbye.

Carter helped her into his truck and drove the short way to the town square. They had to park across the square from the diner since so many parking spots were filled.

He led her inside the diner and said, "Table for two, Nancy. This is Tenley Thompson. My girlfriend."

Hearing him say those words he'd first used last night gave her a thrill.

"It's a pleasure to meet you, Tenley," the older woman said, looking her up and down. Her eyes turned back to Carter. "You certainly work fast, Mr. Clark."

He slid an arm about Tenley's waist. "I know a good thing when I see it, Nancy. And Tenley has been good for me."

The diner's owner nodded slowly. "I can see that. You look happy, Carter." She smiled. "Right this way. I saved a booth for you, since I knew you were coming."

They followed Nancy, and Tenley felt eyes on her. She knew the town would be talking about Carter Clark beginning to date again after so many years of being a widower.

"Here you go," Nancy said, as they seated themselves and she handed them menus. "Coffee for you both?"

"Yes, please," Tenley said, picking up the menu. "Everything looks terrific. What do you usually get?" she asked Carter.

"Bring us two of my usual breakfast, Nancy," he said, when she returned with their coffees.

Tenley poured cream into the mug and sweetened it, stirring and then taking a sip. "Oh, this is good."

Then a shadow looming over her and she looked

up. A woman in her fifties with bleached blond hair styled artfully stood frowning down at her, hostility thick in the air. Tenley glanced quickly to Carter, unsure of what she had done to warrant such attention.

"Wilma," Carter said neutrally.

"Don't *Wilma* me," the woman snapped. "How dare you parade some whore in front of the entire town! Everyone comes to the diner on Saturday morning. You're embarrassing me—and yourself, Carter."

He rose, his features tight. "This is my girlfriend, Tenley Thompson. You need to apologize to her, Wilma."

"I will do no such thing!" the woman shouted. "You should be apologizing to me, young man. Why you thought you could bring her here and make such a fuss is beyond me. Dorothy and Clinton raised you better than this."

"My parents raised me just fine, Wilma," Carter said, standing his ground. "And I have nothing to apologize for. You're only embarrassing yourself, Wilma. Please go."

"You are disrespecting my child, Carter. She was *your wife*. Now you've taken up with some New York trollop. Emily would be shocked. Shocked!"

"Emily would want me to live my life," Carter said firmly. "I loved your daughter. I will always love her. But Em would be the first to tell me I've mourned her long enough. She would encourage me to move on."

"Move on? Move on?" Her eyes narrowed. "You are a sore disappointment, Carter Clark. You never were good enough for my Emily. At least you didn't have any children because I wouldn't want this woman to try and mother my grandbabies."

Carter's face drained of color. "You need to leave, Wilma. Now."

The woman glanced to Tenley. "No, *you* need to leave the Cove."

"Let's go," Carter said, pulling out Tenley's chair.

She stood shakily, upset that everyone was watching this scene play out, knowing they would be the object of gossip for days to come.

Suddenly, her cheek felt on fire. Stunned, Tenley's hand went to her face, and she realized Wilma had slapped her.

Carter leaped between them. "What the hell are you doing, Wilma?" he demanded, quickly turning to Tenley. "Are you all right?"

She nodded and he wheeled, again confronting his former mother-in-law.

"Enough!" Nancy cried, stepping between the woman and a very angry Carter. "Get out, Wilma. Now. Else I'll call Dylan—and you don't want to deal with him and an assault charge."

Wilma sniffed. "You've never taken my side on anything, Nancy Mayfield."

"Because I don't like you *or* your gossiping husband, Wilma Bell," Nancy fired back. "How you gave birth to a sweet girl like Emily is beyond me. Thank goodness she had Carter all those years, because he is one of the kindest men I know. Carter has been alone a good five years now, Wilma. It's only natural he would want to start living again. It's none of your business whom he takes up with."

"You're wrong about that, Nancy. He's my son-in-law. He's family."

"Well, you never treated him as family when Emily was alive. You and Fred never served them a holiday meal. You never spent time with them before or after they married. The two of you are selfish busybodies who tear down everyone. Get out of my diner—and don't come back."

Wilma sputtered a moment, and then Nancy shouted, "Go!"

Tenley watched the woman march down the aisle to the door and slam through it.

Then the entire diner burst out in applause.

"'Bout time someone put that woman in her place," a voice said.

"Good job, Nancy," another added.

A man rose from a nearby booth and came toward them. He looked to be in his sixties and was far too thin for his height. She got the feeling he was ill.

"Sit down, you two," he said, taking a seat at their table.

Tenley hesitated a moment and then Carter nodded. She took her seat and Carter did the same.

"I'm Walt Willingham, the former sheriff of the Cove," the man said.

Immediately, she recognized his name. "I'm Tenley Thompson," she said. "I know you served on Willow's scholarship committee."

"I did. Willow has talked about you before and thinks the world of you. Don't let what Wilma said upset you. She's a vindictive vulture, and her no-good husband isn't much better."

Walt paused, coughing into a handkerchief. "Excuse me. I just wanted you to hear that you and Carter aren't doing anything wrong. This man here was a good husband to Emily, and we were all sorry to see her pass so suddenly. But there's a time to mourn and a time to start living again. Carter's found a good one in you, Tenley. Don't let anything come between you, least of all a mean-spirited, malicious gossip like Wilma Bell."

"Thank you," she said softly.

Carter took her hand. "Thank you, Sheriff. Tenley needed to hear that. I have spent a lot of years alone. I realize now why I did so." He smiled at her. "Because I was waiting for this woman to find her way to me."

Walt Willingham smiled and pushed against the table, coming to his feet. "I'm glad to hear that, son. Nice meeting you, Tenley. Tell Dylan and Willow I said hi."

The old man ambled back to his table, and she looked to Carter. "I think all my life was a warm-up that led to you. I know that it's too early to say it, but I can't hide my feelings from you." She swallowed. "I love you, Carter."

He squeezed her hand. "I've been terrified, thinking I'd slip and tell you that I loved you. I was afraid you'd run all the way back to New York if I did." He paused. "But I do love you, Tenley. Yes, I loved Emily. A part of me will always love her. I hope you'll be able to accept that. What I feel for you is very different, though. It's all-consuming. It's as if I've always known you. I want to spend my life with you, Tenley.

"I want to marry you."

CHAPTER 17

Her last marriage proposal had been completely staged. She later learned that Theodore had been too busy to bother with the details and hired a marriage proposal firm to handle everything for him. The company gave them private access to a rooftop with spectacular views of the Manhattan skyline. They provided a table for two with champagne and roses. It included a violinist who serenaded them and a photographer who captured the moment. Everything had been picture-perfect—and yet even as she had said *yes* to Theodore, Tenley felt out of place, at a moment where she should have been overjoyed.

A second proposal had been the farthest thing from her mind. That it was occurring in a busy diner, with the smells of frying bacon and fresh coffee, and tables full of patrons around them, should have been off-putting.

Instead, it was absolutely perfect.

She saw the earnest, worried look on Carter's face, knowing he had doubts as to what her answer might be. After all, they had known each other for such a short time. Anyone in his right mind would slam on the brakes.

But Tenley wasn't anyone. She was an adult who had been through a tumultuous time. So had Carter, losing his wife so suddenly. They both understood that Latin phrase *carpe diem*—seize the day.

The tears in her eyes blurred Carter's image as she said, "Yes. I want to marry you, too."

Suddenly, he was kissing her and she heard the hum of noise about them, but Tenley was caught up in Carter's arms. Joy filled her. Pure, unadulterated joy. This man brought her happiness. Love. Fidelity.

"If you two can stop kissing, your breakfast is here," Nancy said drily.

They sprang apart as the patrons of Sid's Diner roared with laughter. Tenley felt her face flame, but as she looked around the diner, she saw only smiles.

Carter seated her as Nancy set down platters on the table. She saw eggs, pancakes, strips of crisp bacon, and fluffy biscuits. Her stomach grumbled in anticipation.

Nancy placed two tall glasses of orange juice in front of them. "You two enjoy, okay? Then we can go upstairs and look at the apartment."

She bit into a piece of bacon. "Perfect."

"I like my eggs over-easy," Carter said. "Sorry I don't know how you like them."

"Pretty much any way," she told him. "Scrambled. Like this. Sunny side up."

"We'll get them the way you want them next time," he promised. Glancing around, he said, "I know the entire diner saw us kissing. I don't know if anyone overheard my proposal, though."

"I wouldn't care. As Goldilocks would say, it was just right."

He slathered jam onto his biscuit. "Not the most romantic one. I should've waited. We should have been alone. Sipping champagne. Soft music in the background."

"No. This is so... *Cove*. Your proposal was unique. One I'll never forget."

"You said Cove. You usually say Maple Cove."

Tenley grinned. "I guess I'm going native."

They ate and as they did, he pointed out various people in the diner. Gradually, a procession started coming by their table, starting with the mayor, and including a real estate agent, a teacher, an insurance agent, and the town attorney. She thought she might ask him to read the contract Elmo Nichols had sent, in case Willow's brother was too busy to do so.

When they finished, Nancy topped off their coffee and told them she would be available in five minutes.

"Do you even want to look at the apartment now?" Carter asked. "You could just move in with me. I know we haven't talked about a date yet, but I'd be happy to have you."

Tenley took a deep breath. "No, I don't think that's a good idea. I understand how you'll always have feelings for Emily. I know they're very different from what you feel for me. I think, though, that we need to make a fresh start and live together somewhere new to both of us."

He nodded slowly. "That makes sense. And the place is small."

"I think I'll go ahead and take the apartment upstairs. Maybe a short-term lease? Three months or so. I'd like to finish my novel." She paused. "I have a *lot* to tell you about that."

"I think that's a good plan. I can put the bungalow up for sale. We can start looking for something that would suit us both." He gazed deeply into her eyes. "And our family."

"I do want children," she said fervently.

"Same. And maybe a dog or a cat, or a dog *and* a cat." He smiled at her, and Tenley felt on top of the world.

"Ready?" Nancy asked.

"Sure," Carter replied.

They went outside and up the stairs, with Nancy saying, "There is a way to get to the apartment from the kitchen, but that door is kept locked. You'll be entering from an outside side entrance if you take the place, so I wanted you to come this way."

Entering it, Nancy walked them through the place, pointing out a few features, including the new couch Dylan had told her was a must if she intended to rent the place again.

Tenley knew it would suit her in the short-term. "I'd like to lease it, Nancy, but only for three months."

The older women nodded approvingly. "I suppose you and this one will be keeping house after that."

Carter laced his fingers through hers. "We will. We want to find something larger than what I have now. Tenley's working on a novel and needs to finish it up. Then we'll talk wedding."

"No," Nancy admonished. "You can talk wedding now so that it can take place when you're ready. Go ahead and set a date. Do the planning. It can be simple. Or do what your friend Dylan did. Elope and have a big party after."

"Not a bad idea," Carter mused and then looked to her. "Do you want a big wedding?"

She had experienced a big wedding the first time around, even if it didn't legally count. Over eight hundred guests had attended, with another three hundred invited to the reception that followed the ceremony. Tenley, being on her own, had very few friends in attendance and no family present at all. The evening had been a blur of faces, most of whom she didn't know, and smiling until her cheeks ached, not remembering much of anything.

"No," she said softly. "We can talk about it when we leave." Looking to Nancy, she asked, "When can I move in?"

"Whenever you like. I cleaned it yesterday, knowing you'd be looking at it today. Even made the bed with fresh sheets and a thick blanket."

"Then I'll move in tomorrow. I don't have much so it won't take long."

Her new landlady removed a key from her pocket. "Then here's the key. Rent will be due first of the month."

"I'll pay all three upfront now," she said.

"That's even better. The kitchenette is small but functional. Dylan would call down a few times a week and order dinner. I would lump that in with his monthly rent. For you, I can run a tab, payable at the end of the month, if you'd like."

"That would be wonderful," she said. "I'm not much of a cook, and I want to spend most of my time working on the book."

"Or with me," Carter piped up. "And I can feed her on my days off."

Tenley had brought a check with her, anticipating she would lease the apartment. "This still has my Brooklyn address, but the bank has branches all around."

Nancy accepted the check Tenley wrote out after naming the monthly rent on the place. "It's yours now. If you and Carter can't find what you want, you're welcome to keep the apartment longer. Just give me a heads up."

"Will do," she said.

Nancy left and Tenley walked through the place again, noting the linens and towels in a small closet, as well as plates, silverware, and glassware in the kitchenette. One pot and one pan were tucked inside the small oven.

"This will be perfect for me. I can even set up at that small desk in the corner or write sitting on the sofa."

"When you're not with me." Carter pulled her into his arms. "No excuses. I expect my fiancée in my bed on a regular basis, Miss Thompson." He gave her a lingering kiss.

"Let's sit a minute," she suggested. "It's quiet—and I have a ton to tell you."

Tenley took her time, explaining how she had e-mailed the same pages Carter had read to Diane, and how Diane had raced through them, even forwarding them to her cousin.

"I know you said she had some people she knew, but she should've asked your permission before sending the manuscript on."

"Normally, I would agree with you. The partial went to her cousin, though. Elmo Nichols. One of the biggest agents in the literary world." She smiled. "I spoke with him, and he wants to represent me, Carter. We spoke of publishing houses where he wants to land a deal. He thinks he can even create a bidding war between a few of them."

Carter framed her face in his hands. "I told you it was good. Better than good. This is amazing."

He kissed her and for a moment, Tenley thought of nothing but her future with this man.

Breaking the kiss, he asked, "Did he send you a contract?"

"He did. Elmo suggested I have an attorney look it over. I was going to ask Willow's brother. I've met him once. Or I thought about Clancy Nelson. Willow mentioned him to me when she was dealing with Boo's will."

"Clancy's still got it going on at his age, but he's never dealt with anything that big. What about your New York attorney? The one who helped get your annulment so quickly?"

"Oh, Sylvia. I hadn't even thought of her. Her specialty is divorce, but she would have to know something about contracts. Elmo—and the houses he's pitching to—are all located in New York. That might be a better idea than Jackson taking a look."

"I think so. Plus, Jackson is about to wrap up a murder trial. From what Dylan has said, it has been consuming Jackson's every waking moment."

"Then I won't ask Willow for that favor. I do want to go ahead and give Elmo an answer regarding the contract."

"Call this Sylvia now. Then I have somewhere I want to take you."

Curiosity filled her, but Tenley brought her phone from her tote and scrolled through her contacts, touching Sylvia's name.

After three rings, she heard Sylvia's husky voice. "Don't tell me you need another annulment, sweetie."

She laughed. "No, but I could use some legal advice. Remember how I told you I was working on a novel?"

"Yes. You finish it?"

"No, but I'm getting close. I've had an offer from Elmo Nichols to represent me. He's e-mailed a contract for me to read over and recommended I have a lawyer peruse it. I know this isn't your specialty—"

"It's close enough," Sylvia interrupted. "Forward it to me. I can read it by tonight and get back to you."

"Thank you, Sylvia. I really appreciate it."

The attorney cackled. "Oh, you'll get my bill. But you know I'm worth every dime."

Once off the phone, Tenley told Carter she would know something from Sylvia by tonight.

"Good. That gives us the rest of today to enjoy. There's someone I want you to meet. My mom."

Nerves rippled through her. "Your mom?"

The thought of meeting Carter's mom made everything between them suddenly seem incredibly real.

"Will she be upset?"

"About what?"

"About... you getting married again. And doing it so quickly."

Carter shook his head. "Mom is the best. You'll see what I mean."

Despite her new fiancé's assurances, nerves built within Tenley as they returned to Carter's truck, and he drove less than two miles from the square to a large, two-story house with a wraparound porch.

"You didn't call her and let her know we were coming," she said, as he came around and helped her from the truck.

"Mom doesn't need advance notice for a visit. If the house is upside down, she doesn't care. She has company drop in all the time."

"But... this is different. We're sharing big news with her, Carter."

He laughed and pulled her close for a quick, hard kiss. "It's fine, Tenley. Come on."

They went up the stairs to the porch, which had a

swing on one side of the door and wicker furniture with colorful cushions on the other side, giving it a homey feel.

"Did you grow up in this house?" she asked, as he rang the doorbell.

"I did."

The door opened, and Tenley saw an attractive woman in her mid-fifties with brown hair shot through with gray. She had Carter's same chocolate-brown eyes and was even taller than Tenley, probably an inch under six feet.

"Carter, darling. Hello. And you must be Tenley. My son has been telling me about you. Come in."

"Thank you," she said shakily, glancing over her shoulder at Carter with a questioning look.

"I just finished baking some oatmeal raisin cookies," Mrs. Clark said. "Shall we go to the kitchen and sample a few?"

"Define *a few*," Carter said, laughing. "Your 'few' and my 'few' are probably worlds apart."

Tenley followed the older women through the house, which looked comfortable and lived-in. The kitchen was large and obviously updated, most likely by Pete Pulaski. The freshly baked cookies sat resting on wire racks on the large island.

"Milk? Or hot tea?" Mrs. Clark said.

"Tea, if it's not too much trouble," Tenley told her hostess.

"Not at all. I'd already put the kettle on and just added the tea ball to it, so it won't be long."

"Milk for me," Carter said, going to a double-door stainless-steel fridge and removing a gallon of milk.

His mother took a glass from the cupboard and handed it to her son. "Drink up. It goes bad in another two days. I should buy quarts of milk since it's just me these days, but I do like to have it on hand for company."

"Carter says you have company drop by frequently, Mrs. Clark. I wanted him to call before we stopped by."

"Not necessary, Tenley. And please, call me Dorothy. I'm either Dorothy to family and friends, or Miz C to former students. I don't remember the last time I was addressed as Mrs. Clark."

Dorothy tore off paper towels and placed cookies on them, taking them to the kitchen table. She indicated for Tenley to join her. Tenley liked that they would eat off paper towels.

"I do have people pop by all the time. Carter teases me about it. But I just know so many after living in the Cove my entire life. I met Clinton, Carter's father, at Portland State, and the first time I brought him home to meet my parents, he fell in love with the Cove. Insisted we move here after we both graduated and married, although I was a year behind him. He did his firefighter training while I completed my education degree. Of course, Clinton had visited here before, because his parents brought him up in Crescent Cove, just the other side of Salty Point. Have you been to see either town yet?"

"No, but Carter said it was a tradition for the Clark men to be firemen serving at Salty Point. I'm eager to see his fire station and meet some of his fellow firefighters."

Carter joined them, quickly downing half his glass of milk and eating three cookies.

Dorothy's brows rose. "I would tell him to slow down, but he hasn't listened to my advice for his first thirty years. Why would he start now?"

Tenley laughed. "Your son has a zest for life."

"I like the fact that he's quite handy. Carter, my shower is dripping. It's driving me crazy when I'm trying to go to sleep at night. And I also need my Christmas decorations taken up to the attic." She looked to Tenley. "I'm a purist and leave them up through Epiphany on January sixth."

"I'll do it now, Mom." He rose and kissed the top of her head. "Just text me when I've been gone long enough and you've pumped Tenley dry."

"I am a subtle gatherer of information," Dorothy protested.

"Well, I want to share some with you now before I leave." Carter placed his hand on Tenley's shoulder. "We're getting married."

Tenley watched for Dorothy's reaction, expecting shock, anger, or doubt. Instead, the woman beamed at her only son.

"That is wonderful news," she declared, quickly standing and embracing Carter. Then she bent and hugged Tenley, as well. "You definitely need to leave us now. I need full details, Tenley, dear. Carter would merely tell me, yeah, I asked. She said yes."

She burst out laughing. "I think most men are alike, Dorothy."

"Go," Dorothy said, flipping her hand dismissively.

"I'm going," Carter complained good-naturedly.

When he had left the kitchen, Dorothy turned her gaze back to Tenley. "I already know you're the best thing that's happened to my boy in ages."

"I know this seems sudden," she began. "But we'll—"

"No explanation needed," Dorothy assured her. "When it's right, it's right. I know Carter must have told you about poor Emily and how quickly he lost her and the baby."

"The baby?" she said dully.

Worry filled Dorothy's eyes. "Oh, goodness. I'm sorry I spoke out of turn."

"Emily was... pregnant?"

"Yes. She wasn't very far along. No one knew but Clinton and me. And Dylan. Not even Emily's parents." Dorothy frowned. "I try my best to never speak ill of anyone, but Fred and Wilma are poor excuses for human beings."

"I've met Wilma," Tenley said, still reeling from the news that Carter was to have been a father with his first wife. "At the diner this morning."

"Oh, no. She caused a scene, didn't she?"

She nodded. "She did. A pretty ugly one. She said a few cruel things about me and then let Carter know that he should be loyal to Emily's memory."

Dorothy took Tenley's hand. "I hope you aren't still upset by it. Wilma was a terrible mother to Emily. Cared more about her clients at the salon than she did her only child. Wilma and Fred both live for gossip. Why, she never even packed Emily a lunch. That girl made her own from kindergarten on. She didn't know she needed one that first day." Dorothy paused. "When I saw her sitting in the cafeteria with nothing to eat, my heart broke for her. I was able to get her a tray, and I watched her closely after that. I made certain she had the supplies she needed, as well as the support every child deserves."

"She sounds as if she were like a daughter to you," Tenley noted, a lump swelling in her throat.

"She was. But many of my students become that to me, Tenley. Please don't think simply because I knew Emily from such a young age that I won't give you a chance. In fact, it's quite the opposite. I've seen how happy Carter is. Heard it in his voice when we've spoken on the phone and observed him when he's dropped by for a quick chat.

"*You* have made him find the joy in life again, Tenley. For that, I will be forever grateful. Carter has been sleepwalking through life for too long. It's Sleeping Beauty all over again, with the roles reversed. You've awakened my son and brought him back to the living."

Dorothy rose, wiping tears from her face. She returned with the tea kettle and two mugs, pouring them cups of the hot tea.

"Lemon? Or sugar and milk?"

"Sugar and milk for me," she replied.

They sipped their tea and ate another cookie, and Tenley found herself relaxing in this woman's company. She realized Dorothy only wanted Carter to be happy.

He finally returned. Reaching for more cookies, he gobbled them down. "We've got to get going, Mom. You two can talk wedding stuff later. We don't want a big fuss. Something small. Maybe even an elopement. We'll talk about it and let you know."

As she rose, Tenley embraced Dorothy Clark. "I'm so glad to have met you."

"I can say the same, Tenley. You'll have to come back when we have longer to visit."

"I'll do that," she promised.

They returned to Carter's truck. Once he was inside, Tenley turned to him.

"When were you going to tell me about the baby?"

CHAPTER 18

Carter gripped the wheel, and Tenley saw his knuckles turn white.

"You don't have talk about it if you don't want to," she said quickly, regretting she had ambushed him with her question. "It's really none of my business."

He turned to look at her. "Everything is your business now, Tenley. I don't want to hide any secrets from you." He hesitated. "Could I take you back to my place? I'd rather have some privacy while we talk about it instead of sitting in front of Mom's house. She would notice sooner than later that we hadn't left and figure something was wrong."

She agreed and he started the truck, driving back to his bungalow. Tenley thought of the layout of the small house, wondering which room had been designated as the baby's.

Carter and Emily's baby.

They went inside and he took her hand, leading her to the sofa. He faced her after they sat—and she saw the tears welling in his eyes.

"I wasn't trying to hide anything from you," he began. "It was hard enough to keep that I loved you from being voiced. Everything has happened today so quickly. I knew it would be a major hurdle after I spoke of my love for you to get you to understand that I will always love Emily. She was a part of my growing up here in the Cove. A part of those wonderful, carefree high school days of baseball games and dances. Then we went off to community college together. She's like Dylan to me, in a way. I grew up with both of them —and became the man I am because of my relationships with the two of them."

He paused, and she knew he was searching for the words to say that were in his heart.

"I did grow up—mature—being with Emily. I don't want to erase that time in my life and the years I spent with her. But at the same time, I want you to know that they are in my past. That I'm looking forward to my present and future with you. My wife has been gone a long time now, and she's a sweet memory, for the most part. Sometimes, a bittersweet memory. And that's where the baby comes in."

His fingers tightened on hers. "We waited a few years before we tried for a baby. We wanted to be more settled in our careers. I guess we wanted to be more grown up than we felt at twenty-two when we married. After three years of marriage, though, we decided the time was right. Emily had just turned ten weeks when the aneurysm took her. We had only told my parents. My sister already had two kids, so it wasn't new for them to have grandchildren. Still, all the same, it would be a little different because it would be my firstborn. Mom and Dad were over the moon for us, and so was Dylan. Emily knew that even though Dylan was half a world away, he was still my best friend, and I wanted to share our news with him."

"You didn't tell her parents. Why?"

"Mostly because Emily was worried about a miscarriage. One teacher friend at school and Emily's college roommate had both miscarried in the year leading up to us getting pregnant. They had both shared their pregnancies around the six or eight-week mark, and then lost their babies. She said both of them talked about how awful it was to have to tell people that they had miscarried. It wasn't just the physical death of the baby growing within them, but the death of the dream of that baby and all he or she stood for. We talked to her OB and read enough about it to feel comfortable sharing when she was twelve weeks along."

He sighed. "You met Wilma today. Her husband Fred is cut from the same cloth. They are the two most ferocious gossips in the Cove. Their jobs make it easy for them to spread any news. Wilma is a stylist and Fred owns the gas station just on the edge of the Cove, where a lot of people gas up before heading toward Portland. They are in the business of spilling secrets. Emily was afraid if we told them, the entire Cove would know within twenty-four hours."

"You don't think they would have honored her wishes? My gosh, Carter, she was their child."

"All I can say is that Emily was never close to either of them. Because of their natures, she didn't want them to know about the baby. They hadn't been loving parents to her, and she didn't want her personal life spread across the Cove before she was ready for others to know."

"Will you tell me anything about that day?" Tenley asked softly. "I don't want to hurt you by making you relive it, but I think it might help me understand you better."

He leaned back against the sofa and closed his eyes, still holding on to her hand.

Finally, he opened his eyes and said, "Emily and I had a tradition of going up to Seattle to see the Seahawks play one home game a year. She was crazy about football. Probably a bigger fan than I was. We flew up on a Friday after she got out of school, staying at a B&B we had found and liked. The next morning, we enjoyed brunch at her favorite spot to eat and then went to Kerry Park. It's in Queen Anne and has amazing views of the entire city."

Carter paused, gripping her hand tightly. "That's where it happened. A sudden headache came out of nowhere, and it wasn't right. We both knew it. I dialed 911 and requested an ambulance as she fell unconscious. I tried CPR but couldn't revive her. The EMTs arrived, and I rode with them to the hospital, where an ER physician pronounced her dead."

"Oh, Carter, I can't tell you how sorry I am. Not only did you lose the only woman you had ever loved, but you lost your child, too. A double blow."

He winced at her words. "A triple blow," he muttered.

"I don't understand."

Tenley watched as tears began to roll down her fiancé's face.

"The doctor gave me a few minutes to say my goodbyes. While I was doing that, Mom called. Dad..." Carter choked—and Tenley instinctively knew what he was going to say.

"Don't."

"No, I want you to know it all. Mom was calling to let me know that Dad had been lost in a fire. A beam fell on him, trapping him in a burning house. I lost my wife, my baby—and my dad that day."

She now felt her own tears coursing down her cheeks. "Oh, Carter."

Tenley curled up next to him, wanting to bring comfort to the only man she had loved, and feeling so inadequate.

They stayed locked together for a long time, and then he said, "Make love with me, Tenley. You've been the one who has healed me. I need you now. More than I ever have."

She kissed him softly, then pushed to her feet, pulling him to his. They went to the bedroom and they undressed one another slowly. She willed her strength to flow into him as they made slow, tender love.

In the afterglow, she lay nestled in his arms, stroking his forearm.

"Thank you," he told her. "For letting me still love Emily. And the baby."

"I understand, Carter. I truly do. They will always be a part of you. That doesn't mean you don't have any room left for me and our children, though. You have the biggest heart of any man I've ever met. I am in awe of how you handled such a tragedy. I love you so much."

Carter kissed her. "And I love you, Tenley."

TENLEY LEFT PORTER WILLIAMS' office, glad that the insurance agent had set her up with both renter's insurance on her apartment and automobile insurance, since she would be purchasing a vehicle today. She walked to Antiques and Mystique, Rylie's store.

Although a closed sign appeared hanging on the door, Rylie had said to come on in, and Tenley did so.

"Hello," she called.

Moments later, Rylie emerged from an opening near the back of the store. "Good morning, Tenley. I'm so excited that you wanted to go into Portland today."

"You're the one who is doing me the favor. When I told Willow I wanted to invest in a car, she insisted that I see Tom Presley. Thank you for driving me into Portland and setting up a meeting with him. Willow has been very pleased with the SUV she purchased at his dealership."

"I'm glad to hear that. Tom and I went to college together, and he's a great guy. He sold my car to me and also one to Ainsley when she returned from her training in Paris. He'll give you the best price possible."

"I was happy you wanted to meet here. Do we have time for me to look around your store before we leave?"

"Let me give you the guided tour!"

Rylie led Tenley about the store, commenting on a few of the pieces, and then showing her an area devoted to consignment and new furniture.

"This area isn't large, but if you ever need anything and want it new, I can order it for you. It would have to be delivered here, but I could get you a terrific price, and then Carter could use his truck to bring it up to your new apartment." Rylie smiled. "I'm so glad you've decided to stay in the Cove, Tenley. I hope you'll be happy here. Let me grab my purse, and we'll head out."

In the car, Rylie asked what kind of music Tenley liked to listen to and found a station on Sirius they both enjoyed.

"Was Willow upset when you decided to move out from Boo's house?" Rylie chucked. "I think we'll all always call it Boo's, no matter how long Willow and Dylan live there."

"No, I don't think she was upset because I'm staying nearby. I just didn't feel I should impose on her and Dylan anymore."

"You weren't," Rylie insisted, sounding like Willow. "I know the two of you are closer than sisters."

"Even sisters need to give each other space. Especially when one of them has married a hot sheriff."

Rylie burst out laughing. "You're right about that. Willow and Dylan can't seem to keep their hands off each other. I'm thrilled for both of them, having this second chance at love."

"Speaking of love," Tenley began, "I have a bit of news. Carter and I are engaged."

Rylie gave an enthusiastic shout of delight, sounding an awful lot like Sloane had when Tenley talked to her friend yesterday.

"That's fantastic, Tenley. I'm so happy for the two of you."

"You don't think it's too soon? I know people will think that."

Rylie glanced over. "No, I don't." Her eyes returned to the road. "Yes, there will probably be a little gossip about how soon an engagement occurred, but I know Carter is thirty."

"So am I."

"You know your mind and yourself by that age. I know after one date—no, ten minutes into a first date —if I want that date to continue and if I see relationship potential in that man sitting across from me. Carter has been married once. He knows what kind of commitment that is. He wouldn't go into it again unless he was certain it was right. In fact, he would have to be one hundred and ten percent certain because he does understand what a commitment marriage is. So if the two of you love each other, ignore what anyone else says. It's none of their business. Yes, there will be some in the Cove that think you've jumped the gun. I'm sure Emily's parents will be two of those people, but stay true to your heart, Tenley. Carter is a wonderful guy. You're great together."

Rylie paused. "Now, let's talk important things. Such as, when is the date?"

Tenley relaxed. "We need to sit down and talk about that. Yesterday was devoted to moving me from Boo's to the new apartment above the diner. I took a three-month lease, which Nancy said I could extend if I needed to do so."

"So, we're talking at least three months."

"Yes, it will give us a little more time to get to know one another and build the foundation of our relationship. Neither of us wants a large wedding."

"I can see that, with Carter having been married before. Are you sure you won't be missing out on anything?"

"Not at all. I'd told you that my marriage was annulled. That was a huge wedding. One I didn't really want and was nudged into. I'd prefer a small ceremony with just a few friends and family or even an elopement. It's working for Willow and Dylan."

"I'm glad you and Carter found each other—and found love again."

They arrived in Portland and met with her friend Tom, who took them back to his office. Over coffee, Tom asked Tenley several questions, trying to establish what she wanted in a car. She knew she didn't want an SUV, as Willow had bought from this sales-man. She wasn't an experienced driver and needed something smaller and compact, like she had driven during her years in California. In New York, she hadn't even owned a car, although she had gotten her New York driver's license for ID purposes. She would need to ask Willow what she had done in regard to getting one in Oregon.

"I have a few models I'd like to show you, Tenley, and then you can test drive whichever ones speak to you. And yes, I do think a car lets an owner know to choose it. One of my little quirks," Tom revealed.

They followed Tom to the showroom floor, where he indicated three different models he thought would suit her needs best. Not only was she more comfort-able in a sedan, but Carter had the large truck, which would be something they would use most likely on weekend outings together. Tenley had decided to buy a new vehicle, though, something she had never done in the past because she hadn't had the money during her lean years.

Tom was right. One car seemed to shout Tenley's name. She walked around the four-door, maroon sedan and then climbed behind the wheel.

"It feels right," she told the salesman.

"What about the color?" he asked.

"I like this color quite a bit."

"We have one of these in stock in this same shade. I'll have it brought around for you to take out."

During the test drive, Tenley made up her mind that this would be the vehicle for her. They returned to the dealership, and she told Tom she wanted to pur-chase the car.

"Come back to my office and we can talk details," he told them.

They discussed financing, and Tenley decided she didn't want to take on a monthly payment. She wanted to enter her new marriage debt-free and so after calls to her bank and a short delay, she and Rylie left the dealership, Rylie in the lead, with Tenley following her.

They drove to an Italian place Rylie had mentioned which was nearby and enjoyed a leisurely, celebratory lunch. Over the meal, she told her new friend about her book and how she now had an agent, explaining how her old boss and friend had brought her and Elmo Nichols together.

"He sent me a contract, and I forwarded it to the lawyer who handled my annulment. I told Sylvia I knew this wasn't quite in her wheelhouse, and she laughed, telling me she handled prenups all the time and made sure those were ironclad contracts. I heard from her last night."

"Did she recommend any changes in what Elmo sent to you?"

"A couple of minor ones and one major one—Elmo's cut. I knew from research that agents usually take fifteen percent from their client and the top ones twenty. Elmo's contract called for twenty-five percent."

"Whoa. That's a hefty chunk to pay out."

"I agree. But Elmo is in the top three literary agents in the business. He can command that because he produces fantastic results. I gave Sylvia permission to discuss it with him. She used the word 'haggle.' We were on a three-way phone call last night."

"Did he go for a lower take?"

"He did. While he pointed out he could have doors opened to me simply because of his name, Sylvia told him the huge earning potential from not only this book but the entire trilogy would benefit him. She stressed he would more than make up that missing five percent in sales, but that he would have to drop to twenty percent if I would be hiring him as my agent.

"In the end, Elmo folded. Later, Sylvia told me she had doubted he would, and so she was incredibly pleased at the outcome. She also believes, as does Elmo, my work has film potential. That Elmo was also considering his profits from that."

"You mean your book might be made into a movie? This is really exciting. Why, you could be one of those people attending a movie premiere—with your dashing new husband, of course. Carter would look amazing in a tux."

Tenley mentally pictured her fiancé in one—and then her taking it off him—and grinned.

"You're thinking about sex, aren't you?" Rylie teased.

She felt the hot blush spill across her cheeks. "Maybe. But on the small chance we did sell the film rights, it doesn't mean a movie gets made."

"What do you mean?"

"Books are bought all the time, along with spec scripts. Speculation scripts."

"Oh, you mean like spec houses. Built with the hope that someone wants a house like that."

"Exactly," Tenley confirmed. "Just because a book or script is purchased by a studio doesn't mean that it makes it to the screen. Once it's bought, a screenplay has to be developed and written. Then a director hired. Casting needs to take place. Then filming. By the time all of that occurs, several years might pass."

"That could be a good thing," Rylie said. "By then, you might have written the second and third books. The entire trilogy being out could drive ticket sales to the first movie and even help see a second and third brought to the screen."

"*If* that first film did well. We're getting way ahead of ourselves, though. Elmo does want me to come to New York soon. He is shopping my partial manuscript around this week and hopes to narrow it down to two or three publishing houses. When he does, I'll fly in and meet with him and the editors at each house that would oversee this project."

"This is pretty exciting news for a new resident of the Cove. A marriage and a book deal. I feel like I should get your autograph now."

Tenley laughed. "We'll see. There are a lot of *ifs*. In the meantime, I need to get back to the Cove and finish up my latest scene."

They went to their cars, and Rylie told Tenley to follow her back.

She got behind the wheel of her new vehicle, inhaling deeply, enjoying that wonderful new-car smell. She didn't know how long it would last, but the feeling of owning her first new car gave her a thrill. As she followed Rylie back to the Cove, she deliberately focused on the road and not her characters. Instead, she sang along to songs on the radio, and the time passed quickly.

The only thing that bothered her was as they entered town and she saw the gas station that was owned by Emily's dad. She would wind up purchasing gas here many times and hoped it wouldn't be awkward. While she could avoid Wilma's hair salon and find another place to have her hair cut, buying gas on a regular basis would be another matter.

She waved to Rylie as her friend turned in a different direction from Tenley. She parked on the side street next to her apartment. Dylan told her the spot was usually available, and its proximity to the stairs leading up to the apartment was convenient.

Entering the apartment, she texted Carter, letting him know she had arrived home with a new car and that she'd be writing the rest of the afternoon. Though she would prefer spending time with him on his final day off before his next four-day shift began, she had to get busy on her manuscript. With an agent shopping it now, the pressure to complete it was definitely on.

Her phone rang and it was Carter. She picked up. "Hi."

"Hey," he said. "I know you said you need to work this afternoon, but I'd like to cook dinner and bring it over to you. Do you have time to eat if I bring something by?"

"I'll always have time for you," she told him, still amazed that she was going to marry him. "Plan on staying and having dinner with me."

"Okay. What time do you want to eat?"

"How about seven?"

"Sounds good. I'll plan accordingly."

Tenley went to her laptop and brought up her document, soon losing herself in her world.

CHAPTER 19

Tenley entered the skyscraper that housed Elmo Nichol's offices and took the elevator to the fourteenth floor. She had flown in yesterday for the meetings she and her agent would have with three publishers today. She had arrived in time to have dinner with Sylvia Driver, who caught her up on the drama surrounding Cecilia's and Theodore's divorce. Tenley had deliberately kept from searching for news accounts online regarding the couple.

Sylvia had let her know that the divorce should be granted today, and that by the end of the week, Cecilia and Theodore would be sentenced on the bigamy charges, which both had already pled guilty to.

The attorney told Tenley that Cecilia was still designing her handbags with a vengeance amidst boosted sales, while Theodore had taken a leave of absence from his Wall Street firm and was licking his wounds. Sylvia promised to keep Tenley in the loop on the progress of the case, but Tenley had declined, telling her lawyer she had moved past all that.

Sylvia had understood Tenley's reasoning and told her to keep her head down while she was in town this week. Reporters knew she had left the state, but none of them knew she was back in town. Unless some eagle-eyed spotter had seen her at JFK's terminal yesterday.

She stepped from the elevator and to the receptionist's desk and provided her name. The woman's eyes lit up.

"Right this way, Miss Thompson."

Tenley followed the woman to a small conference room lined with shelves of books, noting they were all written by authors her new agent had represented. She declined an offer of coffee or tea and waited only a few minutes before Elmo Nichols appeared. It was obvious he was related to Diane since he had the same hazel eyes and friendly smile.

She stood. "It's nice to meet you in person, Elmo," she told him, shaking the hand he offered.

"Have a seat, Tenley," he said. "I want to go over our schedule today."

The agent had already e-mailed her a list of the various publishing companies he had spoken with the previous week. With his advice, they had narrowed it down to three publishers, two of the Big Five ones and a third rising company which looked as if it would become a player in the next couple of years. Already, *Publishers Weekly* had written about the bidding war going on over her manuscript. Elmo had let it leak that the manuscript was part of a trilogy that was being shopped, telling Tenley he wanted additional pressure put on each publishing house.

"I'm glad you went with the three choices you did," he said. "I've worked with all three firms, and my clients have nothing but good things to say about their experiences with each of them. Do you have any preferences going into our meetings today?"

"No, I don't. I have studied each of their websites thoroughly, seeing the kinds of books they publish and who is included in their stable of authors. I'm trying to keep an open mind, but I would like a deal for the entire trilogy locked up. I also want to retain the rights to my characters in this trilogy. If I'm able to continue it as a series or spin it off into something related, I need to own the rights to these characters."

"Understood. Do you have a timeline in mind as to when you'll make your decision? I guarantee they will all ask you that question."

"What do you suggest?"

"I wouldn't drag it out. I suggest a week or less. Your gut, along with my advice, will tell you which house will best suit your needs." He glanced at his watch. "We should head downstairs. A car is waiting for us."

Tenley accompanied the agent downstairs, and they spoke of Diane and how she was Elmo's favorite cousin.

"I have plans to see her for dinner tonight," she revealed. "If you'd care to join us, I'm sure she wouldn't mind."

"I'll have to let you know about that."

They arrived at the first publishing house, one of the Big Five, and checked in with the security guard, who issued visitor passes for them and instructed them on which bank of elevators to use.

In the elevator, Elmo asked, "Nervous?"

"A little," Tenley admitted. "I never thought it would come to something like this so soon. I had dreams of supporting myself with my writing, but I never thought I would be pitching a partial manuscript to such big players."

"You wouldn't be unless you were talented, and

they recognized that," he told her. "You should be brimming with confidence now that you have these meetings today. I haven't asked yet. When do you think you'll finish up this first book?"

"I probably am three or four chapters from the end. I'm still debating on whether to do an epilogue or save things for the second book."

"Write what you need to finish the book. You'll know what to do at that point. So, a week? Longer?"

"I would say two weeks. One to finish and a second to go back and re-read the entire manuscript. I want to check for consistency and pacing."

"Have you outlined your next two books? Or are you a pantser?"

She didn't answer his questions because the elevator doors opened. Soon, they found themselves in the office of an imposing editor whose name was legendary in the business. Max Edgewood had a headful of thick, white hair, and dressed like Cary Grant in a 1940s movie, elegant and dapper. He greeted them and asked them to have a seat. He spent almost half an hour telling them why he liked her book and how he foresaw marketing it. It would be an aggressive campaign, one touching all aspects of the media, from ads in a variety of magazines to a social media blitz through Facebook, Instagram, and Twitter.

"Do you have any questions for me, Tenley?" Max asked, after he finished his spiel.

She asked a few questions about how the editing process would work between them, especially how many passes he would take through the book and the number of rewrites she would be expected to produce. As Elmo had, Max wanted to know when she could get the completed manuscript to him, along with the other two books.

"Honestly, Max, I can get the first book to you in less than a month. I'm not quite sure how long it will take me to write two and three. They are outlined. I am writing full time now. Neither of those were the case when I started the first book. My hope is to be able to finish both of them by the end of this year."

Elmo took over at that point, talking numbers. Tenley sat with her hands folded in her lap, not trying to show her surprise at the figures being bandied about. Her agent did emphasize that Tenley must have control of the characters in case she extended the trilogy or spun off into a different series. Max quibbled a bit, and the two men bantered back and forth over the issue.

Elmo nodded to her and they rose, thanking the editor for his time and sharing they had two more meetings scheduled for today with other houses.

"When can I expect an answer?" Max asked. "Or should I say when will you commit to us?" He grinned shamelessly.

"By the end of this week," Elmo guaranteed. "Tenley wants this part decided quickly."

"I like hearing that." Max offered her his hand, and again she took it. "A pleasure meeting you, my dear. I hope you enjoy your other two meetings—but not too much."

She laughed, being charmed by the legend.

They rode the elevator back to the ground floor without conversation. Only when they were back in their car did Elmo ask, "What did you think of Max?"

"My reaction is mostly positive. He knows his stuff. He's done this for decades and has had too many successes for me to count. I was surprised that no one else was in the room for our meeting, though."

"That's just the way Max rolls. It'll be different at

the other two publishing houses. We'll see attorneys. A team of editorial assistants and marketing people. Perhaps even the publisher himself."

Elmo's predictions proved true at their second meeting. The next company they visited had almost twenty people in a huge conference room. It was a bit overwhelming after her first experience. Their pitch was similar to the one Max gave, only shared by numerous people. Again, Elmo thanked them and said a decision would be made by the end of the week, which seemed to please them.

It was almost noon by this time, and he told her their next meeting wasn't until two this afternoon, with Oakwood Publishing.

"Can I take you to lunch?" he asked.

"I'm famished."

Instead of some expensive, fancy restaurant, Tenley was surprised they went to a small, out-of-the-way place. Apparently Elmo ate here with regularity, because he was greeted by name from everyone, from the hostess to the person setting glasses of water on their table to their server. Even the manager came by and chatted with them for a few minutes. The food turned out to be delicious, Northern Italian in nature. She ordered lasagna and a salad and had to refrain from going back to the bread basket numerous times.

Elmo talked a little about his childhood and how he got started in the business as a literary agent, training under a name Tenley recognized. In return, she told him some about Sutton Press, the publishing house she'd worked for when she first graduated from college, as well as what she had done for the Borough of Brooklyn.

"You were smart to get out of New York when you did," he told her. "Your former husband and his wife have dominated the headlines. I doubt that would have been conducive to your writing."

"I wanted a clean break. A quieter life. My college roommate lives in Maple Cove, a coastal town in Oregon. I decided to visit her after I sold my loft. Actually, I'm staying there permanently."

She left out her engagement to Carter, wanting to keep that and the rest of her life now private.

"I need to set you up with the public relations agency I want you to use," Elmo said. "Dalton International. They're pricey, but they specialize in best-selling authors. We need to work on creating your website and you establishing your brand. They'll also help you set up an author page on Facebook and Instagram, as well as a Twitter account. They also know about TikTok, which I'm clueless about, but I'm told it's a platform appealing to younger people. Your books have broader appeal, but the PR firm will be able to guide you. You'll have final approval on everything. They'll send you example websites of clients they work for, as well as others in your genre."

"Thank you for taking me on, Elmo, and arranging all of this."

"It's my job to not only take care of your book but you, Tenley. I hope we will be in business together for a long time."

He asked for the check and they left the restaurant, heading to their final meeting. The building and its address weren't nearly as fancy as the two Big Five publishing companies they had visited that morning, but she had a good feeling as they entered the lobby. They met with the publisher first, along with the editor that would handle her books, then transitioned to a conference room. A team of four awaited them, and they walked through how to brand and market her.

They even showed her mock-ups of five different cover designs, which neither previous house had done.

They spent an hour with this team, and Tenley felt drawn to their philosophy. They didn't pressure her as to when the book would be completed nor when the other two in the trilogy would be available. The meeting ended on a positive note, with them saying they would stay in touch with her, and Elmo telling them he would notify them by the end of the week as to Tenley's decision.

In the car, he asked her what her general impressions were of this particular press.

"Obviously, they don't have as large a staff as the other two Big Fives. I had already looked at their website before our meeting today, and I believe everyone on their staff was in that room with us. That means the entire company would be involved with my rollouts."

"Are you leaning any one way at this point?"

"Either the first—because of Max—or this third house," she told him. "The second was a little too slick for my taste. I'll need to think on it, Elmo. I'd also appreciate your input."

"I'll write something up and send it to you tonight. I believe either one would be a good fit for you. It all boils down to what you want from your publishing house and your comfort level with them."

"I know this is all so new to me. I do want to mull it over."

"Talk with Diane about it," he urged. "She may not be in publishing, but she's as smart as they come and has good business instincts. So does Sylvia Driver."

"I'll do that."

They pulled up in front of his offices, and he said,

"Have the car take you wherever you like. Back to your hotel. Shopping. I'll be in touch."

He exited the vehicle, and Tenley told the driver to head straight for her hotel. She didn't need to shop in fancy New York stores. Right now, she needed time alone.

To think about her professional future.

CHAPTER 20

Tenley finished dressing and ran a brush through her hair. She stared at her image in the mirror, no closer now to a decision than she had been yesterday when she'd left Elmo.

She'd met Diane Nichols for dinner last night, discussing the pros and cons of going with a larger versus a smaller publishing house. Diane made some good points, but Tenley wasn't ready to commit yet to a publisher. When she'd returned from dinner, an e-mail from her agent awaited her. Opening it, Elmo made some of the same arguments Diane had, further confusing Tenley.

She decided she wanted to talk things over with Carter—and even Willow and Sloane—before she made her final decision. She had sent e-mails to Carter and her two friends, forwarding the list Elmo had sent, asking them to read over it and talk with her when she returned to the Cove. She also included a few of the ideas Diane had mentioned, giving them food for thought.

Her phone rang. She saw it was Sloane and answered. "Hello, world traveler."

"Hello yourself," her friend greeted. "Listen, I got your e-mail and wanted to buzz you now. I'm heading out for assignment and will probably be unreachable for a few days. Just wanted to put my two cents into the mix."

Quickly, Sloane outlined why she thought Tenley should go with Max and his Big Five publishing house.

"It's not that I don't like a smaller outfit. I checked the Oakwood Publishing website and liked what I saw. I just believe a top New York house will give you more opportunities. I liken it to when I was a reporter at a local news station in San Diego versus working for a major network now. I get to cover bigger, better stories. I think a well-known publishing company could open more doors for you. But I think either would be good."

"Thanks for your input, Sloane. I'm trying to decide by the end of the week which to sign with. I want that piece of the puzzle out of the way, so I can focus on my writing."

"The fact that Elmo Nichols signed you speaks volumes about your writing, Ten," Sloane praised. "He'll guide you the right way."

"Where are you headed on assignment?"

"I can't talk about it," her friend said, surprising Tenley because Sloane was always very open about where she went and the news she covered.

"Is it dangerous, Sloane?"

"I can't talk about it," Sloane repeated, giving Tenley a bad feeling.

"Stay in touch," she urged.

"I'll try to. Give my love to Willow when you get back to Oregon."

"Will do. And Sloane—be careful."

Sloane's deep chuckle sounded. "I always am, Ten."

Tenley ended the connection, worry nagging at her. Sloane had gone to some dangerous countries in the past. She was in Africa now, where tribal warfare seemed a constant. It worried her that Sloane was so far away. She wished her friend would take a job stateside so they could see one another more often.

And so Sloane would be safer.

She closed her suitcase and picked up her tote and carry-on bag, heading downstairs to check out and meet Janice Craig, her former boss at Sutton Press. After paying her bill, she asked for her bags to be held while she met a friend for breakfast in the hotel's dining room.

Heading to the restaurant, she spotted Janice and joined her at the table for two. They hugged.

"You look fantastic, Tenley. I was so pleased to hear from you."

"I was glad you had time to meet me before I returned to Oregon."

"That's where you went? Three thousand miles away? You were from California, I remember," her former boss said.

"Yes. I went to visit my college roommate on the Oregon coast and decided to stay. It's a beautiful place. A small, sleepy town. I like the quiet and the people."

The server brought coffee for them, and they took a moment to study the menu before ordering.

"I'm sorry to hear about your divorce. Or annulment," Janice corrected. "I still hate that you left Sutton Press because of the pressure Theodore Fielding exerted."

"I regret that I let him talk me into leaving," Tenley

admitted. "I loved my job and missed it and my fellow workers after I left."

"Would you come back?" Janice asked hopefully. "I know I've heard you're writing a trilogy. It's creating quite the stir in the publishing world. You probably don't have time to work full time and write."

"No, I made a good profit on the sale of our Brooklyn loft in Dumbo. I'm living off that until my book drops."

She discussed the two different publishing houses with Janice, who noted a few things neither Elmo nor Diane had mentioned. Tenley filed Janice's ideas away, knowing she would take the long coast-to-coast flight to think about her decision as to which company to choose.

Their breakfasts arrived, and Janice said, "It's too bad you're not writing non-fiction. You know you'd have a home with us at Sutton Press."

Tenley took a bite of her omelet and chewed thoughtfully, an idea coming to her. "Actually, I may have a tip regarding a new author for you."

"Really? What kind of book? We're still doing really well with self-help books."

"This would be a cookbook."

Janice frowned. "We haven't published anything food-related. Well, maybe a couple of books in our how-to catalog. I don't think we'd be interested in a cookbook author."

She removed her cell phone and pulled up a picture, turning the phone so Janice could see Carter. Tenley had taken it on one of their hikes, and it showed Carter's handsome face and broad shoulders.

"What if this were the author?"

Janice said, "Then I'd go all Rachael Ray on you and say *yummo*. Who is he?"

"My fiancé," she said proudly. "We've been toying with the idea of Carter starting a food blog because he enjoys cooking so much. I've even suggested that he write a cookbook. Here, let me pull up one of the videos we've shot."

She did so and handed over her phone to Janice, who was spellbound for the next several minutes. When the video concluded, the editor handed back the phone.

"He's got oodles of charisma. Has he ever done any vlogging before?"

"No, but you're right. Carter's a natural. He's a fireman. Learned to cook at his firehouse and decided to expand his horizons from the basics of meat and potatoes."

"If he's this good without coaching, imagine what he would be with it?" Janice mused.

"Oh, he wouldn't want to be coached, and I would agree with him on that point. I think his appeal is that his delivery is so natural. I don't think he should sound too polished."

"I like that name—*A Fireman's Guide to Surviving in the Kitchen*."

"He came up with it on the fly. He's smart. Personable."

"And very easy on the eye. You're a lucky woman, Tenley."

She smiled. "I think so. Would you be interested in him doing a cookbook for Sutton Press?"

Janice didn't hesitate. "I'm sold. But would he be?"

She shrugged. "I'm not sure. I think he would. The idea just came to me to approach Sutton Press since a cookbook is non-fiction. Let me talk to him and get back to you."

"That sounds great. If he ever wants to leave fire-fighting, he could have a career with this."

They spent the rest of the meal catching up with one another. Janice had two teenagers, a boy and a girl, and Tenley heard all about their accomplishments. Her former boss also talked about two books she was editing now, one by a newcomer and another by a veteran author.

Janice insisted upon picking up the check. "I can use this as a business deduction. I only hope Carter gets onboard with the idea."

"I do, too."

Tenley promised to stay in touch and keep Janice apprised of Carter's decision. She collected her luggage and took a taxi to JFK, arriving in plenty of time for her Delta flight. She even bought Carter a T-shirt with the Manhattan skyline at one of the gift shops in the airport. Knowing he had never visited the Big Apple, she hoped to bring him here someday. Perhaps for their honeymoon.

During the almost six-hour flight, Tenley opened her laptop and wrote two chapters. She was getting near the end of her book and felt such a sense of accomplishment. Knowing they would be landing soon, she closed out her document and nibbled on a package of peanut butter crackers she had picked up in the airport, hoping to tide herself over. Carter was on his final day off of the current rotation, and she wanted to squeeze in whatever time she could with him tonight.

She texted when her plane landed on the tarmac, and he messaged back, saying he'd just left The Gourmet Chef and was on his way to Portland International. She told him not to park and simply head for the cell phone lot. She'd text him once she claimed her bag, and he could drive up to the door and meet her there.

By the time she stopped at the restroom, dabbing on a little perfume and freshening her lipstick, she arrived at the luggage carousel and saw her suitcase coming out. Quickly, she grabbed it and sent Carter a text. Tenley exited the doors and two minutes later, he pulled up. Hopping out of the car, he took her suitcase and placed it in the back of his truck, before taking her into his arms for a slow, delicious kiss.

"You need to move along, sir," a voice shouted.

They broke apart and saw a grinning policeman gesturing at them.

"Will do, Officer," Carter said, acknowledging him with a wave before opening Tenley's door. She handed him her carry-on, which he placed in the cab behind her, and then she climbed into the passenger seat.

As they pulled out of the airport, Carter took her hand. "It seems like forever since I've seen you. Maybe longer. I missed you."

"I missed you more," she told him.

"Not possible," he declared, flashing her a cheeky grin.

It was half-past three, and Tenley was glad her flight had come in when it did. They should be able to beat the afternoon traffic rush. They did hit a snarl just outside Portland but made it back to the Cove by a little after five. He drove directly to his house, telling her that he wanted to test something new on her.

"I mixed it up before I came to get you. You know —or maybe you don't—that hazelnut is the state nut of Oregon."

She laughed. "Somehow I missed that fascinating fact."

"Well, I've come up with a new casserole. A vegetable casserole that spotlights roasted hazelnuts. It's got carrots, broccoli, spinach, and cauliflower in it."

"Oh, that sounds terrific. Unless it has cheese in it. Then it would be marvelous."

"Hmm. I could add some cheddar to it. Yeah. I like that."

They pulled into his driveway, and she let him come around to help her from the truck. She had noticed that he liked doing little things for her—and she liked having those little things done for her.

Going inside, he turned on the oven and removed an oblong casserole dish from the refrigerator. He put it into the microwave.

"Just going to take the chill off it. Then it'll need to bake for thirty to forty minutes."

She slid a finger down his arm. "I can think of a few things to do while we wait."

He grinned. "You're on. Let me get this in the oven."

Tenley went to the bedroom and removed the blazer, shirt, and tailored pants—but left on the bra and panty set she had seen in the display window of a boutique shop at her hotel and knew she had to buy.

Carter entered—and his jaw dropped. "Black lace looks good on you, Tenley." He came toward her, slipping his arms about her, his hands caressing her butt cheeks. Then his fingers slid between the lace she wore and her skin. "Even better."

He kissed her deeply. Even as he did so, he expertly unclasped her bra and rid her of it, then peeled the scrap of lace down her hips, allowing it to drop to the floor. She stepped out of it and hungrily kissed him, desire spreading through her.

Their coupling was hard and fast, leaving her

breathless. As she climaxed, she told herself she never wanted to be apart from Carter again. If she had business with Elmo, she wanted Carter to come to New York with her. If she was sent on a book tour, she needed him to accompany her.

A chime sounded in the distance. "That's the casserole," he said, bounding from the bed and hurrying from the room.

She stretched lazily. He returned. "It needs to rest a few minutes." His eyes roamed her body. "But you better get dressed. Cold hazelnut casserole would not be appetizing, and if you continue to stretch that way, that's what we'll be eating."

"All right." Tenley rose and redressed as he did.

They returned to the kitchen, and he removed a salad from the refrigerator before dishing up healthy portions of the new casserole. She poured them glasses of iced tea and set them on the café table.

They lingered over the meal, Tenley telling Carter about her impressions of Elmo and the two publishing companies she was interested in.

"I read the list attached to your e-mail. I don't know enough about it to steer you either way. You have your finger on the pulse of that industry since you worked in it. You'll make the right decision."

"Speaking of where I worked before, I want to talk to you about something."

Tenley explained her idea and how she had pitched a cookbook based on his vlog to Janice Craig.

"I don't know," he said, tapping the brakes on the idea. "I haven't even started the blog—or vlog—yet. I'm going to need time to think this through."

"Janice knows you already have a fulltime job. There's no rush on this," she assured him.

Carter took her hand and kissed her fingers tenderly. "There's no rush on this either."

He led her back to the bedroom and made love to her slowly this time. She savored every kiss. Every touch. Tears sprang to her eyes. Tenley didn't know what she had done to deserve the love of this man.

"I probably need to get you home," he told her, helping her to dress again. "I saw that yawn you just tried to hide. You're still running on New York time. It may be eight here, but it's bedtime for you."

"It will take me a day or two to get back into sync with Oregon time," she admitted.

He drove her to her apartment, retrieving her suitcase from the back of the truck and walking her up the stairs.

"I think the casserole was tasty," she told him, kissing him. "Almost as tasty as you."

He kissed her a final time before taking the key from her and unlocking the door. He lifted the suitcase and took it into the bedroom.

"I start my new shift tomorrow. But there's plenty of the casserole left if you want to have dinner tomorrow night."

"I'll stop by Buttercup Bakery and pick up some fresh sourdough," she told him. "I think that would be a nice touch to the meal."

"And an excuse to visit with Ainsley." Carter kissed her again.

"Well, that, too."

"Goodnight." He left her, closing the door softly.

Tenley missed him already. Maybe it hadn't been such a good idea for her to rent this apartment. Maybe she should move into the bungalow with him. But that had been his home with Emily. She would rather start their time living together when they found something new, a place where they could create new memories between them and not have the shadow of Emily's ghost in every corner of the room.

She thought she better charge her laptop so she would be ready to start work again tomorrow and realized it was in her carryon. She hadn't thought to get it from the truck when Carter brought her home. Quickly, she went to her cell and called him, hoping to catch him so he could turn back. No answer. She supposed he had left it at home.

When the voicemail clicked on, she said, "I forgot my carryon in the truck. I'll come get it. Or maybe meet you halfway. I'll be walking. It'll feel good to stretch my legs a bit after sitting on the plane so long today. See you in a few."

Grabbing a jacket and her purse, Tenley moved down the stairs and turned away from the square. Carter only lived four blocks from where she did, and she knew the street he would come back along was the one she walked now.

Sure enough, she had only gone two blocks when she saw headlights approaching her and paused. Carter rolled down his window.

"Got your message when I walked int the door. Hop on in. I'll take you home."

She got into the truck, and they were approaching the square when she saw something odd.

"What's that?" she asked, her heart beginning to race.

Carter's truck pulled up across the street from where her apartment stood. The front window was broken. Flames shot from it.

Quickly, he grabbed his phone from where it rested in the cupholder and dialed 911.

"This is Carter Clark. I'm an off-duty fireman with

Salty Point. We have a fire in Maple Cove on the square, originating above Sid's Diner." He paused. "Thank you."

He drove around the corner and parked the truck, throwing his door open. "Stay here!" he ordered.

Tenley's heart beat wildly as she saw him rush to the diner, kicking in the glass. He entered and came out moments later with a fire extinguisher in each hand.

"Stay!" he commanded again when she started toward him.

Carter raced up the stairs and had to stop a few shy from the top. He set down one of the fire extinguishers and turned the other one in the direction of the apartment's front window, spraying it into the flames.

She heard the sound of a fire truck in the distance and was aware of a few people gathering on the square. When they saw the flames, two of them rushed back to their stores and returned with additional fire extinguishers, racing up the stairs to hand them to Carter. He had cast aside the two he'd used up and started in with the new ones.

By now, the siren wailed loudly. Moments later, it rounded the corner and appeared on the square, stopping just outside the diner. Tenley watched the speed with which the firemen unraveled hoses, racing them to the diner and spraying inside it, as well as up the stairs. Carter retreated, allowing them to jam their hoses into the window and through her front door.

Tenley ran to the stairs as Carter descended them, hugging him tightly. He smelled of smoke.

"I don't understand," she said. "I had barely gotten home. I hadn't turned on anything. The heat was lowered while I was gone. Did something happen to the furnace? Did it explode?"

He shook his head, his features grim. "We won't know until we've gotten in there—but I think it was arson, Tenley. Someone set that fire.

"And I think they thought you were inside."

CHAPTER 21

C arter knew exactly who had set this fire.
Wilma Bell.

He had seen cases of arson before and believed the fire in Tenley's apartment had been the product of a Molotov cocktail. His gut told him that was what the arson investigator would find as the source of the fire.

But should he share his thoughts with Tenley? Accuse his former mother-in-law of trying to murder his current fiancée?

Carter embraced her, holding Tenley tightly to him, thinking how close he had come to losing her. She clung to him, weeping softly, and he felt a blind rage overwhelm him. Tamping it down, he knew he couldn't let Tenley see it—or reveal his suspicions to her. Not yet.

He saw Nancy Mayfield coming toward them and released his hold on Tenley. The diner's owner immediately enveloped Tenley in her arms, cooing softly to her as a mother comforting a baby.

"I'm so sorry, Nancy," Tenley said. "If there's damage inside the diner, I hope you'll let me come and help clean it up. Even pay for it, whatever insurance doesn't cover."

Nancy smoothed Tenley's hair. "There is a little bit. Mostly water damage from the men fighting the fire. I'll have to close for a day or two, but I would appreciate your help in setting things right."

Tenley looked hesitant and then said, "You don't blame me for what happened? Carter thinks someone was trying to hurt me."

"I think the same thing," Nancy declared. "And me, as well. You know who I believe is responsible." It was statement. Not a question.

When Tenley's jaw dropped and nothing came out, Nancy filled in the blanks.

"I put this squarely at Wilma Bell's doorstep. She had a beef with both of us, and I think this was her way of trying to hurt us both." Her eyes flicked to him. "And you, Carter."

Tenley shook her head. "You don't really believe she could—"

"I would believe a lot about that woman," Nancy told them. The diner owner glanced around. "Good. I see Dylan's on the scene." She shouted Dylan's name and waved him over.

So much for Carter sharing his suspicions with his best friend in private.

Dylan hurried toward them. "Is everyone okay?"

"I'd bet my diner that Wilma Bell started this fire," Nancy proclaimed. "You need to pull her in right now for questioning, Dylan."

Dylan turned to Carter, and Carter nodded. "It would be a good idea. Wilma was a pretty unhappy camper when she saw me with Tenley last week in the diner."

"I heard after Wilma slapped Tenley, Nancy told her off," Dylan said grimly. "And banned Wilma from returning to the diner. By now, Fred and Wilma must know you and Tenley are engaged." He shook his head. "I hate to think Wilma would act this maliciously, though."

Dylan looked to Tenley. "When did you get back to the Cove?"

"Tonight," she said quietly. "Carter picked me up at the airport, and we went to his place for dinner. He dropped me off, and I realized I had left my carryon with my laptop in his truck. With him working tomorrow, I decided I should get it back tonight. I left him a voice-mail and then started walking toward his place to meet him halfway."

Tenley visible trembled. "I... only took my keys with me. Everything I own except for my laptop and makeup was in that apartment. I lost everything, including what was in my purse. My passport. Driver's license. Credit cards."

She burst into tears, and Carter wrapped his arms about her. Looking to Dylan, he said, "I know you need a more formal statement from both of us."

"I do. Now would be better than in the morning, since things are still fresh in your minds. If you wouldn't mind bringing Tenley to the station, I'm off to collect Wilma."

Dylan left and Nancy patted Carter's shoulder. "Let me know if you need anything, hon," she said, and then left the two of them alone.

Tenley wiped at her eyes. "I know it's just stuff I lost—but it was mine. Thank goodness I accidentally left my carry-on in your truck, or my computer would have been toast."

Carter didn't mention that if Tenley had the laptop, she never would have left her apartment. The flames would have trapped her inside.

"Do you think you can go to the station now?"

She nodded. "Memory can fade quickly. Dylan needs the best timeline possible while it's still fresh in our minds."

"Let's go to the truck," he urged quietly, leading her away.

Carter nodded to a few of his fellow firefighters, not bothering to introduce them to Tenley, though he'd done nothing but talk about her at the firehouse. He didn't want her to meet his colleagues under such circumstances. They seem to understand and gave the couple a wide berth as they went back to his truck.

He got Tenley inside and came around to the driver's side. The minute he was in the truck, his phone began to ring.

Glancing down, he saw the caller's name light up. "It's Willow," he told her.

Carter answered it.

"Is Tenley hurt?" Willow asked, frantic. "Please tell me, Carter. Tell me she's fine."

"She is. She's right here. Do you want to talk to her?"

"Yes," Willow said fervently.

He handed the phone over, and Tenley softly said, "Willow?" before she broke down in tears again.

He slipped the cell from her fingers. "I don't think she can talk now, Willow. She's pretty emotional. We're heading to the station so Dylan can interview us."

"I'll meet you there."

Carter placed the phone back in his cupholder and started the truck, driving the short distance to the police station.

Usually, it was dead on a weeknight, but a flurry of activity now occurred. Deputy Linda Goodnight met them.

"Come with me," she said, slipping her arm around Tenley's shoulders. "I'm Linda Goodnight. You must be Tenley Thompson. I'm sorry we're meeting under such circumstances."

Linda led them to one of the two conference rooms and asked them to take a seat.

"Is there anything I can bring you? Coffee? Water?"

"Do you have any hot tea?" Tenley asked timidly.

Linda smiled. "We sure do. I'm a chamomile drinker myself. I'll be back with some."

Carter entwined his fingers with Tenley's, and they sat silently until the deputy returned with a mug of steaming tea.

"I'm going to take your statements now, if that's all right," she said. "I'll turn on the camera if you're comfortable with that, Tenley."

Her fingers tightened on his as she nodded.

In an official-sounding voice, the deputy stated her name, the date, and time, then had Carter and Tenley to do the same. She walked each of them through the events separately. Tenley never let go of his hand the entire time.

"Now, I need to ask you about an incident that occurred last week in Sid's Diner," the deputy said. "Do you know the one I'm referring to?"

Carter said, "Yes. We had gone in to have breakfast together, and then we were going upstairs to look at the apartment over the diner. Nancy... Nancy Mayfield was going to give us a tour of it."

"There was a confrontation at the diner?" Linda asked.

"Yes," he continued. "My... Wilma Bell, my deceased wife's mother, came over and spoke to us briefly. She said some pretty ugly things to both of us, having learned of my relationship with Tenley. Wilma even slapped Tenley."

"She called me a whore," Tenley added quietly. "I know... she loved her daughter. But Emily has been gone five years. She shouldn't expect Carter to mourn for the rest of his life."

"Apparently, she did," he said flatly. "Nancy came over and the verbal confrontation escalated between the two of them. Wilma was asked to leave and never come back. She left, still angry."

"Do you believe Wilma Bell had reason to harm Tenley?" the deputy prodded.

"I had never known Wilma to be physically violent until she slapped Tenley, but waves of anger came off her when she spoke to us. In the meantime, she would have heard the news that Tenley and I are engaged and plan to marry soon. She also had to know Tenley was out of town and had only come back tonight. Things like that get out in the Cove. I do believe she's responsible for starting the fire at Tenley's apartment. If Tenley hadn't remembered that her laptop was still in my truck and left to come get it, she wouldn't be sitting here right now. She would be on a table at the morgue."

Carter glanced over and saw fresh tears streaming down his fiancée's cheeks.

"I think we have all we need. Thank you both. I know this was very difficult to talk about, and you're feeling emotionally raw."

Linda switched off the camera. "If you'll stay here for a few minutes, I'll see if you're free to go or not."

Moments after the deputy left the room, the door

flew open. Willow rushed in, and Tenley rose. They fell into one another's arms, both of them sobbing.

Carter felt utterly helpless. He wished he knew what was happening back at the scene. Which arson investigator would be assigned to the case. Everything would have been taped off by now, and the arson investigator would go through the apartment and diner tonight and again tomorrow morning when it grew light.

He stood, indicating for Willow to take his seat, and she did, pulling Tenley into the one beside her.

"You need to come back and stay with Dylan and me," Willow urged Tenley. "You'll be safe there. I know you want to probably stay with Carter, but I think coming back to Boo's would be a better idea. No one is going to attack the house the sheriff of the Cove lives in."

Willow looked to Carter. "You're welcome to come stay, as well. In fact, that would be the best idea of all. I know Tenley would worry if you were in your house by yourself. We don't know what that crazy bitch Wilma Bell is going to do next. I was outside when Dylan brought her and Fred in. Wilma was wearing a smug smile. Fred trailed them, looking like the cat who ate the canary. I know one—or both of them—is responsible for tonight's fire."

The door opened again, and Deputy Goodnight said, "You're free to leave. Sheriff Taylor said he will touch base with both of you again tomorrow morning."

Willow gently clasped Tenley's elbow. "Do you want to ride with me?" She looked to Carter.

"That's a good idea, Tenley," he said, cradling her cheek. "Go home with Willow now and I'll follow shortly. I need to stop at the house and pick up a uniform to wear tomorrow."

"You're going to work?" Tenley asked anxiously.

"You'll be safe at Boo's, and I'll be closer to the investigation. As soon as I learn anything, I'll let you know."

Carter walked them out to Willow's SUV and saw Tenley safely inside the vehicle. He kissed her lightly. "I'll be there soon," he promised.

He watched the vehicle pull away. Instead of heading to his truck, he went back inside the station to wait for Dylan.

And confront Wilma Bell.

Unfortunately, one other person waited. Fred Bell. Carter took a seat as far from his former father-in-law as possible, trying to contain his anger.

Fred turned and faced him. "Sorry about what happened to your girlfriend, Carter." His tone revealed no apology.

"Not my girlfriend, Fred. My fiancée. Tenley is my fiancée. We're getting married."

Fred shrugged. "Maybe."

"What do you mean by that?" he asked sharply.

Fred just smiled mysteriously and turned away, confirming in Carter's mind that his former in-laws had definitely started the fire. He heard movement and glanced up, looking down the corridor. Dylan had emerged from the second conference room, along with Wilma Bell. She didn't look shaken or remorseful. If anything, she seemed... pleased.

Wilma came to her husband and smiled broadly. "We can go now, Fred." She looked to Carter. "You might want to rethink your future plans," she said cryptically and then led her husband from the station.

Carter was ready to explode when Dylan placed a hand on Carter's shoulder.

"Calm down," his friend said. "There's nothing we can do tonight. The two of them alibied each other. So far, we haven't found any witnesses that can place either of them on the square near the time of the fire."

"You're not going to find any damn witnesses on the square at nine o'clock on a weeknight," he said through gritted teeth. "It's not like any shops are open that late this time of year. I don't know of anywhere that even has security cameras outside its storefront. But you and I both know the Bells are guilty, Dylan."

"I agree—but it's my job to collect the evidence which will prove that. I'll meet with the arson investigator tomorrow after he's walked through the scene and filed his report. For now, Carter, go home to Tenley."

"Willow invited us to stay with you," he informed Dylan. "She said it would be safer and that no one would dare attack Tenley or me while we were at Boo's."

Dylan smiled. "I do have a clever wife. Then I guess I'll see you at home."

Carter strode from the police station out to his truck and drove home. He entered the house and his bedroom, looking at the bed, thinking only a few hours earlier how he'd made love twice with Tenley there. He let out a loud string of curses as he packed a suitcase, including enough unfirms for the next four days, as well as civilian clothes. Entering the bathroom, he quickly loaded his toiletries into his shaving kit. He placed his suitcase in the truck and drove to Boo's house, trying to get his emotions under control. It wouldn't be good for Tenley to see him angry, worried, or upset. He needed to be strong for her now.

He pulled into the long driveway and cut the engine. Tomorrow, he hoped they would find the evidence to link the Bells to the fire.

Steeling himself, Carter locked the truck and went inside the house.

CHAPTER 22

Tenley felt abandoned when Carter left the bed. He slipped quietly from it and dressed in the dark so as not to wake her before heading out for his shift at the fire station. She wanted to run after him and cling to him, fighting the urge to do so. He had been wonderful to her these past three days they had stayed with Willow and Dylan. Carter hadn't asked anything of her, just remaining by her side and being the rock she needed.

She was an utter mess. She couldn't think, much less write. It was Friday, and she was supposed to contact Elmo Nichol about her decision regarding which publishing house she wished to sign with. She had delayed thinking about it because her thoughts swirled about the fact that someone wanted her dead.

The preliminary report had come back from the arson investigator, and he ruled the fire in her apartment as arson. The fire originated from two Molotov cocktails, which had been thrown through the window next to the front door of the apartment. She researched Molotov cocktails online and found how simple they were to make. Anyone with Internet access could have easily created one. Dylan's small police force had not been able to locate a single witness to the incident. Whoever had thrown the bombs into her apartment had timed everything beautifully.

Except for the fact that she hadn't been inside.

Knowing how news traveled in a small town, it wouldn't have been hard for Wilma Bell to have learned not only that Tenley was out of town, but when she was returning. Wilma could have waited inside her salon, watching for Tenley's return, and slipped over to Sid's Diner in the dark. She would have seen Carter's truck arriving and then leaving minutes later. With Tenley's car sitting there, she would assume Tenley was inside.

She shuddered, thinking again how close she had come to death. Though Dylan assured her they would find the evidence needed to bring the bomb thrower to justice, Tenley knew that would never happen. The timing had been perfect. With no tourists on the coast this time of year, stores on the square closed early. Every restaurant had also been closed by that time, as well, the Hidden Bear Bar & Grill being the lone exception. Only a few patrons had been inside it, and none had come in or out in the minutes surrounding the bombing.

Dylan had not been able to prove Wilma or Fred Bell had been on the square that night. Though both had cell phones, those phones showed the pair at their residence on the outskirts of the Cove. But phones could be left behind.

Tenley did not want to live the rest of her life in fear, but she worried what would happen after she married Carter. There would be no avoiding his former in-laws because the Cove was simply too small to do so. She had toyed with the idea of seeing if he might want to move to Salty Point or even Crescent Cove, the town on the other side of Salty Point. She didn't know how to broach that topic with him, though, and she knew Carter would be reluctant to leave his hometown, much less be chased away from it. He would not want to be run off by the Bells.

What worried her more was, even if they did move a short distance away, Fred and Wilma Bell would still be nearby. Would they be bold enough to strike again—this time injuring or even killing her and Carter?

She didn't want to take such a risk.

Though she loved Carter more than she had ever imagined loving a man, she thought it might be better if she ended things with him and left the Cove, keeping him safe from the Bells' wrath. She supposed going back to New York would be her best option. She would be a continent away from Carter and close to her publisher and agent. She didn't want to live in Brooklyn again, but there were many other options to consider. The thought of a life without Carter, though, tore at her, bringing a physical pain deep within her.

Tenley rose and showered and dressed, knowing she needed to call Elmo. She didn't even bother with a cup of coffee first, thinking it would be like acid hitting her stomach, making her queasy.

She dialed her agent's direct line, and Elmo answered on the first ring. "Tenley, good to hear from you. I was hoping you would contact me this morning. Have you made your decision?"

She did make it in that moment. "I'm going to go with Oakwood Publishing. I hope that doesn't disappoint you."

Elmo chuckled. "Max Edgewood will be the most disappointed."

"I liked Max. I really did. I know having him in my

corner would be amazing, as well as all of the resources of a mega-publishing house. But I also believe that Oakwood Publishing is on the cusp of making the leap into the big leagues. Yes, they are small in comparison, but they are detail-oriented. I also like how some of their ideas were well outside the box. I think having the entire staff working on different aspects of my books would be a good thing."

"I agree wholeheartedly," Elmo told her. "They are leaner—and hungrier. They will work their asses off for you. I think you will connect with them better than another house. I also believe you will be the client that pushes them over the top. They'll be grateful, and that gratitude will buy a lot of goodwill, Tenley."

"I know their advance wasn't quite as large as the one Max offered to us."

"Don't worry about that. We're going to make up for that in sales. I think you will blow off the roof. I've been working on other ideas for you, as well. This trilogy has incredible film potential. Would you be interested in selling the film rights?"

For the first time in several days, Tenley grew excited by the prospect. "I would definitely want you to explore that option, Elmo, but I wouldn't want to sign anything yet. I think we need to wait until at least the first book has been released and generated interest."

"I agree but will continue to work on that and other avenues of revenue for you. "I'll call Ricki Robins now and give her the good news." He paused. "How is the manuscript coming? You said you thought you might be finished by the end of this week and then look over the entire novel next week."

"I... no, I haven't finished yet. A few things happening in my personal life that caused me to put writing on the back burner. But not for long."

Tenley decided she didn't want to share what had happened with the fire at this time and did not offer a further explanation.

"Just do your best," her agent said reassuringly. "I'll send you digital copies of the contract to sign with Oakwood."

"Should I have Sylvia Driver look this over?"

"You could but it's not necessary. I have in-house legal counsel. They draft all contracts for me."

"Then I'll trust everything to you from this point forward. Thank you again, Elmo, for signing me as a client."

"Thank you for writing an amazing book, Tenley, and for being friends with my cousin."

She laughed for the first time in days. "I suppose I should dedicate this first book to Diane."

"You do whatever you want. Talk with you soon."

Tenley felt a little better having made such an important decision. She did need to work, however. She was so close to the end and needed to push her personal troubles aside.

Carrying her laptop, she went to Boo's library. Actually, the room had belonged to Boo's husband, who was a voracious reader. Three of the walls were lined with shelves filled with hardback books. The fourth wall held a fireplace, and Tenley lit it. Soon, the room was nice and toasty, and she entered her imaginary world again.

"Ten?"

She typed *The End* and looked up, seeing Willow standing in the doorway. "I literally just finished my draft," she said, pride filling her at the accomplishment.

Her friend came into the room and gave her a hug. "That's amazing, Tenley. I'm so proud of you. I know it's been difficult trying to concentrate with everything that's been going on, but you did it. You wrote a book!"

"I also spoke to Elmo Nichols earlier and told him I'm going with Oakwood Publishing."

"I'm glad you made a decision regarding your publishing house. Maybe one day, we'll take a trip to New York together. We'll go to The Runyon Gallery for one of my gallery shows, and I'll return the favor by attending the book-signing of your latest bestseller. We might even arrange it so Sloane was in town and could be there for both."

She smiled. "Who would have thought we would wind up in this position, Willow?"

"I think this calls for a celebration," her friend declared. "Why don't we see if Ainsley and Rylie are available? We could do dinner together."

"I'd like that." Tenley glanced at her watch. "It's almost four o'clock? I've been writing all day and didn't even realize it."

"I'll call Ainsley. You call Rylie. Let's see if they can meet us at Eats & Treats at six."

Both cousins were eager for the impromptu dinner, and Tenley texted Carter to let him know she wouldn't be home when he arrived.

Her phone dinged, and she read his reply.

Have fun going out with the girls. Dylan & I will do our best to scrounge some food. Love you.

Guilt ran through her as she read it. She did love Carter but thought it would be wise to end things between them. If she discussed it with her friends this evening, she was afraid they would talk her out of her decision. She still wasn't sure if breaking her engagement and leaving the Cove was the right thing to do, but not saying anything to Carter and continuing on before ultimately leaving might hurt him even more.

Tenley decided to tell him when she got home that she wanted to end things between them.

She did her best to hide her aching heart, putting on a huge smile as she and Willow entered Eats & Treats. She had yet to visit the café and was surprised at its extensive menu. They ordered food and a bottle of wine for the table. She hadn't eaten anything all day since she'd been so wrapped up in her writing and knew to sip slowly until she got some food in her.

They talked for a bit about the lack of progress on the arson case.

"At least Nancy was able to reopen the diner this morning," Rylie said.

Even though Tenley had offered to come and help clean up, she had been too nervous to leave the house. She had called Nancy and begged off, saying she needed to work on her book. Nancy had been extremely understanding. She had also offered to refund Tenley's rent in full since it would be some time before the apartment was livable again. Tenley had told Nancy to keep the money and put it toward the insurance deductible, still feeling the burden of responsibility fell upon her for what had occurred.

Ainsley talked about some new cupcakes she was testing and asked if they wanted to come over Sunday afternoon for taste-testing the recipes. Tenley planned to be gone by then but said she would be there, feeling awful that she was lying to her friends. Rylie had been to an estate sale the previous weekend and told them about the furniture and antique jewelry she had purchased. Willow discussed the new painting she was working on and how being back in the Cove and taking long walks and runs in nature had fired her imagination.

"How is your book coming along?" Rylie asked.

"Good news on that front," she said brightly, tamping down the sadness filling her, knowing this would be the last meal she would share with this group of friends. "I finished my first draft today and have been reading and tweaking as I wrote. I only have a few chapters to go back and re-read, then I'll do one complete read-through from beginning to end. Then I'll send it to my agent and publisher."

"Did you make a decision on which house to sign with?" Ainsley asked.

"Yes, I did. I spoke with my agent this morning."

Tenley told them about Oakwood Publishing and why she thought it would be a better fit for her in the long run.

"They pitched some really interesting ideas on how to use social media in the ad campaigns, and they were the only one of the three houses to prepare mockup covers for me to view. I like their enthusiasm and drive. I would also work with everyone at the house, so I would be as invested in them as they are in me."

"That's great news," Rylie said. "I think that calls for another bottle of wine."

"I'll tell our server," Tenley offered. "I need to go to the restroom anyway."

She rose from the table and moved toward the back wall where the restrooms were located, passing their server and telling her to bring one more bottle of wine to their table.

Moving toward the double doors, she pushed through them and saw the ladies' restroom on the right. She entered one of the two stalls and heard someone else come in. Then water began running.

When Tenley emerged from the stall, her heart caught in her throat.

Wilma Bell stood waiting.

The water still ran in the sink. Tenley started to move toward the door, but Wilma blocked her way, her eyes narrowing.

"You were lucky," the older woman said. "Very lucky. If you want to hold on to that luck, you'll leave the Cove."

"You were responsible for the fire, weren't you?"

Wilma only smiled malevolently. "I'd hate for anything to happen to Carter." The threat hung in the air. "Of course, accidents happen all the time. Even though he was so good to our Emily, I foresee an accident in his future." She paused. "A deadly one. And no one would ever guess it wasn't an accident." Smiling, she added, "My Fred will always be my alibi."

Tenley gasped. "You would kill Carter?"

"I guarantee you he'll be dead within a week if he continues with his current plan to marry you."

She didn't want to be a coward and have this woman keep her and Carter apart, but Tenley knew crazy when she saw it. If she didn't end her engagement with Carter and leave town, it would be her fault when something awful happened to him. She loved him enough to give him up.

"You don't have to worry about Carter and me," she said crisply. "I'll be leaving Maple Cove this weekend and returning to New York."

Wilma nodded slowly, a satisfied smile crossing her lips. "I think that is a wise decision. Carter will be upset, but he'll get over it."

Tenley hoped he would get over her, knowing she would never get over him.

"I'll be telling him and my friends this news. Please keep this information to yourself for now. I'll be leaving as soon as I can book a flight out."

She figured it would take a day to book a flight and find somewhere to stay in New York, as well as do a little shopping. She'd been wearing Willow's clothes the past few days but would need a few things of her own before she left. The rest of a wardrobe could be purchased in New York after she arrived.

"I can do that. You're making the right choice. A dead Carter would be no good to anyone."

Wilma stepped aside. Tenley quickly moved toward the door and pulled, finding it locked. She turned the lock and hurried from the restroom, stopping in the small hallway a moment to compose herself before she rejoined her friends.

Carter would never understand why she was leaving—but Tenley knew doing so would save his life.

CHAPTER 23

Carter and Dylan were watching a basketball game when Dylan's phone rang.

"Hey, Bear. What's up?" He listened a minute and then said, "Not a problem. Be there in a few."

Dylan looked to Carter. "It seems there was quite a bit of celebrating with the girls this evening, and a couple of bottles of wine were consumed. Willow didn't think it wise to get behind the wheel and wants me to come get her. Would you mind dropping me off at Eats & Treats? I can drive her and Tenley home."

He grinned. "You may drive your wife home, but I'll be the one to make sure my fiancée gets here."

His friend chuckled. "When are you two going to get married? I was a little surprised when Tenley moved into the apartment. I thought she would move straight into your place."

"We both want a fresh start," Carter told him. "That was my house with Emily. We want to find something else and begin married life there. I've talked to Shayla Newton about it. If we have to build, we will, but I'd prefer to find something that already exists."

He followed Dylan out the door, grabbing his jacket as they headed to his truck. A few minutes later, they pulled onto the square and located Willow's SUV. Carter stopped behind it, leaving the engine running.

Dylan glanced at him. "See you at home soon," he said before getting out and heading to the driver's door.

Carter watched Tenley slip from behind the wheel, and Dylan took her place. She headed toward the truck, but her face didn't look like someone who had been celebrating. He got a funny feeling and wondered if something might be wrong.

She climbed into the truck and closed the door. "Thanks for dropping off Dylan. Willow didn't feel she should be driving."

"Not a problem," he told her, putting the truck into gear and leaving the square. He sensed a tension filling the small space between them and needed Tenley to talk it through with him.

"So, you were celebrating tonight?"

"Yes," she said quietly. "I finished my manuscript and also chose a publisher." She didn't elaborate, which surprised him.

He was caught up to where she had written before her trip to New York and said, "I guess I'll have a few more chapters to read. I can't wait to see how you finished it off. Did you go with the epilogue or not?"

She hesitated and then said, "No epilogue. But the way I ended it will be satisfying to my protagonist's story, and yet I hope it will be open-ended enough to make readers want to pick up the second book."

"Hey, you've gotten a non-reader like me to race through it," he pointed out. "Anyone who picks it up will want to finish it—and move to the next installment."

Tenley didn't reply to his remark, and Carter's gut told him there was something seriously wrong. He didn't press the issue, though. He would wait until they got back to Boo's house before pursuing it. He pulled into the long driveway and parked to the right, cutting the engine. Dylan was right behind him, pulling off to the left. Carter sat, waiting to take his cue from Tenley since she made no attempt to unbuckle her seatbelt and leave the truck.

He watched Dylan and Willow enter the house and then turned to her. "What aren't you telling me?"

She flinched at his words, puzzling him. He hadn't spoken harshly to her. He reached for her hand, and she jerked away, unbuckling her seatbelt.

"What's wrong, sweetheart?" he asked. "You know you can tell me anything."

She turned and their gazes met. Immediately, Carter's insides tightened.

"I've decided to go back to New York tomorrow," she said quietly.

"Do you need to sign the contracts with your new publisher? Which one did you go with? Does Elmo need you, or does the publishing house? I know I'm on the schedule tomorrow. It's the last day of my shift, but I might be able to finagle out of that shift and join you."

Tears brimmed in her eyes. "I won't be coming back to Maple Cove, Carter. I'm going to make New York my permanent base." She turned and stared out the windshield.

Her words gutted him.

"What's going on, Tenley? I don't understand any of this. When I left for my shift this morning, things were fine between us. Now, you're telling me you're leaving the Cove—and that means leaving me. Why? You owe me an explanation."

"You don't need to understand any of this. You just need to respect my decision and back off." She refused to look at him as she continued. "I think we let our physical attraction get the better of us, Carter." She swallowed. "I think once the newness wore off, we would find that we're just too different to make it. I belong in New York. You belong here."

Tears stung his eyes as he reached for her hand, entwining his fingers with hers. He could feel her trembling. "I don't believe you, Tenley. Yes, we've got a sizzling physical chemistry that's off the charts, but we also have our core values in common. Something's happened. Something you're not telling me."

She yanked her hand from his. "I want to build a different kind of life than you do, Carter. I went along with everything you said because I was so dazzled by you and how you made me feel. But I don't belong in the Cove."

"You do," he insisted. "You're running from me. Be honest with me, Tenley. We can work this out."

She shook her head. "I don't want to work anything out. I want to end things. Gracefully, if possible. Please respect my feelings and just let it go."

Let go of his dream with a life with this woman?

"No," he said firmly. "There's more to this that you're not telling me. We love each other, Tenley. We belong together."

"It was too much, too soon," she said dully. "I let fantastic sex cloud my judgment of the situation. I'm sorry that I led you on."

"Look me in the eyes, Tenley, and tell me that you don't love me," he demanded.

Carter held his breath as she didn't move. For almost a full minute, they sat in silence. Then she swung her head and met his gaze.

"I like you, Carter. You were a nice distraction. You helped me see that I wasn't worthless because I sure felt that way after my annulment. But I don't love you —and I don't want to be stuck in Maple Cove with you."

She swung her gaze away from his and added, "I'll sleep in a different room tonight. I'll be leaving for New York tomorrow."

Tenley exited the truck, and Carter watched her in disbelief as she walked purposefully toward the house, entering it.

He gripped the wheel tightly, stunned by her declaration. Yes, they had only known each other a short time and their relationship had been intense from the beginning, but he knew she was lying to him. She had felt everything he had. Carter couldn't understand why she was abandoning him and the Cove.

A horrible thought occurred to him. Was Tenley so shallow that her recent success had gone to her head? She had shared with him her agent's thoughts and how Elmo Nichols believed this trilogy would hit the top of the charts, as well as be made into a series of movies. Did Tenley believe if she stayed with him in the Cove that it would hold her back? He didn't want to believe it, but he had no other explanation. He didn't know how to change her mind.

He sat in his truck for a couple of hours, mulling over the situation, still refusing to believe that the woman he loved was leaving him for good, claiming she had never loved him. Finally, he went inside Boo's house and up to the room they had shared. A single lamp glowed on the nightstand. Frustration filled him.

He needed to talk to Tenley. Convince her she was wrong.

Carter went into the hallway and found the bedroom door across the hall closed. He assumed she was inside.

Knocking on it gently, he called, "Tenley? Please. We need to talk."

A long silence followed. Carter waited, hoping she would open the door to him. He thought just one kiss would convince her how much he loved her and break down the wall she had erected between them.

The door suddenly opened, startling him. Tenley's eyes were swollen from crying.

He blurted out, "I love you. I'll go to New York with you if that's what it takes. I've never thought I'd leave the Cove, but I'll do anything—go anywhere—to be with you."

She stared at him, unmoved.

"Perhaps you didn't understand me before, Carter. Let me make myself clear so there will be no more misunderstanding on your part. I don't love you," she said flatly, causing a physical ache to wrench his heart. "I never loved you. Yes, the sex was phenomenal, but I want to move on with my life. Without you. I don't want to live in a sleepy little town that doesn't even have a decent restaurant. I certainly don't want you following me back to New York. Go find some nice, small-town girl and start a new life with her. I'm not whom you're looking for. I never was."

Anger filled him, thinking every moment with her had been a lie. Bitterness caused him to spit out, "You aren't the woman I thought you were. I guess it's a good thing I found that out now. Have a nice life."

He turned and stormed away, entering the bedroom they had shared. Opening the closet, he removed his suitcase, placing it on the bed. He gathered clothes from the closet and the drawers he had been using, throwing it all in haphazardly, then zipping up the suitcase. Carrying it to the door, he stopped, glancing about the room, memories of what had happened in here flooding him. He couldn't believe he had been duped. That he had finally taken a chance and given his heart to someone who stomped upon it so cruelly.

In that moment, Carter vowed never to be vulnerable again.

He left Boo's house, closing the front door as he hoped he could close the door on memories that would be too painful to ever recall again.

CARTER TOSSED BACK the covers and stumbled into the bathroom, splashing water on his face. He hadn't slept a wink. Instead, he had lain in bed, with a physical ache so great that he thought he might be having a heart attack.

His life felt as if it were over.

While he had grieved over Emily's death, hurting not only for the loss of his wife but the baby, as well, at least he understood what had happened. An aneurysm had ruptured. It was nothing they could have predicted, and he'd had no way to save her or the baby. But this breakup with Tenley had torn him apart. He had been lonely for so long, and when he met her, it was as if he had been gifted with his soulmate, a woman who understood him. One who had also had her share of sorrows and had come out stronger for all she had been through. They had instantly clicked, and Carter had easily foreseen the future they would share.

Nothing made sense about her leaving him. Leaving the Cove. Tenley hadn't faked the feelings she'd had for him, and he didn't believe she had been swept up in nothing but lust. No, real love existed between them.

Then why had she suddenly pushed him away?

A thought occurred to him.

Could it have to do with Wilma Bell?

They all believed the hairdresser had started the fire, but her husband wouldn't budge from his alibi. Fred insisted he and Wilma had been watching TV together, an old rerun of *The Carol Burnett Show*. The couple had always talked about their love for the comedienne and her variety series. Carter knew they had watched every episode hundreds of times.

Had Tenley run into Wilma at Eats & Treats last night? Had Wilma threatened Tenley?

His gut told him Wilma lay at the heart of Tenley's sudden resolve to end their engagement and leave the Cove. But his fiancée had emerged from her annulment a stronger woman than before. Together they had forged a bond he had thought was unbreakable. Then why would Wilma be able to chase Tenley out of town?

Carter realized *he* was the key.

Just as he would do anything to protect Tenley, he knew she would do the same for him. Somehow, Wilma Bell had made a threat—not against Tenley, but him. Instinctively, Carter knew the woman he loved was protecting him the only way she knew how.

By leaving the Cove.

He had to be right. Nothing else made sense. He hurried to his cell and dialed Tenley's number even though it was barely six in the morning. It rang several times and went to voice-mail.

"Tenley, I know why you're leaving. You're trying to protect me. Please. Don't go. Don't leave until we've talked in person. I've got to head to the station soon. Call me back. Don't go. Please. Don't go."

Carter made coffee, needing the shot of caffeine, and then took a quick shower and dressed in his uniform, keeping his phone close by in case Tenley returned his call. He even held it in his hand as he drove the short way to Salty Point.

Tenley didn't call.

He prayed she would listen to his message and not leave. That she would give him a chance. Hear him out. Talk to him and let him share whatever burden she was trying to carry on her own. He desperately wanted to call Dylan and urge his friend to try and talk some sense into her, but it wouldn't be right to involve others. If Tenley left Oregon, then he would follow her to New York despite everything she had said.

Pulling into the station's parking lot, he exited his truck and locked it. As he entered the firehouse, he greeted those who were about to come off the night shift and others who were arriving for Day One.

Heading to the kitchen, he poured himself another cup of coffee as others began gathering. Cooking would help take his mind off things, and he moved toward the refrigerator to pull out eggs and bacon.

Suddenly, the alarm sounded. Everyone rushed from the room, scrambling into their gear. Carter finished dressing and grabbed his EMT kit, heading for the truck, leaping onto it just as it pulled from the station. The driver turned in the direction of the Cove, and he hoped that his friends and their stores were all safe.

The truck ran full speed, sirens blaring as it turned on several streets before making a familiar turn to its final destination. He saw the flames, and reality set it. Carter steeled himself as the truck slowed and then stopped.

At Fred and Wilma Bell's house.

The fire crew leaped into action like a well-oiled machine. Carter pushed aside his feelings that roared inside him. He was a trained professional and would perform as one. Quickly, hoses were unraveled and water sprayed.

People had gathered on their lawns, watching the action. One man raced over and got Carter's attention.

"I saw Fred leave for the gas station, but Wilma must still be in there. Her car's in the garage." He pointed to the open garage door, where an old Cadillac sat.

"Thanks. Stand back, sir," Carter told the concerned neighbor. He signaled to his chief that he was going in, motioning to the nearest fireman, holding up a single finger to indicate one citizen still inside.

As a team, they rushed to the open garage. The fire hadn't reached there yet, and Carter kicked in the door that he knew led to the kitchen. Again, he motioned right and the firefighter accompanying him moved that way as Carter headed left.

He came upon Wilma Bell's still form lying in hallway, quickly checking for a pulse. It was faint but present. He hollered but doubted he would be heard over the fire. Bending, he rolled Wilma onto her stomach and knelt by her head. He lifted her dead weight, dipping his head under her right armpit and squatting, placing her over his shoulder in the traditional fireman's carry.

By now, the thick smoke made it hard to see where to go. His lungs burned with each breath he inhaled, and he slowed his breathing. He caught sight of his partner and they headed back the way they had come.

Suddenly, a burning beam fell directly in front of him, the fire spreading, cutting him off from his partner. Carter took a final breath and leaped over the beam, rushing through what remained of the kitchen and out the door leading to the garage. It was empty now, and he knew Wilma's car had been pushed from the burning structure by his fellow firefighters.

He stumbled as he crossed the lawn, bringing Wilma Bell to the waiting ambulance. Paramedics lifted her from him.

"Faint pulse," he managed to say, before a coughing fit struck.

They loaded her into the ambulance and a paramedic tapped him. "Get in, Clark. You need oxygen."

He followed the stretcher in as someone slammed the doors. One paramedic began CPR on Wilma as the other jumped behind the wheel. The ambulance pulled away, sirens blaring.

Carter located the oxygen and placed a mask over his face. The first responder working on Wilma did the same.

"Her heart stopped," the man revealed. "I got it started again."

He only nodded, closing his eyes, which burned. He closed them, seeing the flames raging, wondering if Wilma would survive.

They pulled up to the emergency room, and he remained in the ambulance, allowing them to remove Wilma from it before he slipped off his oxygen mask and followed them inside. Since it was early on a Saturday morning, the ER was empty. No one there from sports injuries or falls from ladders, the typical weekend wounds.

A nurse he knew approached him. "The guys said you have smoke inhalation damage, Carter. Follow me."

He did so, and she started him on oxygen, saying, "Nod yes or no. Are you having trouble breathing?"

He shook his head.

"Coughing?"

He nodded yes.

"Any confusion?"

He shook his head again.

"Stay here. I'll bring some eye drops. We only have one doctor on duty. He'll be in as soon as the patient that came in with you is stabilized and transferred upstairs."

Carter gave her a thumbs up. Then he began to grow dizzy and leaned his head against the wall. He tried to take deep, even breaths but felt himself floating away.

Into nothingness.

CHAPTER 24

Tenley sat in a chair throughout the night, crying softly. At one point, she went to the bed and collected a pillow when her sobs grew louder, forcing her face into the pillow in order to muffle the noise.

The sun would rise soon, and she returned to the room across the hall. The bed was still made. She knew Carter hadn't slept in it because she had heard him leave last night, guessing he had returned to his house.

Her heart had shattered into pieces as she had cruelly told him that she had never loved him. Lie after lie poured from her mouth, and she watched his heart break before her very eyes. A thousand times during the night, she had forced herself to keep from reaching for her phone to call him and beg for his forgiveness. Leaving was the only way to protect him, though, from the insanity of Wilma Bell. Eventually, Tenley would tell Willow the story and have her warn Carter about his mother-in-law. For now, though, it was best to leave because it would keep Carter safe.

She took a quick shower, hoping it would ease the

pounding headache at her temples and disguise her puffy eyes. It did neither. She dressed in the clothes she had worn home from New York, the only ones she possessed. She had no suitcase to pack, simply slipping her laptop and makeup into her carry-on, along with chargers for the computer and her phone. Tenley took her things downstairs.

The house was still, and she guessed Willow and Dylan were out for a run with Shadow. She hated to leave without saying goodbye but decided she should because she knew they would try to talk her out of her decision. As she went to her car, she realized she needed to do something with it. She decided to park in long-term parking at the Portland airport and leave the parking slip in the glove compartment. She could Fed Ex the keys to Willow and ask her to pick up the car and sell it. The proceeds could go toward the next recipient of Boo's art scholarship. Tenley wouldn't need a car in New York.

She loaded her suitcases into the rear, along with her computer, and closed it. She hadn't booked a flight yet, thinking she would take the first one available at the airport. If no direct flight had seats, she would city-hop until she wound up back in New York.

Getting behind the wheel, she took out her cell to text Willow, feeling she owed it to her friend to give her some kind of goodbye. Her heart lurched again as she saw she had a voice-mail message. It had come in early this morning. She had seen Carter's name light up her screen, and she had refused to answer it. She decided to listen to it now, though.

Tenley, I know why you're leaving. You're trying to protect me. Please. Don't go. Don't leave until we've talked in person. I've got to head to the station soon. Call me back. Don't go. Please. Don't go.

Her throat thickened with unshed tears as she listened to his voice. Had he figured out why she was leaving? It sounded as if he had an inkling about her reasons. It didn't matter, though. If she were gone, Wilma would back off. Carter would be safe.

She would keep the message, though, and listen to it when loneliness burned into her soul. She would remember the incredible man who had been hers for a short while and how he had brought love and laughter into her life.

Dropping the phone into her cupholder, she took a deep breath and wiped away the tears that continued to fall.

Her phone rang, startling her. Tenley glanced down, not recognizing the number. She started to ignore it, but for reasons she didn't understand, she reached for the phone and tapped it.

"Hello?"

"Is this Tenley Thompson?" a deep voice asked.

"Yes," she said hesitantly, a sense of dread filling her.

"I'm Arnold Poth, fire chief at the Salty Point station. I'm calling—"

"Is Carter all right?" she asked quickly. "Has he been hurt?"

"He's suffered some smoke inhalation from a fire we fought this morning. He's asking for you."

Despite her resolve to leave the Cove, Tenley wouldn't turn her back on Carter now. "I'll be right there. Where do I go?" she asked anxiously, tremors overtaking her body.

"He's at Salty Point Memorial."

"I'm on my way."

Tenley disconnected the call and quickly opened her map app, typing in the hospital's name. She dropped the phone twice because her hands were shaking so badly. She tapped to start the directions, her insides churning. She knew people could die from smoke inhalation. In one of her old favorite shows, *This is Us*, the lead character had suffered from smoke inhalation after racing back inside to save the family's dog. He had seemed fine once he arrived at the hospital but died of a sudden, catastrophic heart attack. Tenley had wept at that episode long after it ended since Jack was her favorite character on the show.

What if Carter died as Jack had?

She burst into tears as she pulled out of Boo's driveway, leaving the Cove and heading toward Salty Point. A constant prayer echoed in her mind on a loop.

Please don't let Carter die. Please don't let Carter die. Please don't let Carter die.

Tenley reached the hospital and parked, hurrying inside the building to the admissions desk.

"I'm here for Carter. Clark. He's a fireman. He has smoke inhalation."

"Are you a relative?" the clerk asked.

"No. I'm his fiancée," she told the woman, swallowing the bitterness at using the word. "The fire chief, Arnold something, he called me. Carter is asking for me."

"I'm sorry, but we can't—"

"Tenley?" a voice called.

She turned and saw Dorothy Clark hurrying toward her. Relief poured through Tenley as Dorothy enveloped her in an embrace. Then Dorothy pulled away and smiled at the clerk.

"Hello, Melinda. It's so good to see you."

The woman beamed. "You, too, Miz C."

"My son was brought into emergency. Carter

Clark. He's a firefighter. He should have been assigned a room by now."

"Yes, ma'am." Melinda tapped a few keys. "Carter is in Room 424."

"Thank you, dear." Dorothy slipped her arm through Tenley's. "Let's go upstairs."

In the elevator, Tenley broke down. Dorothy held her tightly, murmuring encouraging words. The doors opened, and Dorothy led them to the nurse's station, where again she greeted the nurse sitting at the desk by name.

"The doctor is with him now, Miz C. You can wait in the lounge. It's right around the corner."

Dorothy thanked the nurse and took Tenley's elbow, guiding her to the lounge and into a seat. They clasped one another's hands tightly.

"I'm so glad you're here," Dorothy said. "The last time I did this, I was alone. It's nice to be with someone."

Tenley remembered Carter telling her how his father had died fighting a fire, a burning beam striking and then pinning him to the ground. She couldn't imagine what Dorothy had gone through.

Dorothy gripped Tenley's fingers. "They didn't tell me he died at the scene. I was just called to the hospital. To the ER. I thought Clinton had been injured and brought in so they could tend to him. I didn't know he had been trapped in the fire and died. Bringing him here was merely a formality so he could be pronounced dead."

Dorothy sighed. "The ER was packed that day. There had been a wreck on Boxboro Highway. A school bus on the way to some band contest had been hit and toppled over. So many injured students. So many worried, crying parents trying to find out how their child was." She shook her head. "In the chaos, I got lost in the shuffle. It was hours before a nurse approached me and said the doctor wanted to see me. He told me how Clinton had been struck by falling debris. He assured me the smoke inhalation took him before the fire ever did. I like to hope that was the case."

Tears welled in her eyes. "I'm so sorry you lost him, Dorothy. I wish I could have met him."

"He was the love of my life, just as Carter is the same for you. I only hope Carter will be fine." Tears rolled down Dorothy's face and she wiped them away with her free hand.

"He will be," she told the older woman. "He will be," she repeated, wanting to believe it will all her heart.

"Tenley? Mrs. Clark?" a voice in the doorway asked.

"Yes, that's us," Dorothy assured the doctor as they came to their feet and hurried toward him.

"I'm Dr. Knowles, Mr. Clark's physician." He paused, his face serious. "Let's go have a seat."

He led them back to the chairs they had been sitting in.

"Is it bad news?" Dorothy asked pointedly. "If so, tell us up front. My husband was a firefighter, and I lost him in a fire. If I'm going to lose my son, just say so and let us spend what time is left with him."

Dr. Knowles looked taken aback. "No, Mrs. Clark. Your son is going to be fine."

Tenley burst into tears, clutching Dorothy. They both clung to one another a moment before Dorothy said, "Young man, you need to work on your delivery. By the look on your face, I thought my son might already be dead."

"I'm sorry," the physician apologized. "My wife tells me I'm too serious. I didn't mean to alarm you. Let me share with you all we've done, and then you can go see him."

"Thank you," Tenley managed to get out, holding Dorothy's hand tightly.

"Mr. Clark does have some damage from inhaling smoke. His biggest symptom is a cough. The mucous membranes in his respiratory tract were irritated by the smoke, which causes increased mucus production. The muscles lining his airway have also tightened due to this irritation. His mucus is a light gray. If it were darker or black, I'd be more concerned because that would mean many more burned particles were lodged inside his trachea or lungs. Still, it is causing him to cough, and I've addressed that issue.

"On the other hand, he is showing no signs of shortness of breath, which is a very good sign. He does have a headache, due to his exposure to carbon monoxide, but he's experienced no nausea or vomiting, another positive. He is hoarse, however. That shouldn't last beyond a few days. His eyes will look bloodshot when you see him. Smoke definitely irritates eyes and causes redness."

"I saw that frequently with my husband," Dorothy said. "Anything else to be concerned about?"

"No, ma'am," Dr. Knowles said. "We did chest X-rays to check for lung damage. He isn't experiencing any decreased alertness, which can occur with low oxygen levels. Mr. Clark does have swollen nostrils, but the swelling will go down in the next day or so."

Tenley spoke up. "What about chest pain?"

The physician shook his head. "You must be a *This is Us* fan. I've gotten that question for years since Jack Pearson died of a heart attack. Let me assure you, Mr.

Clark has been adamant that he has no chest pain. I've established how long he was exposed to the smoke. I've already mentioned his X-rays are clear. I also had blood tests run and read those results before I came out to visit with you. His red and white blood cell counts, as well as his platelet count, are fine. No signs of carbon monoxide poisoning are evident. His ABG test was normal. Mr. Clark is on oxygen now, strictly as a preventative measure. No breathing tube inserted in his throat, just a nose tube.

"In other words, I'll keep him today and overnight for observation, but he'll be free to go home tomorrow."

"When do you suggest he returns to work?" Dorothy asked. "That's the first thing Carter will be itching to do."

The thought of Carter returning to active duty and being in danger caused Tenley's heart to race.

"I'd give it a week. He can walk a day or two at first for exercise, then return to light weights after that. Mr. Clark told me that he would have to be cleared by the department's physician before he can return to duty, so I won't need to see him for a follow-up." Dr. Knowles paused. "Any more questions, ladies? If not, you are welcome to visit with him."

Tenley wiped her eyes. "Thank you, Doctor."

"He is very eager to see you."

She swallowed the lump in her throat.

Dr. Knowles left, and she said to Dorothy, "You should see him first. I know how worried you've been, especially since you went through such a painful time with your husband."

Dorothy embraced her, kissing Tenley's cheek. "I'm going to be a selfish old woman and take you up on that, dear. I promise I won't stay long, and you can see him soon."

Tenley watched Dorothy Clark leave the waiting room and stood there. Hesitation filled her.

Should she stay and see Carter—or should she slip away?

CHAPTER 25

Carter was happy to see his mom, who burst into tears the moment she entered his hospital room. She rushed to the bed and hugged him tightly. He thought of her waiting in this same hospital five years ago, only to receive the news that her husband had died. But as happy as he was to have her with him, he wondered if Tenley had come.

His chief had appeared shortly after Carter entered the ER. Though Carter wore an oxygen mask, he had lifted it and asked that Arnold call both Tenley and his mom and let them know he was in the hospital. Arnold had remained with Carter during the examination Dr. Knowles gave him before he got the numbers from Carter's phone and then stepped outside, making the calls as requested. Arnold assured him that he had reached both women and they were on their way.

Dr. Knowles had put a rush on the X-rays and blood results and shared those with Carter before going to search for Tenley and his mom. It worried him that only his mother had entered his room.

She stepped back, brushing away the tears. "It's so good to see you, Carter. You had me worried."

He took her hand and squeezed it. "I'm sorry, Mom. I know you worried every time Dad left for a shift, and doubly so for me after Dad's death. I'm fine."

"Yes, Dr. Knowles gave us a thorough rundown regarding your condition."

"Us?" he asked.

"Tenley is here," his mom assured him. "She was gracious enough to give me a few moments alone with you first." She smoothed his hair and then framed his face with her hands. "Oh, Carter. I'm so glad you're fine. What happened?"

He frowned. "I was trying to carry Wilma Bell to safety."

His mom's eyes widened. "Wilma Bell? The fire was at her house? Or the salon?"

"Her house," he confirmed. "I don't know the cause. A neighbor had seen Fred leave for work earlier. I found Wilma on the floor, overwhelmed by smoke inhalation." He paused. "I'm not certain she made it, Mom. Her pulse was barely registering when I found her. They did CPR on her in the ambulance. I've been tied up with tests, so I have no idea."

"I know none of us are fond of Wilma, but I would hate to see her gone."

"Dylan and I believe she started the fire at Tenley's apartment," Carter said. "I know I sound bitter, but she was never a mother to Emily—and I believe she wanted Tenley dead." He kept silent about his suspicions regarding Wilma threatening Tenley.

His mom kissed his brow. "I'm going to let your fiancée have time with you now. I'll make a few calls and let everyone know you're on the mend."

"Call Dylan and Willow first," he urged.

She smiled. "I will."

He watched her leave and waited, his heart in his throat, his gaze fastened on the door.

"Please come," he whispered.

The door opened again. Tenley stepped inside. She stood a moment, biting her lip, and then rushed to him, wrapping herself around him, sobbing loudly.

"I'm okay, baby," he told her, smoothing her hair. "I'm fine."

She pulled away and stared at him, as if he'd come back from the dead.

"You look a mess," he said, grinning. "A beautiful mess."

His hand cradled her nape, drawing her to him, and Carter kissed her. He hoped he conveyed his love to her. His promise of their future together.

She broke the kiss. "I was leaving. My bags were packed. And then your chief called." Her voice trembled as much as her body. "I knew I had to come."

"I know why you were leaving," he told her. "Somehow, Wilma Bell got in your head. She threatened you—or me."

"You," Tenley confirmed. "She wants to kill you. She said she could make it look like an accident. That her husband would alibi her. The only way I could protect you is by leaving." Tears slid down her cheeks. "But then you could have died in the fire today. I decided I was wrong. That you were right. That we should capture the moment. Grab the brass ring. Wring out of life what we can, when we can—because we don't know what tomorrow brings. If we have a day, then I'll have those memories. If we are lucky enough to have a year or five or a decade or more? Then we'll have those together.

"I can't be without you, Carter. I need you in my

life. I was foolish to push you away. We can go to Dylan. Take out a protective order. Hell, I'll volunteer to wear a wire and confront Wilma and try to get her to voice the same threats she's already issued to me. But I can't go this alone. I love you too, too much."

Tenley kissed him, and Carter found tears spilling from his eyes.

He broke the kiss. "We'll figure it out. From now on, we do everything together. Agreed?"

"Agreed." She kissed him again. "I guess I shouldn't be doing this. After all, you're on oxygen. I'm probably sucking the life out of you," she teased.

She continued to hold his hand, sitting on the bed, and they talked a few minutes. He told her that it was Wilma he had carried from the burning house.

"Is she alive?" Tenley asked anxiously. "Oh, it's hard to believe it was you who went in to save her."

"I believe my English teacher would call that a fine example of irony," he quipped.

The door opened. Dorothy appeared again, this time with Dylan and Willow in tow. He was happy to see his friends and assured them he was fine, only staying in the hospital as a precaution.

"I can leave tomorrow," he told them. Glancing to Tenley, he added, "Tenley was already packed up. She had planned to move in with me while we're trying to find a bigger place."

His fiancée squeezed his hand, silently agreeing to the small white lie he had just told.

"I don't know if you know, but Wilma Bell died," Dylan said.

Carter stiffened as Tenley gripped his hand. "Is that so?"

"Yes. I'm going to give Fred a few days and then speak to him again about his alibi," Dylan continued.

"You think he'll fold?" he asked.

"Wilma always wore the pants in that family," his friend said. "I think there's a good possibility that with her gone, Fred will finally tell the truth."

They stayed a few more minutes, and then Willow said, "You must be exhausted. We should let you get some rest." She kissed his cheek. "We'll let everyone know you're fine and that you'll be home tomorrow. Don't worry about meals. We'll take care of that for you."

"I wouldn't mind Ainsley bringing over some cannolis," he said. "But Tenley has all the makings of a good cook. I'll walk her through things."

Carter thanked them for coming. His mother stayed another hour and then said, "You need to get some rest. I know Tenley wants to stay with you. I'll be back later. Anything you want?"

"A cheeseburger?" he joked.

She smiled. "I'll be back." To Tenley, she said, "Call if you need anything."

"I will."

"Your mom is right. You've been through a lot."

"I know. A brutal breakup with my fiancée. A night without any sleep. A dangerous house fire. A reunion with my fiancée. Yeah, I could use a nap." He grinned up at her. "But I'll sleep better if you're cuddled next to me."

"Carter, I don't think—"

"Now, that's where you went wrong. You don't have to think about it. Just climb into bed and snuggle next to me."

She giggled. "You're on."

Tenley slipped off her shoes and joined him in the narrow bed. Carter turned on his side and draped and arm about her, drawing her close. He breathed in the scent of her shampoo and sighed.

"This is a good Saturday," he murmured, dropping into sleep.

~

THE DOORBELL RANG. Carter shouted, "I'll get it."

He went to the door and opened it, greeting Dylan and Willow. Dylan carried four large pizza boxes from Stuff 'n Crust.

"Come on in, guys," he said, stepping back and letting them inside.

"Wait for me," called Rylie, who hurried up the steps after them. She gave Carter a huge hug. "Looking pretty good," she told him.

"Actually, I'm feeling pretty good," he replied, closing the door.

It had been six days since the fire at the Bells' house. He had been discharged from the hospital after twenty-four hours, just as Dr. Knowles promised, and had scheduled an appointment for Monday with the county's firefighter physician to see if he could be cleared for duty.

Carter wasn't certain he was going to keep that appointment.

The doorbell rang again, and he opened it to find Ainsley and Gage on the porch.

Ainsley smiled brightly at him and held up a Tupperware container. "Your beloved cannolis." She nodded her head to Gage, who also bore a Tupperware container. "He's got custody of the brownies. I'm not sure if or when he'll relinquish them."

As they came through the door, Gage said, "I deserve every brownie in this box," he declared. "I started a new class for women over fifty this week. They are demanding."

They all went into the kitchen, and Carter asked, "Are they whiners?"

Gage chuckled. "Far from it. The want to push themselves—and me—probably further than they should go. I've never seen a group of women more determined to get into shape. We're meeting three days a week at five in the morning, and your mom is the ringleader of their pack, Carter."

"Really?" he asked. "She hasn't mentioned it to me."

Gage grinned. "Probably because she's too busy bossing me and the others around." He set down the two six-packs he carried while Willow opened wine for the women.

Gage pulled off a beer from the pack and handed it to Carter.

"None for me yet," he said. "I'm still drinking a lot of water and working on building my lung capacity through cardio."

"Are you doing any light lifting?" Gage asked.

He nodded. "Very light. I'm beginning to feel like myself, but I don't want to rush things."

"I can understand that," Rylie said. "I broke my leg once playing basketball. After the leg healed, it took me a while to enjoy running again, much less build my stamina to run up and down the court again."

"Here are the wines for the women," Tenley said, and the ladies claimed their glasses. "We'll have to eat gathered around the coffee table in the den since we don't have a table large enough for all of us."

"Everyone grab slices of pizza, because Tenley and I have some news to share."

Ainsley's brows shot up. "This sounds interesting. One question—are you married yet?"

He and Tenley laughed. "No," he told them. "Not yet. Soon."

The group grabbed plates, piling pizza slices on them, moving to the small den. Carter had already placed the two chairs from the café table in the room, as well, so there would be enough seating.

Once everyone was situated, plates on their laps or the coffee table, Willow said, "Okay. Spill. What news do you have?"

Carter laced his fingers through Tenley's and said, "We put in a bid on a house, and it was accepted. The Garners' house."

Willow squealed. "That's about a quarter mile from us! I didn't know that Mr. Garner was selling."

"He's decided to retire from the bank in Salty Point," he told them. "You know that he lost his wife a couple of years ago. His only daughter lives in Arizona now, with his three grandchildren. He decided he wanted to be closer to them and a whole lot of sunshine so he could play golf every day."

Tenley took up the story. "Shayla Reynolds called us before it even went on the market. Mr. Garner was friends with Carter's dad, and Shayla told him we were in the market for a home similar to his. He agreed to have us come in and look at it before he even listed it. It will take some fixing up, but it's roomy and we love the layout."

"Pete walked through the place with us this morning. Mr. Garner had already vacated it as of yesterday. We're actually going to keep a few pieces of furniture. The moving van will arrive on Monday to take what he wants to bring with him to Scottsdale."

"What did you and Pete discuss doing?" Dylan asked.

"The floors are in good condition but definitely need to be sanded. Tenley and I agreed that the entire inside and outside of the house needs to be painted. She's already gotten with Pete and chosen colors."

"Without my input?" Willow teased.

"You can look over my choices," Tenley said, "but I think I did a good job on color selection."

Carter said they would remodel both bathrooms, and he detailed the updates that would occur in the kitchen.

"I think we're going to be spending a lot of time in the kitchen," he said. "More on that later."

"Ooh, a man of mystery," Rylie said. "I look forward to hearing more about that."

As they ate, they caught up with one another. It was an enjoyable evening, one which Carter believed would be one of many to come through the years with this group of friends.

Tenley and Rylie gathered their plates and took the empty pizza boxes away as Ainsley opened the containers bearing the desserts she had brought and distributed them.

Over dessert, Dylan said, "I have news for Carter and Tenley, but I don't think they would mind me sharing it with all of you here."

Tenley said, "You've talked with Fred Bell."

Dylan nodded. "After the funeral on Wednesday, I gave him my condolences and told him anytime he was ready to talk to me, I was willing to listen." Dylan paused. "He knew exactly what I meant. Fred came in to the station this morning and asked to meet with me privately. Behind closed doors, we had an interesting discussion."

"Did he admit he and Wilma started the fire at the diner?" Carter asked.

"Fred isn't the nicest of guys," Dylan said, "but I don't believe he has the capability to lie to me effectively. He admitted that Wilma had gone out the night of the fire and come home in a very excited state, telling him that if anyone asked—especially Sheriff Taylor—that they had been at home all evening watching Carol Burnett reruns. Fred didn't know why she told him this, only that she was adamant that he back her up. Once I brought them in for questioning, he understood how serious the charges were.

"Fred felt pretty bad about what Wilma had done and tried to talk to her about it," Dylan continued. "According to him, he said she acted a bit crazed. Like she had gone off the deep end. She was talking wildly about what she would do to Carter—and Tenley—unless she could chase Tenley out of town. Fred tried to get her to let it go, but she was like a dog with a bone."

Carter placed his hand on Tenley's knee and could feel the tremors running through her.

"Fred said that Wilma came home last week and told him that Tenley was leaving town and it was a good thing she was, because if she didn't, Wilma said she was going to kill Carter."

Everyone gasped. Carter tightened his hold on Tenley's knee. She placed her hand over his.

"Fred had mulled over coming to see me when he was notified about the fire at his house," Dylan said. "I don't know if you've heard yet, but it was started by faulty wiring in a bathroom. Fred said he wanted to come clean with me about what had happened and Wilma's role in things. He wanted me to let Carter and Tenley know that he has no problems with them and wishes them the best."

"I always thought Wilma had a screw loose," Ainsley said. "She just seemed off to me."

"Will Fred be held responsible for anything?" Gage asked. "After all, he lied about his wife's alibi."

"I hope not," Carter spoke up. "Fred was only trying to protect the woman he loved, no matter how wrong she was." He glanced to Tenley, and she nodded. "Don't press charges against him, Dylan."

"If you think that's wise," Dylan said, "I'll put the matter to rest and let Fred know. I told him I'd be speaking with you about things."

The group stayed another few minutes, and then Ainsley said, "We need to leave before we tire out Carter."

"Hey, I'm not some baby," he protested. "I'm feeling fine."

Mischief gleamed in Ainsley's eyes as she added, "You might want to save what strength you have to entertain Tenley after we leave."

Everyone hooted with laughter, and Tenley blushed a pretty shade of pink.

"Why didn't I think of that sooner?" he asked. "Out. Everyone out! I need my rest."

They said goodbye to their friends and collected the empty glasses and dirty dessert plates, taking them to the kitchen and loading them into the dishwasher.

Carter took Tenley's hand and led her not into the bedroom but back to the sofa in the den. They sat and he put an arm around her. She rested her head against his chest and took his free hand in hers.

"That was a nice night," she said. "We have some amazing friends."

"That we do." He hesitated and then said, "I have

something I want to talk over with you. In part, it's about the renovations that Pete will do."

"I'm intrigued. Go on."

"What would you think if I left firefighting?"

She sat up and faced him. "Are you serious? What brought this on, Carter?"

"Although I love what I do, I love you more," he said honestly. "I think about how I rush into burning buildings and worry now about if I don't come out. I do have my EMT certification and could try to get on fulltime with the hospital if we needed a steady, dependable income."

Tenley studied him a moment. "But you have something else in mind, don't you?"

"I do. Cooking. It's become more than a hobby to me. It's my passion. I would love to be able to help others learn how to cook. Whether it was through this vlog you've talked about or if I found a place to hold group classes, similar to what Gage offers. Maybe even work out of our new home. That's why I wanted the huge island and Viking ovens. For lessons or filming. What do you think?"

The backs of her fingers brushed his cheek and then she kissed him tenderly. "I think it's a terrific idea. What about the cookbook we talked about? You know my old boss, Janice, went wild over it, especially the name—*A Firefighter's Guide to Survival in the Kitchen*. She thinks it would be a great cookbook series and wants Sutton Press to have first dibs on it if you ever decided to put one together."

Though he had put the thought of a cookbook on hold, his imagination now caught fire. "I could do a book of basics to begin with. Then branch out into specialty books. Italian cuisine. Japanese. Mediterranean. Or categories such as desserts. Even holidays."

Enthusiasm brimmed within him. "Do you think I could make a living off this?"

"I really do, Carter. I think we need to go on and claim a website domain and start getting some content out there. We can use the couple of videos that I've already shot. I'm sure we can bring in a professional at some point. Who knows? As much as high school kids know about technology, we might even be able to hire a few locals to produce and direct your videos."

She smiled at him. "I like this new beginning for us. Two writers in the family."

"That's what it is, isn't it? A new beginning," he agreed.

He kissed her deeply and then broke the kiss. Grinning, he said, "I think I could use a final workout before we go to sleep."

Her eyebrows arched. "You think so?"

He rose, bringing Tenley with him. Leading her into the bedroom, he slowly undressed her, marveling at this angel who had come into his life. As Carter gathered Tenley in his arms and kissed her, he knew their future would be bright.

EPILOGUE
NINE MONTHS LATER—NEW YORK CITY

Tenley awoke to Carter nibbling her nape. The usual, wonderful sensations from his touch began rippling through her. He made love to her slowly and tenderly. Every kiss—every touch—from her husband caused her to fall even more deeply in love with him.

They climaxed together, and Carter collapsed atop her. Tenley nuzzled his neck, and he rolled to his side, keeping her close to him.

"That was pretty much perfect," he told her.

They had spent the past week in New York, playing tourists since Carter had never visited the city before. Besides taking him to familiar attractions, such as the Statue of Liberty and Rockefeller Center, they had also visited museums, including the 9/11 Museum, where Carter was moved by how well the museum honored those first responders who had given their lives that dark day. She had them stroll along the High Line and even take the tram over to Roosevelt Island, as well as hit up some of her favorite restaurants. He had enjoyed the pizza in Brooklyn the most, and they had walked across the Brooklyn Bridge after that dinner, seeing the Manhattan skyline lit up in all its glory.

Yesterday, they had fulfilled the ultimate tourist fantasy by attending the Macy's Thanksgiving Day Parade. She had never gone in person, despite living in New York for several years, and was happy to accommodate her husband's request to view the parade in person. They marveled at the size and color of the many balloons and then enjoyed a wonderful brunch at Tavern on the Green.

Today, they got down to business, the heart of why they had taken this trip. Elmo Nichols had signed Carter as a client, arranging the deal for a cookbook series with Sutton Press. The agent had also helped Carter launch a line of cooking utensils, pots and pans, and aprons that sold exclusive on Carter's website. His You Tube Channel had proven to be popular and already helped drive sales of his first book. Gillian handled the bookkeeping for the growing empire, and they were thankful she handled all business transactions for them.

Starting at ten this morning, Tenley and her husband would be part of a joint book signing at the largest bookseller in Manhattan. Carter's first cookbook had released a week ago, as had her first book in her fantasy trilogy. She had worked with Elmo, Oakwood Publishing, and Dalton International to arrive at the perfect time to release her first novel. They all thought it would be the runaway hit of the Christmas season.

Tenley had actually finished writing both the second and third installments of her trilogy during this past year. Having outlined each story before she began writing made the process flow more quickly. Having Carter's input was also invaluable. He had contributed a great deal to the storylines in both books.

Oakwood now had those two books in hand, and Tenley had completed edits on the second one, though she still awaited editing notes on the third in the trilogy, since she had only turned it in the day before they left for New York.

After today's joint book signing, she was meeting with the entire Oakwood team all afternoon. Tomorrow morning, she would accompany Carter, along with Elmo, to her old stomping grounds at Sutton Press. Janice wanted to discuss with Carter his next cookbook. He had also received interest from the Food Network, as well, and there was a strong possibility that he would tape a pilot in their kitchen early next year. Her husband had insisted if the pilot succeeded, and they received a green light for the series that he would insist it be shot at their home in the Cove.

"I suppose we should get moving," he said, pressing his lips to her temple. "Do you want the shower first?"

"No, you go ahead. I have some e-mails to answer. I'll also order us breakfast from room service."

"Good. I'm starving," he informed her.

By the time Carter had finished showering, shaving, and dressing, their meal had arrived. Tenley ate hers and then retreated to the bathroom to get ready for the book signing, while Carter perused the newspaper that came with their breakfast.

Elmo texted, letting them know the car would be at their hotel within ten minutes, and she and Carter went downstairs to the lobby. As they stood waiting, three women rushed over to them.

One exclaimed, "Carter Clark? It's really you!

We've all bought your cookbook and watch you on You Tube. Could we get a selfie?"

He gave them that engaging smile of his, the one which continued to take her breath away.

"Let me take it for you," she offered, holding out her hand for the fan's phone.

The women grouped around Carter, beaming, and she took a picture of the group and then individual shots, each of them posing with him. They thanked Cater profusely as Tenley returned the phone.

"Let's go outside," he suggested when they left. "I'm sure the car must be here by now."

They stepped through the hotel's front doors just as a black town car pulled up to the curb. The window went down, and Elmo waved at them. They hustled to the vehicle before anyone else could recognize Carter.

After they climbed in, he said, "You're going to be even more famous than me. People are just recognizing me because I'm online."

Tenley chuckled. "That's a slim possibility. Besides, I'm not a hot fireman. You'll always be the one everyone wants a picture with."

"Ex-fireman," he said, entwining his fingers with hers. "Best decision I ever made."

Tenley had worried slightly that it would take Carter a while to gain his footing, leaving the close-knit, regimented world of firefighting and becoming his own boss. He had surprised her at how well he adjusted, organizing his time and schedule with ease, juggling various projects. The Garner house had now become the Clark house, with all renovations completed, and it felt like home. Though they hadn't talked about specifics, they were both eager to start a family, and Tenley hoped by this time next year, they might be welcoming their first baby.

They arrived at the bookstore, and Elmo told them to wait in the car while he went in and made sure everything had been set up to his liking.

After Elmo closed the car door, Carter asked, "Are you ready for this? Our first joint appearance."

"Both publishing houses and the PR people at Dalton have assured me that our books will hit *The New York Times* bestseller list, as well as *USA Today's* list."

The PR firm had wanted to set up other joint book signings, and Tenley had agreed to an additional week beyond today. From New York, they would fly to Boston, Miami, Dallas, Chicago, and L.A. Pretty much a flight a day and one signing in each city, except for L.A., where they would make appearances two days in a row. She and Carter had talked it over and decided that would be enough for a first book tour, especially since Christmas approached, and they wanted to deck their own halls for the holidays and be home with family and friends.

Her husband gazed into her eyes and smiled. "So much has happened during this past year. It's been all the more special because I'm going through this with the love of my life."

As always, Tenley felt cherished by this man as Carter gave her a lingering kiss.

The car door opened, and Elmo asked, "Ready to rock and roll?"

They smiled at one another. Together, Tenley and Carter replied, "Ready."

**READ COMING HOME,
BOOK 3 IN THE MAPLE
COVE SERIES!**

If you enjoyed Carter and Tenley finding love with the support of their close friends Dylan and Willow, you'll want to read *Coming Home, Book 3 in the Maple Cove series!*

In this romance, Willow's brother Jackson leaves his high profile law practice in L.A. and returns to his boyhood home, being embraced by his sister Willow's friends—and finding love with one of them.

On the edge of burnout, attorney Jackson Martin returns to his hometown of Maple Cove for a simpler life. Ainsley Robinson, who had a girlhood crush on Jackson, lands on his radar and sparks fly as the pair find themselves in love for the first time.

Just when it seems everything is falling into place for the happy couple, one of Jackson's former clients decides to upend their world.

Will Jackson be able to protect Ainsley from a deranged psychopath—or will he lose the only woman he's ever loved—along with his own life?

ALSO BY ALEXA ASTON

MAPLE COVE
Another Chance at Love

A New Beginning

Coming Home

The Lyrics of Love

Finding Home

HOLLYWOOD NAME GAME:
Hollywood Heartbreaker

Hollywood Flirt

Hollywood Player

Hollywood Double

Hollywood Enigma

LAWMEN OF THE WEST:
Runaway Hearts

Blind Faith

Love and the Lawman

Ballad Beauty

SAGEBRUSH BRIDES:
A Game of Chance

Written in the Cards

Outlaw Muse

KNIGHTS OF REDEMPTION:

To Win a Widow

<u>THE ST. CLAIRS:</u>
Devoted to the Duke
Midnight with the Marquess
Embracing the Earl
Defending the Duke
Suddenly a St. Clair

<u>THE KING'S COUSINS:</u>
God of the Seas
The Pawn
The Heir
The Bastard

<u>THE KNIGHTS OF HONOR:</u>
Rise of de Wolfe
Word of Honor
Marked by Honor
Code of Honor
Journey to Honor
Heart of Honor
Bold in Honor
Love and Honor
Gift of Honor
Path to Honor
Return to Honor
Season of Honor

<u>NOVELLAS:</u>

Diana

Derek

Thea

The Lyon's Lady Love

ABOUT THE AUTHOR

A native Texan and former history teacher, award-winning and internationally bestselling author Alexa Aston lives with her husband in a Dallas suburb, where she eats her fair share of dark chocolate and plots out stories while she walks every morning. She enjoys travel, sports, and binge-watching—and never misses an episode of *Survivor*.

Alexa brings her characters to life in steamy historicals, contemporary romances, and romantic suspense novels that resonate with passion, intensity, and heart.

KEEP UP WITH ALEXA
Visit her website
Newsletter Sign-Up

MORE WAYS TO CONNECT WITH ALEXA